THE EMPEROR'S MASK

BEN S. DOBSON

CHAPTER ONE

————

TANE CARVER SPRINTED along the busy Porthaven waterfront, breaking through the linked hands of a goblin couple as he shoved his way past. He ignored the indignant cries behind him, only glancing over his shoulder to see if he'd lost his pursuer.

The dwarf was closing in on him.

Thorick Irondriver stood out even among the eclectic Porthaven rabble of gnomes and dwarves and sprites and ogren and more. He was no more than four and a half feet in height—average for a dwarf—but his shoulders looked near as broad across as he was tall, and the biceps beneath were as big as Tane's head and covered in ugly black tattoos of iron spikes and wire. The tattoos stretched across his chest, too, exposed beneath a stained leather vest. Above a thick black beard and a twisted scowl of a face, his bald head was inked in the same pattern. He charged down the street in a straight line without regard for the people in front of him, and he didn't need to shove them aside like Tane did—most got one look at the furious rail-engine of a dwarf bearing down on them, and cleared the way.

Tane gripped the stolen artifact tighter in his hand and pushed himself faster, weaving among the people on the street for cover. Irondriver was a mage, which meant giving him a clear sightline could only lead to pain. *Not that he needs magic to break me in half. Spellfire, this had better work.* It wasn't the best plan he'd ever had, but stealing something—and making sure he was seen doing it—had been the easiest way to lure Irondriver out of his heavily warded black market workshop.

The alley he and Kadka had agreed on was just ahead on his left, a narrow path between low warehouses. Tane tried to shoulder past a lovely nine-foot ogren woman, and the impact shook his teeth like he'd collided with a stone pillar at speed. He bounced off, gripping his arm, and stumbled toward the mouth of the alley.

"Oh dear, I'm sorry," the woman said in a melodious voice—just like an ogren to apologize to him for running into her—but Tane didn't have time to answer. The heavy thud of Irondriver's feet was close behind as he darted into the alley. It went perhaps forty feet back before turning sharply to the left, just a narrow space out of the way of the crowd. If things went badly, it was best not to have bystanders around.

Halfway down, Tane slowed and turned, holding up his hands. "Wait. I'll give it back."

The scowl across Irondriver's thick jaw rose into a cruel smile. "Too late for that, thief. Shouldn't have robbed me if you don't want to pay the price." He advanced on Tane, and pulled a short blade from behind his back. Mage or no, apparently he preferred to hurt people the old fashioned way.

Tane backed away slowly, and slipped two fingers into his waistcoat pocket to rub the battered brass watch case there. An old nervous habit. "For a man selling faulty artifacts to people who can't tell the difference," he said, "you're surprisingly passionate about criminal justice." He glanced down at the artifact he'd stolen: a brass tube just wide enough to fit a rolled charm, sealed on one end with a small button on the side. A flash-tube, devised to launch colorful flash-charms into the air—though it could be used with more dangerous charms as well. Illegal without a license, but hardly worth so much trouble. "I wonder: if I press the button, do you think this thing would work, or explode?" He pointed the open end at the dwarf.

Irondriver hesitated, flinching, and then narrowed his eyes. "It ain't even loaded." He furrowed his heavy brow. "Who are you, then? Someone send you after me?"

"A client didn't care for your work on her stove. Specifically, the fact that you overlooked some common safety glyphs. She was burned quite badly." If Tane backed off much further, he'd be against the wall where the alley turned. He was far enough from the street now. This was the place. "I'm really hoping that this is the part where you swear to change your ways and make things right with Miss Eutrice."

"Bitch shouldn't have tried to buy cheap. The price I offer, they ain't all going to be perfect." Irondriver shrugged his massive shoulders. "Should have paid someone bigger to come after me, too. Talking's done, thief." Tossing his knife from hand to hand, he started forward once more.

This time, Tane didn't retreat. Instead, he reached into his pocket and crushed the seal on the charm inside.

A translucent dome shimmered to life around Tane and Irondriver, glowing a faint silver-blue.

Irondriver glanced back at the silvery barrier just behind his shoulder, and laughed. "Too late to keep me out now."

And finally, Tane allowed himself the smile he'd been holding back. "Oh, it's not meant to keep you *out*."

———

Kadka crouched atop the low brick warehouse on the south side of the alleyway, waiting for Carver to give the signal. As usual, he was talking too much. Which was often amusing, but there was a mage to fight, and waiting on a rooftop was almost as boring as watching closed doors at the University. There was a reason she wasn't a guard anymore.

The tattooed dwarf advanced, tossing his knife back and forth.

A shimmer of silver, then, and the shield was up.

There it was. The signal.

Kadka backed off a few steps, launched herself into a run, and vaulted over the side of the roof, snarling for effect.

Irondriver looked up at the sound, saw her falling. His eyes widened, and he started to turn. Too late. She passed easily through the shield and hit him hard from near twenty feet up, sending him sprawling to the ground on his back. His knife flew free of his hand, skittered across the ground, and struck the inside of the shield with a silver flash.

Even with the dwarf to break the momentum of her fall, the impact still knocked Kadka to her hands and knees. She and Irondriver both gained their feet at the same time.

Kadka flashed Irondriver a sharp-toothed grin. "Should have sent someone bigger, you said?"

He stared at her bared teeth. "Half-orc," he spat, somewhere between disgust and fear. His eyes went to Carver, and then back to Kadka again. "You... you're the Magebreakers, ain't you?"

"I hate that name," muttered Carver.

"Is not wrong, though," said Kadka, still grinning. She took a single step toward the dwarf.

Irondriver turned and ran.

Or tried to.

He hadn't gone more than two feet before he struck the translucent barrier. A flash of silver sent him stumbling back. Carver had scribed the charm and commissioned it from Bastian—a reversed shield, made to keep things in rather than out. Kadka never understood much when he talked about magical theory, but he'd been clear enough that it wouldn't last long.

Which was fine by her. A time limit made things more interesting.

Irondriver broke right, going for the knife he'd dropped. She moved to intercept, kicking the blade away and tackling him against the shield. He grabbed her arms, pried them off with an angry grunt. He was stronger than she was used to—ogren aside, there weren't many in Thaless who could grapple with her.

A pleasant surprise. She laughed as he shoved her back.

Taking advantage of the space he'd created, Irondriver started to chant in the magical language Carver called the *lingua*. He was already raising a hand. Kadka regained her balance and charged. A fist to the throat usually stopped a spell, but she could already tell she wasn't going to make it.

"Hey!" Carver's voice, and then a brass tube struck Irondriver in the side of the face. The dwarf's head snapped to the side, and a wave of silver force surged high from his outstretched hand, striking the ceiling of the shield-dome over Kadka's head. The artifact Carver had thrown clattered to the ground.

Kadka was on Irondriver before he could open his mouth again. She wrapped her leg behind his and shoved him hard; he toppled backward to the cobblestones. Following him down, she landed with her forearm across his throat, cutting off his breath and his voice. With her free hand, she pinned one of his heavily muscled arms to the ground. Irondriver clawed at her eyes with the other, his face flushed red beneath the iron-black tattoos on his scalp.

A moment later Carver was beside her, putting his full body weight against the grasping hand to hold it down. "Inside his vest, right side. I saw him tuck it away when he was showing me his wares."

Kadka nodded. "No spells," she said to Irondriver, and lifted her arm from his throat.

"Bitch," Irondriver croaked, and immediately began to mutter in the *lingua*.

She grinned. She'd been hoping he'd do that.

She slammed her forehead against his face, and felt something crunch. Blood gushed from Irondriver's broken nose; he kept chanting in a choked, gurgling voice. Kadka headbutted him again, and this time his eyes rolled back and he went still.

A moment later, the shield flickered out of existence.

She glanced at Carver with a grin. "Told you: is more time than I need."

"Can't argue with results." Carver's eyes went to her forehead, and he made a face. "A bit… messy, though."

Kadka rubbed her brow, and her fingers found blood, warm and sticky. But not *her* blood, which was the only thing that mattered. She wiped an arm across her face to clean the rest away, staining the white fur on the back of her hand red. "Messy is what works, sometimes," she said. With her other hand, she dug inside Irondriver's vest until she found a coin-sized badge etched with glyphs, and held it up for Carver to see. "This will get us into workshop?"

"It should," said Carver, rising to his feet. "And the artifacts inside will be all the evidence the bluecaps need to arrest him. Fraud, negligence, illegal artifice." He glanced down at Irondriver's bloodied face and broken nose. "Better roll him onto his side, or he'll choke on the blood before they get the chance."

"Or we could just take him now." A woman's voice, and one Kadka knew. She stood and turned to see a slim brown-skinned half-elf entering the alley, dressed in a charcoal topcoat and trousers, black hair bound back from her face in a simple bun. Constable Inspector Indree Lovial. Even out of uniform, she had the air of a bluecap, a certain self-assured authority over the situation despite only now walking into it. A half-dozen others of various races and sizes flanked her, all in plainclothes, but Kadka knew a constable when she saw one.

"Ree," said Carver. "How did you find us?"

"Finding people is my job," said Indree. "And as usual, you left a trail of angry people behind you." She glanced at the bloody fur on Kadka's hand, and then tipped her head at the motionless dwarf sprawled on the ground. "Is it too much to hope that you had some reason for beating this man senseless?"

Carver spread his hands indignantly. "You say that like we don't always have a reason."

Indree cocked an eyebrow. "What about last month, when you broke into that artificer's house? She hadn't done anything."

"Was easy mistake," Kadka said mildly. Carver and Indree could squabble for hours if she didn't mediate. "Her sister sells dangerous spells with her name. We find one because we chase other first. You know this."

"*I* know it," Indree allowed. "But that didn't make it any easier to keep you out of a cell."

"This is different," said Carver, "Nobody's framing Irondriver. If you come with us to his workshop, there's proof—"

"You can explain later," Indree interrupted, and motioned for two constables to see to the unconscious dwarf. Kadka stepped aside to give them room. "Right now, you two are coming with me."

"Now?" Kadka liked Indree, but this felt wrong—it would have been far easier to summon them with a sending. Tracking them down like this implied she wanted to catch them off their guard. "Why?"

Indree let out a heavy sigh and rubbed the bridge of her nose. "Because," she said, "you might be murder suspects."

CHAPTER TWO

————

TANE FOLLOWED INDREE through the streets of the Gryphon's Roost, surrounded by an escort of four plainclothes constables—two humans, a three-foot-something gnomish man, and a towering ogren woman guarding the rear. Kadka walked at his side, eagerly examining the opulent homes of the Roost.

Elaborate magelight lamps lined the road—unlit in the afternoon sunlight—and high gates loomed all along both sides. In front of every gate a pair of hired guards stood watch in expensive uniforms; behind every one was a massive estate, all open grass and elaborate hedges and elegant statuary. Each estate had an enormous manor house at the center, all of them unique in architecture and design—and yet somehow the same as all the others, in a fundamental way that Tane recognized but couldn't explain. Horse-drawn carriages waited at the ready by most houses, or expensive ancryst carts with loud, ponderous engines. This place was so far removed from the cramped streets and joined brick-front homes of Porthaven that it might as well have been a different world.

"You're obviously not taking us to Stooketon Yard," said Tane, "so we must be going to the crime scene. Someone was murdered in the Roost? I can't remember the last time that happened." There was no district in Thaless more secure than the Gryphon's Roost. The constabulary responded far more diligently to any hint of criminal activity here than they did in places like Porthaven or Greenstone, and every manor had hired guards and thorough wards. "What's going on, Ree?"

"You'll see when we get there," said Indree, and increased her pace.

She was hiding something—he could tell. "You can't *really* think we killed someone."

"If I did, you'd be chained up in a cell right now. I only talked Chief Durren out of having you arrested by convincing him I'd learn more from your reactions to the scene, and those won't matter much if you already know what you're going to see."

Tane raised an eyebrow. "Why does our reaction matter at all? Why would either of us have anything to do with a murder in the Gryphon's Roost? We don't exactly spend much time here."

"Orcs are not so welcome in fancy houses," said Kadka, peering through the bars of the nearest gate at the elaborate hedge sculptures beyond. She glanced at Indree then, with a slight frown. "Is this why? You think killer is orc?"

"Like I said, I can't tell you anything yet." A familiar exasperation crept into Indree's voice. "I need to do this the way I've been ordered to do it. No special treatment. It hasn't exactly helped my career bailing the Magebreakers out of trouble every other week."

"Don't call us that," Tane protested reflexively. "'Magebreakers' sounds like a penny dreadful from some basement ancryst press."

Indree rolled her eyes. "Good luck stopping it. It's already all over Thaless. My point is, you two haven't been at this more than six weeks and most of the constabulary already thinks you're a public menace. Half of Findel Avenue is still caved in from your little adventure underneath the bank last month."

"That wasn't our fault," Tane said. "We didn't *dig* the tunnel. We were just trying to get Mrs. Dookle's husband back for her. Which we did, by the way."

"Yes, you did." Indree's scowl softened at the corners. "You usually manage to help someone underneath all the chaos. That's why I keep defending you. But I won't be able to do that if I'm demoted back to patrol constable."

That was hard to argue with, and Tane knew how much Indree cared about her position in the bluecaps. "Fair enough," he said. "No more questions. Lead the way."

She pointed up the street to the next estate. "Come on. It's just here."

She led them to a huge wrought-iron gate that towered over even Kadka by her height again—large even compared to the ones that had come before. There was no family name on the gateposts, only a number—21—but a pair of guardsmen stood outside in uniforms of deep red and green that Tane recognized immediately.

House Rosepetal. The only sprite house with a seat in the Senate.

"Someone was killed *here?*" Tane peered through the iron bars at the vast grounds beyond. "The Rosepetals are a great house of the Senate! Who would—"

Indree turned a glare on him that he knew all too well.

"Right," he said. "No more questions."

The guards at the gate—two large human men— stood to attention as Indree came near. "Constable Inspector," one of them said. "We haven't let anyone in since you left, as ordered." His tone was surprisingly crisp and formal for a hired man.

Indree nodded her approval. "Open the gates," she said. "If anyone else comes asking around after we're in, don't let on that anything is out of the ordinary. And notify me if anyone shows unusual interest."

One of the guards turned and laid his palm against a glyphed copper panel set into a gate pillar. The glyphs flared silver-blue—checking his Astral signature, Tane surmised—and then the huge gates swung inward with a loud creak. Indree led them through, and the slight tingle of a ward ran over Tane's body as they passed into the estate. Apparently the bluecaps had already added their names to the list of exemptions. On the other side, a long hedge-lined road led toward the manor house.

"Those weren't Rosepetal guards, were they?" Tane said, glancing over his shoulder. "You've got constables on the gate in borrowed uniforms. And you're all in plain-clothes. The bluecaps must really want this kept quiet." Now that he was looking, he noticed a dozen other men and women scouring the grounds among shaped hedges and magically-landscaped ponds and the like—also constables, Tane was sure, despite the lack of signature blue caps.

"Not just us," said Indree. "Like you said, the Rosep-etals are a great house of the Senate. This is a sensitive matter."

"And Chief Durren assigned it to you?" Tane raised an eyebrow. "I thought you were on the verge of being demoted."

"Lady Abena personally requested I lead the investi-gation. I suppose she trusts me, after the… the Nieris matter." She swallowed there, and looked down. She and Tane had both lost a friend to the former University chancellor's conspiracy, but Indree had taken it much harder—she'd known Allaea all her life. "He didn't like it, but the Lady Protector outranks the chief constable."

"Is good woman, Lady Abena," Kadka said. "Knows talent. You are best choice."

"Thank you, Kadka." Indree gave her a slight smile.

Kadka shrugged. "Is true. Most bluecaps I meet are stupid *poskan*—"

"*Thank you*, Kadka," Indree said again, and glanced pointedly at the constables escorting them.

Tane chuckled under his breath. *Better change the subject.* Kadka didn't *always* take the hint, although she was improving. He gestured ahead. "Are we headed for the main house, or somewhere else on the grounds?"

The manor towered just ahead now, a four-story home with huge gabled windows along the roof and a great marble stairway leading to a front door large enough to admit a full-grown manticore. Everything on the Rosepetal estate was oversized, it seemed. Sprite homes were usually built to accommodate guests larger than their hosts, but this seemed like overcompensation.

"Inside," said Indree. She led them up the stairs to another pair of guards, who threw open the doors at her order.

No telltale tingle of a ward prickled Tane's skin as he passed inside, which was inconceivable for a Senate house. The Rosepetals could afford far better than the simple protections around the outer estate. *They must have taken the house wards down for the investigation.* It was the only thing that made sense.

There was no one inside but more out-of-uniform bluecaps, scouring the house with detection spells and divinations. The Rosepetals and their servants would already have been taken to Stooketon Yard for questioning. As far as Tane knew, both Elsa Rosepetal, the senior senator of the house, and her son Byron, the junior, lived on the family's main estate. It was strange to think of either one sitting in a shabby interrogation chamber at the Yard. *But maybe they aren't. I don't know who the victim is yet.*

Following Indree through the house, Tane couldn't help but note the juxtaposition of large and small occupying the same space: ornate nine-foot tall doors with smaller sprite-sized ones cut into their centers; a massive curving stairway to the upper floors with perches along the railing for the tiny and winged; a study containing a great oaken desk beside its miniature twin on a raised pedestal, so that whoever occupied them would be at eye level with one another. All of it was illuminated by silvery magelight—not the simple globes Tane had become accustomed to at the University, but chandeliers and wall sconces of sculpted bronze and artfully shaped glass. The manor had clearly been designed and decorated to show that the Rosepetal's wealth and importance far outmeasured their diminutive stature.

On the third floor, yet another pair of guards met them outside one of the manor's huge doors. It was closed—along with the smaller opening at its center—but Tane had glanced into some of the rooms along the hall, and it wasn't hard to guess that this door led to someone's personal chambers, just like the rest.

"No one's disturbed the scene?" Indree asked.

"No one, Inspector Lovial," answered one of the guards, a white-haired elven woman. "Only the diviners have been inside since you left, and they didn't touch anything."

"Good," Indree said. "We're going in." She motioned them aside, and pushed open the door, holding it for Tane and Kadka. "Just me and the Magebreakers." She smirked at Tane, there. "The rest of you, wait here."

Tane stepped inside, with Kadka just behind. The door opened into a small outer chamber that lacked the rest of the manor's concessions to the larger races. Save for a single full-sized chair against the wall, the furniture was all sprite-sized, sitting on raised platforms. A desk, a reading chair and book table, a reclining couch by one window, all small enough to seat a child's doll. Recessed into one wall was a little bookcase filled with quarter-sized books.

"Looks empty," said Kadka. "Like someone leaves too fast, forgets some things."

She was right. It was the smallest room they'd yet seen, but even so none of the furnishings took up much space—it had a certain abandoned look to it.

"Probably hard to avoid when you're a foot tall and insist on living in a house this size," Tane said, still looking around. A painting of two dragonfly-winged sprites hung above the tiny fireplace—a younger man and an older woman with similar features. Byron Rosepetal and his mother Elsa, almost certainly. *The room must belong to one of them. The victim. But which one?*

There was no sign of a murder, though. He raised an eyebrow at Indree.

"He's in the bedroom." Indree pointed at the doorway across the chamber. "Go ahead."

He. So it's Byron. With growing unease, Tane strode through the next doorway, Indree and Kadka just behind.

He wouldn't have thought so much blood could come out of a man so small.

Byron Rosepetal lay on his small bed on a dais at the far side of the room, but he was unrecognizable as the man in the painting above the fireplace. A bronze spike had been driven down through his face, pinning it against the pillow. On a larger man, it might have left the facial features intact, but a sprite's head was small enough that the inch-wide spike had crushed it almost from ear to ear. Some death-spasm had crookedly unfurled one dragonfly-like wing from his back, its natural iridescence masked by the matte wine-red of dried blood. The same color stained the sheets and the mattress and the dais, running over the edge to pool on the floor below.

Tane's stomach heaved, and he looked away.

But not before noticing one last detail: the spike through Byron Rosepetal's face wasn't a spike at all.

It was sculpted into the shape of an archaic mage's staff, with a crown encircling the head.

The sigil of the Knights of the Emperor.

CHAPTER THREE

———

TANE COULDN'T MAKE himself look any closer. *Spellfire, there's nothing left of his face.*

Kadka was less squeamish. She stepped up to examine the body, and out of the corner of his eye, Tane saw her bend down to peer at the staff-spike jutting from the victim's head. "Is same symbol on Nieris' badge, yes?"

"It is," Tane confirmed, swallowing against nausea. "The Mage Emperor's sigil. Or it was, once. Now the Knights of the Emperor are using it. If we believe they even exist." The ex-chancellor had supposedly been one of those Knights, and killed Allaea for them in an attempt to sabotage the Protectorate's first airship. He'd claimed there were more who would carry on the work, but after the incident aboard the Hesliar, neither Tane nor the constabulary had been able to trace the order any further. To find any sign that they existed outside of Nieris' broken mind.

Until now.

Still trying to avoid the grisly scene at the far end of the room, Tane glanced at Indree. "Is this why you brought us here? I thought you said *we* were suspects. I never found anything more than you did about the Knights of the Emperor."

"It's more than that," Indree said. She stepped forward to grab Kadka's arm, preventing her from touching the spike. "Let me show you. Tane, you're going to have to look."

Reluctantly, Tane turned toward the body once more. If he unfocused his eyes, it almost looked unreal, like a toy—a scene laid out by some deeply disturbed child. He wasn't sure if that made it better, or worse.

Indree took a handkerchief from her breast pocket and covered her fingers, then reached out and gave the crown at the end of the spike a half-turn. It moved easily at her touch, clearly designed to do so. A band of copper ran around the outside of the crown, etched with a series of glyphs that flared a sudden silver-blue.

A face appeared, suspended in the air above Byron Rosepetal's ruined one. Or rather, a mask. It was metallic, probably brass, featureless but for two slitted eyeholes that glowed from behind with silver-blue light. Etched down the middle, the Mage Emperor's crowned staff stretched from chin to forehead, separating the smooth oval into two halves. The eye-slits appeared to be staring directly at Tane. He took a step to one side, and the mask shifted to follow his movement. *An illusion. It has to be.* Even as he thought it, Kadka swept her fingers across the space, and they passed freely through.

Suddenly, a deep, distorted voice boomed from behind the mask. *"The Emperor Who Will Be is soon crowned. And on that day, it is not the mages who will break."*

The mask flickered out of existence.

Silence for a long moment, and then Tane said, "'Not the mages who will break'. You think that's about us. Some kind of taunt for the Magebreakers." He scowled, and not only because he'd said 'Magebreakers' aloud. He didn't much like the idea that a man might have been murdered to send him and Kadka a message.

"I think so," said Indree. "There are rumors about what you did to Nieris, and if these Knights of the Emperor are real, they can't be pleased about it. But all my superiors can see is that you're involved somehow. Chief Durren wants you brought in. I hoped you might know something, or find something I didn't. Something to send the investigation in another direction."

"So our reactions pass muster, then?" Tane asked, quirking up an eyebrow.

"I never really thought you'd killed someone, Tane. You know that. But I had to do this right, for appearances."

"And real killer doesn't turn so green at sight of blood, I think," said Kadka, with a toothy grin that was far from appropriate for the situation.

Tane shot Kadka a glare, and then looked back at Indree. "Fine. I don't have the first idea who did this or why, but if there's something to find we'd better find it before some idiot decides to arrest us." *Ugh, that means I'm going to have to get closer, doesn't it?* Reluctantly, he approached Byron Rosepetal's bed. "What have you got so far?"

"His mother came to check on him when he didn't come for breakfast this morning, and found him like this," said Indree. "Divinations on the body say he was killed last night, about an hour before midnight. But that's all. He was asleep when he died, so no final memory. And our diviners can't find a trace of anyone on the murder weapon at all."

There wasn't much to see in the bed or on the floor. Just blood. "None?" Tane looked over his shoulder at Indree with a raised eyebrow. "You mean it was masked, or…"

"Not masked," said Indree. "There's just nothing there, like no one had touched it before it went through the victim's head."

"Mask is meant to hide traces, yes?" Kadka asked with a furrowed brow. "This is different? How do you know?"

"It's hard to erase the past," said Tane. "Masking traces on an object usually just means blurring Astral signatures so they're hard to follow. In the black market they'll purposely pass goods between enough hands that any meaningful signature gets lost in the noise. But if there's no signature but the victim's... either no one has touched this thing for a long while, or whoever did is somehow invisible to divination."

"Like you," Indree said, looking thoughtfully at Kadka.

Kadka raised her hands. "Not me. Was with Carver."

"No, of course you didn't kill him," Indree clarified. "But we could be looking for someone *like* you. Full-blooded orcs are hard to divine, but I've managed it before—it would have to be another half-orc."

"Possible," said Tane, "but where did they come from? I've never even *seen* one besides Kadka. Or heard of one, for that matter, outside a few undetailed accounts in texts at the University. And I get the impression there aren't many even in Sverna. Isn't that right, Kadka?"

Kadka nodded. "Happens, but rare. I never meet another."

"So for all we know, the Astral invisibility could be a random fluke of birth, unique to her," said Tane. "And even if there's another half-orc in Thaless with the same ability, it would only explain getting by detection spells. Physical wards still stop even Kadka when she lacks the right permissions, and I promise you no half-orc has open access to a Senate house." Tane wasn't entirely sure how Kadka's magical elusiveness worked, but it only seemed to apply to Astral detection. A ward didn't need to search the Astra—if a creature was physically touching it, it didn't need to know anything but that they *lacked* proper permission.

"I suppose it's not very likely," Indree admitted. "Look, I'm grasping for any lead at all. We haven't found anything remotely solid. That's why *you're* here."

Tane gestured at the staff-spike jutting from Byron Rosepetal's body, and winced again at the sight. "What about the gem?" There was a small topaz embedded in the handle, mostly unclouded. "You have to be able to divine the mage who powered it. There's no hiding that."

"We followed it up," Indree said. "A bulk supplier from the Stooketon Circle markets. We're questioning her, but most likely it's just one of thousands like it sold every day."

"So you really haven't found *anything?*" Tane asked. "No witnesses, no triggered detections?"

"No one in the house heard anything," Indree said. "None of the guards saw anyone enter the grounds or the house. No detection spells were triggered. By all appearances, nobody was here at all. But *someone* killed this man, and it certainly wasn't a suicide. And whoever did it, they passed through formidable wards around the house and the estate. The Rosepetals can afford the best."

Tane glanced over his shoulder at Indree. "Portals are blocked on the grounds too, I assume." That was standard practice for any suite of security spells—portals were exceptionally dangerous. And in the wake of the Nieris scandal, wards against them had been tightened all over Thaless.

"They are," Indree confirmed. "Not even the family can open one, unless they lower the blocking spells."

Tane nodded. "So the question is, how did the killer get in?"

"Here," said Kadka. She was peering at a large window that opened onto a lower section of gabled roof. "Came in here. Sill is scuffed." She tested the lower pane; it lifted easily. "And unlocked."

"Of course it is," Tane muttered. "Why bother to lock things when you have wards? Magic*never* fails."

Indree ignored him and gave Kadka a nod. "I noticed the same thing. But there are guards all over the estate in addition to the detections and wards. How anyone *got* to this window unseen, I haven't the faintest idea"

Tane glanced around the walls, noting the ward glyphs near the ceiling. "The wards are keyed to Astral signature?"

Indree gave him a short nod. "They're down for the investigation. You probably noticed when we came in. The outer estate wards work off a simple guest list, which is easy enough to manage, but this one is too much trouble to add permissions to."

"I use something like it for my office," said Tane. "As close to flawless as it gets. No badges to steal or semantics to abuse." Spells and wards worked by making requests of the Astra, the plane of magical energy that lay behind the physical world, and the Astra interpreted instructions very literally. Precision and specificity were key. In this case, the ward was set to allow passage only by specific Astral link. Every guest had to provide a divination focus—hair, blood, fingernail clippings—to be added to the ward's exemptions.

"I always wonder with powerful wards, why do they not stop more? Air." The corner of Kadka's mouth turned up to reveal her teeth. "Clothes."

"Anything worn reasonably close to the skin is folded into a person's Astral signature unless a spell is specifically told otherwise," said Tane. "Largely because of the problem you're alluding to so tastefully. The Astra is fairly literal, but it does obey certain conventions if they become common enough. As for air, wards are usually keyed to sentient things. That glyph there"—he pointed to the ward glyphs, at a circle with the upper arc of a half-circle inside it—"basically means 'everything sentient'. There are refinements from there, and inclusions. Let through harmless animals, keep out obvious dangers like fire and lightning. But for anyone capable of higher thought, there's no way around a ward like this. If it doesn't recognize your Astral signature, you're not getting in. That's a distinction used often in spellcraft—sentient versus non-sentient. Wards mostly care about the former, but the latter is a standard safety precaution. There are plenty of spells and artifacts you don't want to be able to hurt people."

"Like Irondriver's stove," Kadka offered.

"Right," said Tane. "If he'd used the proper restrictions, Miss Eutrice couldn't have been burned. It's actually interesting: the glyph for 'all things', or 'everything', is a plain circle, and originally if you wanted a broadly targetted spell you refined from there. But the distinction between sentient and non-sentient came up often enough that mages got into the habit of short-handing the glyphs. An inner half-circle, upward"—he nodded again toward the same half-circle within a circle on the ceiling—"for 'all things sentient', and downward for 'all things not'. Which is convenient enough, but in some ways it's an example of why magic can be so unreliable. Like I said before, common enough conventions become ingrained in the Astra, so even a language designed for precision like the *lingua* can morph through—"

"It never ceases to amaze me," Indree interrupted, "that someone who distrusts magic so much always sounds so happy talking about the minutiae of magical process. But perhaps this isn't the time?"

Tane flushed slightly. He'd almost managed to forget, for a moment, the grisly scene in front of him. "Sorry. My point is, the strictness of the ward should narrow things down. The voice behind that mask had to be on the list of ward exemptions. Probably someone who was in the house already. The window sill could have been scuffed as a mislead."

"That's where it gets complicated," said Indree. "This wasn't the only murder."

"What?" Tane whirled to face her. "When?"

"The night before last. Ulnod Stooke."

Tane knew the name—the junior senator of House Stooke, the Senate's sole gnomish house. Who, as it happened, had something very important in common with Byron Rosepetal. "Another non-magical member of a Senate house. And let me guess: the similarities don't end there."

"I can show you," Indree said. She didn't wait for an answer; her eyes went unfocused for an instant.

And then Tane was somewhere else. Through Indree's eyes, he could see the scene of the Stooke murder. A young gnomish man, lying in his bed with a bronze staff driven through his face, just like Byron Rosepetal. But unlike the sprite, Ulnod Stooke's features were largely intact. The spike went through his forehead, slightly off-center to the left, and just below it a pair of empty green eyes stared sightlessly at the ceiling. He had the broad face common to his people, with small round ears, a large nose, and a wide mouth. Rivulets of blood ran down his temples, forked around his nose and ears, stained his lips. The bed beneath him was soaked crimson. There was no denying the similarity between the two crimes.

Tane had to swallow back another wave of nausea, even as the image faded. "Spellfire, give me some warning before you do that."

"You'll live," said Indree.

Kadka was looking at him impatiently. "What is it? I don't see sending." Her Astral invisibility meant even a divination as simple as a sending couldn't find her without a focus--inconvenient, sometimes.

"I was right," said Tane. "They were both killed in the same way."

Indree nodded. "Both in their sleep, so we have no final memories to work with. Both with a bronze staff like this one, driven through the skull, without a trace left on it for divination."

Tane couldn't help but shift his eyes to Byron's bloody bed, there. A question came to his lips, one he wasn't sure he wanted to know the answer to. One he *had* to know the answer to. "Was the illusion set into the crown the same? Do you think… was it a message for me and Kadka?"

Indree shook her head. "The same image of the mask, but a different message. No reference to the Mage-breakers, at least not that I could see. Here."

She muttered in the *lingua*, and suddenly the image of a faceless mask bearing the Mage Emperor's sigil was hovering before her—an evoked illusion, this time, so Kadka could see. That strange distorted voice intoned, "*The time of the magical draws near. All praise the Emperor Who Will Be.*"

Nothing about Magebreakers. Which meant the message here at the Rosepetal manor could just be unfortunate wording. Considering two men were dead, Tane felt a little bit guilty over the surge of relief that came with that. If the Stookes were involved, he very much didn't want to be. Didn't want to reopen old wounds.

Kadka cocked her head. "The Emperor Who Will Be. Same in both. Who is this? Man behind mask?"

"I don't think so," said Indree. "These messages talk about him in the third person, like the masked man is some sort of herald. But whose, I can't say."

"Maybe no one's," Tane said. "We can't be sure it's more than some lunatic's wishful thinking. But I have a bad feeling that our killer has someone specific in mind." He looked to Indree. "What do you think?"

"I'm not certain of anything yet," said Indree. "But Byron Rosepetal and Ulnod Stooke didn't have much in common beyond a lack of magic. Their families aren't known for seeing eye to eye." That was true enough—the Stookes were bankers and merchants with a reputation for fiscal responsibility, and they tended to oppose the Rosep-etals' frequent and extravagant proposals in the Senate. "And when two non-magical junior senators are murdered in two days, it suggests a certain pattern."

Tane nodded. "You might be dealing with a magical extremist targeting candidates for Protector of the Realm, you mean." The highest office in Audish government could only be held by those without magecraft, chosen in the Senate from candidates put forward by the great houses. Most houses used their junior senator appointments as a way to groom such candidates for leadership. "But are you looking for an agent of a vast shadowy order, or just a random fanatic with a Mage Emperor obsession?"

"All I know is that I can't waste any time," said Indree. "We've managed to keep both murders quiet for now, but that won't last. When word gets out, it's going to be a mess. And until we know how it happened, we don't know how to stop the next killing."

"I still don't see how two murder scenes overly complicates things," said Tane. "Compare the exemptions on both sets of wards and look for overlaps. That shouldn't be a very long list of suspects."

"It isn't," Indree agreed. "But whose names do you suppose are on it?"

And then he understood. "Oh. Right."

Kadka looked between the two of them with a raised eyebrow. "I don't see. What is problem?"

"The only people likely to be on the guest list for multiple Senate houses are members of *other* Senate houses," Tane explained. "And investigating families that powerful…"

"It's not easy to get access," Indree finished. "If I make so much as an implication without rock-solid evidence, I'll be looking for a new line of work very soon. And now that you two are involved… rumor has it that you can walk right through wards, or break them wide open with a trick of logic. I have colleagues who would be happy to find a way to put this on you rather than offend a senator."

"So we find something to prove is not us, yes?" said Kadka. She looked at Tane there; so did Indree.

"It's not just about that." Tane glanced back at the lifeless body of Byron Rosepetal, and fought down another wave of nausea. "It could just be coincidental phrasing, but if this message really *is* aimed at us... we might be targets. And I don't like thinking that someone is murdering people in answer to something I did."

"*We* did," Kadka corrected, and crossed the room to grip his shoulder. "Killer taunts us both. We find who is behind this mask together."

"I hope so," said Tane. "But I don't see many answers right now." He gestured to the staff-spike protruding from Byron's broken skull. "All I have is that the placement of the staff is strange, if this is a pro-magical killing. Which doesn't get us any nearer to a suspect."

Indree glanced at the spike. "Strange? What do you mean?"

"Astralites and magical fanatics tend to agree that a person's Astral link is anchored in the heart. Symbolically, at least. If I was trying to make a point about magical superiority, I'd have planted my spike there. Not the face." Tane shrugged. "It isn't much. Maybe our killer just doesn't have a theological bent."

Indree was silent a moment, prodding the inside of her cheek with her tongue, and then, "You're right. It isn't much. That's all you have for me?"

Tane spread his hands helplessly. "Right now it is."

She sighed. "I was afraid of that. I suppose there's no helping it, then."

He knew what that meant without asking. "Do what you have to. We won't put up a fight." He looked pointedly at Kadka. "Will we, Kadka?" A small part of him hoped she'd resist, but there wouldn't be any point. Not with so many bluecaps on the estate.

"Depends on fight." Kadka raised an eyebrow at Indree. "What does he mean?"

Tane answered first. "She's going to have to take us to the Yard."

CHAPTER FOUR

―――――

"WHAT AREN'T YOU telling me, Carver?"

Chief Constable Andus Durren leaned forward over the table in the small interrogation room, his thick mustache inches from Tane's face. A sturdy middle-aged human, Durren's interrogation technique largely hinged upon loudly demanding answers until his cheeks turned as red as the half-circle of thinning hair about his temples.

"Not a thing, Chief Durren," said Tane. "I have nothing to hide. Haven't your divinations told you that yet?"

"We both know that wouldn't stop you from lying." Durren had cast a truth-spell, at the start—like all constables, he was a trained mage—but Tane had a reputation for evading divinations. A fact that was apparently very frustrating for a man used to getting information the easy way.

And equally frustrating for Tane, when he didn't actually have anything to lie about. "Look," he said wearily. "That message *might* have been aimed at me and Kadka, but it might just as easily have been an unfortunate phrasing. And if it *was* for us, why should that mean we're involved? We can't control who hears about the 'Magebreakers'"—he grimaced as he said it—"or what they decide to do about it." He already knew it wouldn't work. He'd been under interrogation for more than an hour, and explained his position too many times to count.

"You're always involved!" Durren barked. "You and that orc of yours."

"Half-orc," Tane corrected. "Her name is Kadka. And she's not 'mine'. We're partners." Presumably she was undergoing similar questioning in one of the other rooms. *And probably making it more difficult than I ever could.* Kadka's Astral invisibility meant none of their truth-spells would work on her. She'd just give them whatever answers amused her most, and grin that unsettling grin that showed every one of her sharp, lupine teeth. Tane smiled slightly, imagining some high-ranking constable squirming in discomfort at the sight.

Durren snorted. "I don't care what her name is. What I care about is how often you two happen to be nearby when something goes wrong. You've done more than enough damage to this city already. You aren't talking your way out of trouble this time."

He's never going to listen. He wants to believe he has something on us. According to Indree, Durren had resented Tane and Kadka since the incident with Nieris and the airship—a high-profile case they'd solved when his constables couldn't. It wasn't supposed to be public knowledge, but rumors had spread, and the chief constable wasn't a man who took well to being upstaged.

But the last thing Tane wanted was another hour of this. He had to try. "I know you think we're a menace, but most of that damage wasn't our fault. How many times do I have to tell you that Kadka and I didn't dig that tun—"

The door to Tane's right swung open, and a familiar voice interrupted him midsentence.

"Chief Durren," said Lady Abena Jasani, Protector of the Realm. "I hope you'll forgive my intrusion."

What is she doing here? It couldn't be a coincidence—the Lady Protector didn't just walk into random interrogation rooms on a whim.

Lady Abena wore a topcoat as black as her short, tightly curled hair, with trousers and boots to match. Her deep brown skin made her Anjican heritage obvious—House Jasani's roots were in Estian occupied territories on the southern continent from before the Mage War. Unlike Durren, she didn't demand attention with red-faced bluster; she simply entered a room, and all eyes went to her before she said a word. Tane hadn't met very many people with that kind of presence, and fewer still with the wisdom to use it well. Abena Jasani, in his experience, had both.

Durren and Tane both rose in their seats as the Lady Protector stepped inside. One of her Mageblades—devoted protectors of all who held her office—stepped in after her, a lithe elven woman wearing a brass cuirass over a crisp blue and white uniform. The Mageblade moved to stand at attention just beside the door, her hands never straying far from the glyph-etched saber and dual ancryst pistols at her waist.

"Never an intrusion, Lady Abena," Durren said, unconsciously smoothing down the front of his uniform with one hand. "At your service, always. What do you need?"

"I understand you've been asking Mister Carver and Miss Kadka some questions." Lady Abena greeted Tane with a nod there. "Admirably thorough, given the message found at the scene. I'm sure they've been very cooperative, given their past service to the Protectorate."

Durren looked sidelong at Tane, a slight frown beneath his bushy mustache. "Yes, well—"

"Excellent. In that case, I do need to speak to Mister Carver, and I'm sure you were just finishing up. Mister Carver, you've shared everything you know, haven't you?"

"Of course, your Ladyship." Tane flashed Durren a quick smirk.

"Then I'm sure Chief Durren has more important things to do," Lady Abena said, in a tone that made it clear she wasn't asking. "Let me take him off your hands, Andus."

Durren's cheeks flushed, but he was trapped. It went against the man's nature to argue with anyone more wealthy and powerful than he was, and even if he'd decided to be stubborn, he had no strong evidence against Tane. "Yes, your Ladyship," he said with obvious reluctance. "Is there anything else?"

"Yes," said Lady Abena. "I would appreciate it if you gave us the room for a moment. And please, have Miss Kadka brought to me as well." Behind her, the elven Mageblade was already pushing the door open.

"It would be my pleasure, of course." Durren's face was an angry red from his neck to the bare expanse of his scalp, an absurd contrast to his ingratiating tone. "And if you need anything else from me before you go, I'll be in my office." With a final, furious glance at Tane, he strode out the open door.

When the door had swung closed again, Tane bowed his head to Lady Abena in gratitude. "Thank you, your Ladyship. He would have kept me in here until I admitted to every crime in Thaless for the last six weeks."

Lady Abena regarded Tane for a moment before answering, and then, "You *did* tell him everything you know, I hope. Audland owes you a debt, and I believe Inspector Lovial when she tells me you are innocent, but you do strike me as someone who might find it tempting to frustrate Chief Durren."

"There was nothing to tell," Tane said. "I don't know anything."

"And yet the killer's message *could* have been directed at you and Miss Kadka. The wording was… unusual."

"Trust me," said Tane, "the possibility looms fairly large in my mind just now. I'm not thrilled at the thought of a murderer taking a personal interest in me."

A knock at the door before Lady Abena could answer, and then Indree's voice from the other side: "Your Ladyship?"

Lady Abena motioned for her Mageblade to open the door once more, and Indree led Kadka in.

"Inspector Lovial," Lady Abena said with a welcoming nod. "You two can thank her for this reprieve. She contacted me on your behalf. You're very fortunate I was able to get away from preparing for my trip to the Continent." The Lady Protector was following the success of her airship treaty with a diplomatic tour of the Calenean continent aboard the Hesliar. It had been a popular talking point in the streets and taverns of Thaless in recent weeks.

"Lucky us," Tane said wryly. "I owe you a favor, Ree."

Indree smirked at him. "You owe me a thousand. I'm not holding my breath on repayment."

"I did offer you that dinner," he countered. "Which you still haven't taken me up on."

"Well," Indree said, "maybe if you two stopped breaking the city every week, I'd have time."

A loud crack from Kadka's neck headed off Tane's response. "Is good you get us out," she said to Indree, rolling her head from side to side. "Hear same questions much longer, maybe I break little gnome woman's nose on table, get thrown in cells." She grinned. "Better this way, but not so satisfying."

"I'm sure Inspector Gabbins appreciates your restraint," Indree said dryly, and then dipped her head to the Lady Protector. "Lady Abena, thank you for coming. I'm sorry to bother you with this, but I don't like to see time and resources wasted on a dead end. Chief Durren…" She hesitated there, and shook her head. "I'm sorry. I shouldn't… it's not my place."

"You need not censor yourself in front of me, Inspector Lovial," Lady Abena said with a small smile. "I haven't yet clapped anyone in irons for speaking honestly. And I assure you, I am well aware of the chief constable's shortcomings. But with his political allies… suffice it to say, I am doing what I can. For now, I can only ask that you do the same. Word of the murders will be on the streets by tomorrow at the latest, and I fear the connection to the Knights of the Emperor may lead to panic. The demonstrations these last weeks have caused enough unrest in the city already."

"You mean Silver Dawn?" Kadka asked. "You think they have hand in this? Usually they just yell." The Silver Dawn was a loosely organized group of protestors emboldened by the recent decision to allow non-magicals to attend the University. Their criticism of the inequalities in Audish society was seen by some as close to treasonous, and a number of their demonstrations of late had taken a turn toward angry confrontation.

"They haven't hurt anyone yet," Indree said. "And they're in favor of non-magical rights. These murders don't seem to fit their agenda."

"I have no reason to believe they're directly involved," Lady Abena clarified. "They have the right to their protests, of course, so long as no one is harmed, but their presence has already invited counter-protestors. Tensions between the magical and non-magical are already high, and word of a killer who may have pro-magical motives will only fan the flames. I am in the midst of certain diplomatic negotiations, and it will hardly strengthen our position if the citizenry or the Senate are losing their heads over—" She paused there, frowned. "A poor choice of words, given the circumstances, but true all the same. I have already assigned my Mageblades to patrol the Roost, but I would prefer they not be necessary. The person behind this mask must be apprehended before anyone else dies. And if Nieris' phantom knights are in fact real, they need to be stopped."

Indree stood tall and gave a firm nod. "I will do everything in my power to make that happen, Lady Abena."

"I expect nothing more, or less," said Lady Abena.

"Mister Carver, Miss Kadka, I must ask you not to insert yourselves into Inspector Lovial's investigation except where she asks. Your past service is greatly appreciated, but this *is* a sensitive matter, and you two do have a history of… somewhat less than sensitive methods. After tomorrow afternoon, I will be unavailable to extract you from any trouble you might find yourselves in for some time."

"Listen," Tane said defensively, "we didn't *dig* that—"

"They'll be good, Lady Abena," Indree interrupted. "I'll make sure of it."

"Very well." Lady Abena gestured to her Mageblade, who opened the door for her. She fixed Indree with one last solemn look. "I am placing a great deal of faith in you, Inspector Lovial. I cannot delay my tour, so I must leave this matter in your hands. Please don't disappoint me." With that, she strode out of the room. The elven Mageblade followed after her, letting the door swing closed once more.

"Rather make killer angry than her, I think," Kadka said, and flashed Indree a grin. "Best solve this, yes?"

"That's the plan." Indree sounded confident enough, but Tane could tell Lady Abena's last words had shaken her. The Lady Protector had been very generous with the three of them, but she was still the most powerful woman in the Protectorate. "Although I wouldn't mind a little bit more to go on."

Kadka clapped Indree on the shoulder. "We will help. If message is for us, is our problem too. Right Carver?"

"That depends on Indree," Tane said, and looked to her with a raised eyebrow. "You heard Lady Abena: this is her investigation." He kept his tone controlled and his breathing even, in case she tried a truth-spell. He wasn't about to let this go—not until he was sure the killer hadn't aimed that message at him and Kadka.

Indree rolled her eyes. "Right. I'm sure if I said so you'd just go home and forget all about this."

Kadka cackled at that. "Knows you too well, Carver."

So much for that. "There's a first time for everything?" Tane ventured.

"Don't try so hard," said Indree. "You'll break something. Look, I don't *want* to cut you out of this. I have two candidates for our next Protector dead, and someone found a way to bypass a lot of wards and divinations to do it. I need to know how, and you're the expert on that. Can we agree that if I keep you two involved, you'll follow my lead and try to keep yourselves beneath Chief Durren's notice?"

"I'll take that," said Tane. "Kadka?"

Kadka nodded. "Is fair."

"It's a deal, then," Indree said, and pulled open the door. "Come on, I'll see you out for now. I'm going to have to spend some time reassuring Chief Durren that he's still in charge before anything else."

They'd barely stepped out the door when a trembling, high-pitched voice pierced the air.

"*You!*"

A blur of motion, and then something struck Tane in the chest. A blonde woman, no more than a foot tall, fluttering on iridescent dragonfly wings. She gripped Tane's collar in one fist and battered his chest with the other, tears rolling down her face.

He knew who she was. Her deep red and green dress was too finely made and expensive for anyone else. And besides, he'd seen her picture hanging above the fireplace just outside the murder scene.

Elsa Rosepetal. The senior senator of House Rosepetal, and one of the most powerful women in the city.

Tane took a startled step back; she moved with him, still clutching his collar. "Senator, I—"

She beat her hand against his chest once more. "This is your fault!" Rage glinted in her teary eyes. "That message was for you! You *Magebreakers!* My son is dead because of you! Both of you!" She cast her glare towards Kadka, but didn't let go of Tane's shirt.

Kadka reached out for the furious sprite, but Tane held up a hand to stop her. "If this *was* a message for us, I'm truly sorry, Senator Rosepetal," he said. It was hard to meet her eyes without imagining Byron Rosepetal's head crushed under a brass spike, but he forced himself to do it all the same. *I owe her that much.* "I promise you, I'm going to do everything I can to help—"

"*Help?*" Elsa laughed bitterly. "My son is already dead. There is *nothing* you can do for him now." Finally, she released his collar and fluttered back a short distance. "Consider yourself lucky that this place is warded against unauthorized magic, or I would kill you where you stand."

"I…" But Tane couldn't find an answer to that. *Is someone killing people to get my attention?* He didn't *want* to believe it, and as far as he knew there had been nothing at the Stooke manor to suggest a pattern. But it had been easier to deny when the consequences had been distant, abstract. Before a grieving mother had grabbed him by the collar.

I need to know there was nothing at the other scene. I need to be sure.

Several constables were closing in around them, and Indree stepped between Tane and Elsa. "You're upset, Senator," she said, "so I'm going to let that threat pass. I wouldn't suggest saying anything else of the sort in the middle of Stooketon Yard." She beckoned to an approaching sprite in bluecap uniform. "Constable Sweetleaf will see you to your carriage. And while it may not come as much comfort now, know that we *will* find the person who did this."

"You're right," Elsa said in a dull, flat voice. "It's no comfort at all." But she went with Constable Sweetleaf, and didn't look back. Tane watched them go until they passed around a corner and out of sight.

"I know that look," Indree said after a moment. "The deal's off, isn't it?"

Tane turned to her with his best innocent face. "I don't know what you mean."

"Don't bother, Tane. I know you. A bereaved mother tells you it's all your fault and I'm supposed to believe you're still willing to wait on procedure? You've already decided you owe her this. And you're not going to listen when I tell you any guilt is on the killer, not you. I'm not going to be able to keep you in line short of throwing you in a cell."

Astra, she does *know me too well.* He could lie well enough to fool spells, but Indree saw right through him. Tane offered her his wrists. "If that's what you think you have to do."

Indree sighed, and reached into her pocket. But she didn't come out with handcuffs. Instead, she drew out a small artifact—a brass locket-like enclosure with a glass front. She grabbed Tane's wrist, turned his palm upward, and pressed the little device into it. Through the glass, he could see a small lock of her hair, held in place by a copper clasp.

She wasn't locking him up. For some reason, she was giving him exactly what he wanted.

"I can't let you into the scene at the Stooke manor without supervision, but the family is staying at their townhouse off Stooketon Circle while we investigate," Indree said. "Number 9 Oolai Street. Maybe something they saw will mean more to you than it did to me. You can use this to contact me, day or night."

Kadka leaned over Tane's shoulder to look at the locket. "What is it?"

"A sending locket," he said. "It lets people who can't use magic contact those who can. When I squeeze it, the person the divination focus inside belongs to—Ree, in this case—feels a sort of tingle through the Astra. An indication to open a sending between us." Tane couldn't think of any particular reason for Indree to have one on hand unless she'd made it particularly for him. Which was either flattering or patronizing—he couldn't decide which.

"So we can go?" Kadka asked, cocking her head at Indree. "Without bluecaps watching? You don't worry that we break another street?" She half-grinned, exposing sharp teeth at one side of her mouth."

"Oh, I worry," said Indree. "But you'll find a way to cause trouble no matter what I do. And the truth is, I... I need you." Her eyes darted to the side there, away from Tane's. "Whether I can control you or not. I've got nothing to go on right now, and there's no reason to believe the killer won't go after someone else very soon."

"Well that can't have been easy for you to admit." Tane knew he shouldn't gloat, but it was hard to resist.

"Shut up, Tane." Indree fixed him with a glare as hot as spellfire. "Don't forget, I could lock you up for the night instead."

Tane just held up his hands in surrender. *Better not push her. She might actually do it.* He needed to hear what the Stookes had to say, and he couldn't do that from a cell.

"Smart," Indree said. "Now go find me something. And when you do, I'd better be the first person you tell. Or if you get in any kind of trouble. *Anything* happens, and I want to know before anyone else. If Chief Durren learns I gave you free rein..." She looked between the two of them, prodding her cheek with her tongue, and then, "I'm going to regret this, aren't I?"

"When have we ever let you down?" Tane asked with a slight smile.

Indree gave a resigned shake of her head. "Just go," she said. "Before I change my mind." Then, to their backs as they hurried down the hall:

"And this ought to go without saying, but *try* not to get yourselves killed."

CHAPTER FIVE

THE STOOKE'S TOWNHOUSE wasn't far from Stooketon Yard. Both were in the Stooketon district of Thaless, a center of trade and commerce named for the powerful merchant house itself. Some of the neighborhoods were more affluent than Tane was used to, home to successful traders and speculators, but even so he felt more at home here than he did in the Gryphon's Roost. This was wealth on a level he could *almost* understand—no manor estates, just tall joined houses with gabled roofs, clean and well-maintained.

The townhouse was on an expensive residential street just off the markets of Stooketon Circle at the district's center. Each house was uniquely designed and appointed, and few were smaller than four floors, but they bore some distant relationship to the single-room brickfront rows in Porthaven—like wealthy third cousins, long estranged but related all the same. Tane supposed the Stookes kept the place for visiting family and guests, because no one in the order of succession of a Senate house would settle for such modest accomodation under normal circumstances. *Modest.* He snorted. *My office would fit twice over on the bottom floor alone.*

"Is this one," Kadka said as they drew near. 'Number 9." The number was wrought in brass and affixed above the townhouse's letterbox.

It was easily the nicest house on the street, a tall off-white facade with a deep green door and matching green shutters and gables on the upper floors. A brass badger's head protruded open-mouthed at the door's center where a knocker should have been, but it lacked a ring to knock with. There were no guards, which was curious, given the circumstances, but a family like the Stookes could afford powerful magical security—perhaps they thought hired men unnecessary.

"Let me do the talking," said Tane. "I think they'll let us in if they know it's me." His fingers moved to his waist pocket and brushed over his dented watch case. His father's. It didn't tick under his fingers—there was no clockwork inside, not since the ancryst rail accident that had taken his parents from him.

"You know senators?" Kadka raised a bushy eyebrow. "You never say this before." She grinned. "And you have not so many friends."

"I don't *know* them, exactly. But we have… history." History he'd been happy never to leverage before. He wasn't particularly eager to do it now.

Kadka shrugged. "Fine. But you tell me this story."

"I don't want to get into it twice," said Tane. "It will be obvious enough in a moment or two. Come on." He marched past her and up the short stair leading to the door. There was no visible knocker, but a small copper plate sat on the right side of the doorframe with a glyph engraved at its center. Tane pressed his thumb against the glyph, and heard a bell chime inside the house.

"Who's there?"

A young male voice, but it didn't come from the other side of the door. Rather, it issued from the mouth of the brass badger. A simple voice-casting artifact, not uncommon for those who often received unwanted guests.

"My name is Tane Carver. I'm here with my partner, Kadka. We want to talk to you about the… the recent tragedy. We might be able to help."

"Carver?" the voice repeated, with a trace of recognition. A short pause, and then, "You're the ones they're calling Magebreakers."

Tane grimaced at the use of that title, but he didn't fight it. This wasn't the time or place. "Yes. But that's not where you know my name from." He was taking a chance, there—this might be some servant who had no idea what that meant. But he didn't think a servant would have said his name that way.

"No," said the voice. "It isn't. You and I have things to talk about besides my… my brother, don't we?"

"We do. Will you let us in, Endo?" There was only one person that voice could belong to: Endo Stooke, the younger son of Umbla Stooke. His mother was the head of the house and senior senator, and his elder brother the junior senator and a potential candidate for Protector of the Realm, but it was Endo who most interested Tane. He'd heard that name a great many times when he was younger.

Too many times.

No answer for a moment, and then, "I have to check with my mother. Please, wait in the receiving chamber."

Tane heard the lock click, and then the door swung open under an invisible force. There was no one behind it, just a small white-walled room, empty save for the cushioned benches on either side. At the far end, another green door stood closed—and locked, Tane assumed. Beside it at eye level, a brass panel on the wall drew his attention. A lens of blue glass or crystal sat in the center of the panel, surrounded in engraved glyphs, and below it was what looked like a small drawer with no handle. He had no idea what it was for, and he could usually identify an artifact on sight.

But it didn't matter, just then. He stepped inside,

through the tingle of a ward, and beckoned for Kadka to follow.

She did, and closed the door behind them. "Is farther than I think we get," she said with a grin. "Shouldn't wards be stronger? Like one you say checks Astra, at Rosepetal house."

"The real ones start on the next door, I'd guess," Tane said. "I've heard of wealthier families doing this— minor wards on the receiving chamber so guests can sit while they wait on being added to the exemptions on the stronger ones. I imagine a servant will be along shortly to take divination foci from us. If they decide to let us in."

"You think they will," said Kadka. "Why? Why does this man know your name?"

"Like I said, you'll understand soon enough." Tane sat himself down on a green cushioned bench and stretched out his legs.

Kadka didn't press the issue, just walked over to the strange brass panel and leaned in to examine the inert blue lens. She tapped a thick half-orc fingernail against it. "What is this, then?"

"I don't know," said Tane. "I've never seen one before."

Kadka looked over her shoulder at him. "Magic you don't know? First time I hear you say this."

"Umbla Stooke's son Endo is supposedly quite the artificer," said Tane. "This is probably his work. Not much of it ends up out in the world. From what I hear, his inventions are brilliant but far too expensive for anyone with less money than a Senate house."

"Drawer here has no handle." Kadka pried around the edge of the little brass drawer with her claw-like nail. "How does it open?"

"Kadka, don't play with it."

The warning came too late. A chime sounded from the panel, and silver-blue light lit the lens from behind. A brass iris flared out behind blue glass as the lens focused on Kadka like an eye. Tane heard metal moving on metal from the other direction, a bolt sliding into place. The outside door locking.

That can't be good.

Kadka took a step back. "What is—"

Before she could finish, a spider the size of Tane's head dropped onto her shoulder from above.

"Spellfire!" Tane leapt to his feet; an instant later another one of the things fell on the bench where he'd just been sitting. And it wasn't a spider, not like he'd thought.

Not a living one, at least.

An oblong brass body with several panels set into the sides sat atop eight brass legs, each hinged and jointed into three segments. At the center of the body, surrounded in etched glyphs, a lens like the one on the wall panel glowed silver-blue. A brass iris narrowed and dialated behind the light.

An automaton. Artificers had been experimenting with such things for centuries, trying to make automated artifacts, or even golems—humanoid automatons that could operate independently. But Tane had never seen any as advanced as this. The spells behind such a thing usually only allowed the most basic function, and then not for long without incredibly expensive gems for power. They were a novelty, a dream.

But this one was very real. It gathered its legs beneath it and leapt at Tane, and he stumbled backwards with a terrified cry.

Not fast enough. Its legs caught in his vest, and it started climbing towards his face. One of its side panels opened, and a copper-tipped wand extended on a segmented brass arm. He very much didn't want to learn what its function was.

"Kadka!" Tane shouted, grabbing the brass spider on his chest and trying to yank it free. Its legs undulated wildly, another hooking into the fabric of his vest each time he dislodged one. The wand-arm jabbed at his face, but he craned his neck away and held the thing just out of reach.

Kadka palmed the spider on her shoulder in one hand and hurled it against the wall. One of its legs broke off at the second joint, and it fell upside down onto the bench below, struggling to right itself. Two more leapt onto her back to replace the one she'd torn free—they were coming from a pair of hatches in the ceiling that Tane hadn't noticed until now. Kadka slammed her back against the wall to dislodge them, and then grabbed the spider on Tane's chest and ripped it away with one hand. His vest tore in several places as the legs lost purchase.

Two more spiders approached, skittering along the walls—they must have had some spell engraved some-where that let them keep purchase on the vertical surface. Kadka raised the spider she'd just torn from Tane's vest and threw it. Her aim was true, striking one automaton from the wall; both it and the one she'd thrown tumbled to the floor, their legs in a tangle.

But more were coming, climbing out of their hatches and moving upside-down along the ceiling. Several had their wand-arms out, and more than a few had exposed sharp-looking three-pronged pincers at the end of similarly jointed arms.

Kadka put herself between Tane and the automatons. "We need out, Carver!" she shouted over her shoulder.

"I know!" But there was nowhere left to retreat, just the door behind them. Tane grabbed the handle and tried in vain to open it. It was locked, just as he'd feared.

I should have brought more charms. He'd used the last on Irondriver, and that one wouldn't have been any use here in any case. He needed a standard shield, something to give them time to force the door. Or maybe just some-thing to blast it off its hinges. But he had nothing. And there were at least ten of the spider-automatons now, crawling along the walls and ceiling.

The spiders swarmed at Kadka, advancing from all di-rections; one leapt down from the ceiling toward Tane, bypassing her altogether. He dodged out of the way, kicked it across the floor. Grabbing the door handle once more, he tugged at it with all his might. "Let us out! She was just looking, she didn't mean anything—"

Cold metal jabbed against his shin, and his whole world went away.

CHAPTER SIX

_____

"I AM *SO* sorry!"

Tane awoke to an unfamiliar voice—almost certainly gnomish, by the pitch—and found himself lying on the floor with Kadka's heavy torso across his legs. She stirred at the same moment, propped herself shakily on her elbow, and looked up at him with unfocused yellow eyes.

"What... what happened?" Tane raised a hand to rub at his face. The movement felt sluggish, like his body was responding to commands a second too late.

"My crawlers got you with their daze-wands," the gnomish voice said, and now Tane recognized it as the one that had greeted them at the door. Endo Stooke. He had to be the man behind the automatons, if his reputation could be believed. "I can't apologize enough." His voice came from the panel by the door—the glowing silver-blue lens set into it appeared to be focused on Tane and Kadka.

"They are... gone?" Kadka shifted her still-bleary eyes to the closed hatches on the ceiling.

Endo spoke through the wall panel once more, timid and abashed. "I called them off. They really shouldn't have attacked you like that."

"Well I suppose I'm grateful," said Tane, "but why *did* they attack, if they weren't meant to?"

"After what happened to Ulnod…" Endo's voice caught there, audible even through the wall panel. "Mother says she can't trust any of the servants or guards until we know who did it. I've been trying to handle the wards and security myself. I haven't… quite calibrated the crawlers correctly. Did one of you try the door, or tamper with anything?"

Kadka looked a little bit sheepish, at least. "Tried little drawer on wall." She pushed herself up, freeing Tane's legs, and then stood, supporting herself against the wall.

"Ah," said Endo. "That's only meant to be opened from this side. They must have seen it as an intrusion attempt. I'm going to have to tighten the wording on their control spells."

"They're automatons, aren't they?" Tane tried to stand, his legs shaking; Kadka offered a hand and helped him up. The lens on the wall shifted and adjusted its brass iris to refocus on them now that they were both standing. "I've never seen one so advanced. Those spells must be incredibly complex."

"Not so much that they don't try to kill us," Kadka said, one corner of her mouth lifting to show her teeth.

Tane shrugged. "No point holding a grudge. It was an accident." And then, in a whisper that he hoped only Kadka could hear, "We still have to get him to let us inside, remember?"

She just grinned wider. "Who says anything about grudge? Metal spiders are magic I don't see before. Was *exciting.*"

"Even so, I *am* sorry," Endo said. "I'll add a warning into the spells so it doesn't happen again."

"It's fine, Endo," said Tane. "It's no wonder these 'crawlers' of yours need fine-tuning. They must have pages on pages of nested spellwork behind every action. That kind of magic would take an attention to detail most people don't have. I'm impressed that they work as well as they do."

"Oh, it's nothing," Endo said through the wall panel, a shy tone in his voice. "I can show you, if you like."

"Does that mean we can come in?" asked Tane.

"Oh, of course!" Endo said. "I'd almost forgotten. I have to apologize again—I shouldn't have made you wait. Mother wants to talk to you. Please, if you would each supply a focus, I can add you to our ward exemptions." As he said it, the little drawer below the lens—the one Kadka had tried to force open—slid out under its own power. Inside were a half-dozen small vials.

"Convenient," said Tane. He reached up to pluck a hair from his head, wincing at the quick stab of pain. "I've never seen one of these panels before. Is it your design?" As he spoke, he took one of the vials, slid the hair inside, and replaced it in the drawer. Following his lead, Kadka did the same.

"It is," Endo said. "I just installed it today. Without a footman to greet guests and retrieve samples, we wouldn't have been able to let guests through the wards unless I did it myself. And Mother wouldn't allow that. I'm all she…" His voice caught in his throat, there, unmistakable even through the panel. "It's just the two of us, now."

"I'm sorry, Endo. I didn't mean to upset you. I was just impressed by the clever design." Tane watched the drawer slide back in, taking their divination foci along with it.

"It's not your fault. And thank you, but I don't know how clever it is. There really isn't much to it." That hint of shyness was back in Endo's voice. "Just give me one moment, and then I can let you in." The lens on the wall went dark—presumably he was seeing to the wards.

"Is nice enough, for rich boy," said Kadka.

"Seems that way," said Tane. He'd imagined what Endo Stooke would be like more than once—polite and humble hadn't been at the top of the list. "But let's not jump to conclusions too quickly. His automatons did just attack us."

"Thought you don't hold a grudge," Kadka said, raising an eyebrow.

"I just didn't want *him* to think I do." Tane knew that wasn't entirely fair, but old habits were hard to break, and youthful grudges tended to linger—no matter how irrational.

A click came from the inner door that had to be the lock opening, and then the lens on the wall glowed once more, just long enough for Endo to say, "Please come in."

Kadka didn't hesitate, just pushed right through the door into the next room—a small entry hall with stairs leading to the upper levels of the house. Taking a deep breath, Tane followed. Gooseflesh rose on his skin as the powerful house wards allowed him through.

Endo Stooke waited on the other side, a gnomish man of perhaps twenty. He sat in a wheeled chair of wood and steel and copper and brass, etched all over with glyphs in the *lingua*. Sitting up with his back straight, his head was just barely above Tane's waist. He was brown-haired and green-eyed, with a broad, pleasant face and the large nose and small round ears common to his people. Tane had known what to expect—Endo's condition was no secret—but even so, he couldn't help but glance down.

Endo's legs ended at the knee. A dark green blanket was draped across his lap, but no feet came out below the bottom edge, and the way the fabric draped limply over the front of his chair made it obvious there was nothing there.

Endo noticed them looking—Kadka was even less subtle about it—and self-consciously adjusted his blanket. "I understand you have some scars of your own," he said to Tane. "I wish I could hide mine so easily."

"I suppose fair is fair," said Tane. He undid the top button of his shirt and exposed his collarbone, where the scars began. They ran all down his torso, souveniers of the ancryst rail accident that had changed his life.

"So it's true," said Endo. "I heard about you after they kicked you out of the University. The Gazette talked about you, the way you used the accident in your dissertation. I thought about coming to meet you, but... I never did. I suppose I was worried we'd just end up arguing over who lost more in the accident."

"You're probably right," Tane admitted. *More right than you know.*

After the accident, the only thing anyone in Thaless had cared about was that a young scion of House Stooke had lost his legs. The Gazette had run dozens of stories about Endo's injuries and recovery, ignoring everyone else who had died. No one had cared that it could have been prevented, if the men and women maintaining the train had possessed a modicum of the magical knowledge reserved—until very recently—for mages. For a long time, Tane had resented the lack of attention to the *true* injustice.

And he'd resented the boy who'd stolen that attention away.

That resentment felt petty now, looking at this shy little man and the terrible injury he'd lived with for all these years. Tane's wounds had been severe, but the mage-surgeons had been able to put him together again. Endo hadn't been so lucky.

"Wait." Kadka looked from Tane to Endo, her eyes widening slightly. "You are in same accident? Carver's accident?"

Endo smiled slightly. "Well, I don't think of it as *his*, but yes." He glanced over his shoulder, down a short hall that led to a closed door. "Mother is waiting. Please, follow me." He twisted a small lever on the arm of his chair; several glyphs engraved in the copper base-plate glowed briefly, and the entire chair swiveled toward the staircase with a strange whirring noise. It had to be magically powered, but Tane had never seen an ancryst vehicle that size.

The smallest ancryst engines were nearly as large as Endo's entire chair.

Kadka was staring at Tane with a hundred questions in her eyes, but he just beckoned for her to follow and strode down the hall after Endo.

"The chair—did you make that too?" Tane asked, watching glyphs on the wheels and around the steering lever glimmer and fade as Endo moved.

"I did," said Endo. "When I was younger, I had a non-magical one. I had to be pushed around everywhere I went. I... didn't like that very much."

"Is it ancryst powered?" Tane asked. "It seems small for that. So did your crawlers, for that matter."

Endo shook his head. "No, I couldn't make an engine small enough. This is entirely spellwork. The crawlers too." Which meant they moved under the power of direct spells rather than engines.

"That must be... expensive," said Tane. Ancryst engines turned magical energy into mechanical by using basic spells to push a piston—the translucent green stone called ancryst reacted to the presence of magic by moving in the opposite direction, which allowed simple magical fields to power complex machinery. Maintaining specific movement and control spells throughout the day would take far more Astral energy, and far more expensive gems to store it.

"It is," said Endo. "Very. I'm still working on making it more efficient. There are people with injuries like mine who can't afford what my family can, and I'd like to help them."

"That's... generous of you." Tane rubbed the back of his neck, feeling particularly churlish for how angry he'd been with this man for so much of his youth.

"How do you use stairs?" Kadka asked bluntly. Tane elbowed her in the side; she didn't even flinch.

If Endo was offended, it didn't show. "That is a difficulty. I've worked levitation spells into the chair, but they take too much power to use very often. We've built ramps into the manor, but here at the townhouse... I tend to stay on the ground floor." He reached the door and pressed his palm against a glyph-engraved copper panel beside it, set low enough for his hand to reach. The door swung open. Another bit of artifice he'd designed himself, Tane assumed. Opening a door by hand would be difficult from the chair.

They entered a sitting room, not overly large but lavishly furnished. The chairs and couches weren't as varied in size as in the Rosepetal manor, but they were enough to accommodate all manner of guests. In a small chair at the far end of the room sat a gnomish woman with features similar to Endo's, her greying brown hair done up in a hasty bun. She was dressed entirely in black—mourning garb for a murdered son—and her eyes were red-rimmed from crying. In her lap, she held a small painted dragon, a child's toy, turning it over in her hands.

"Mother," Endo said softly.

Umbla Stooke looked up at the sound of her son's voice, but her eyes went to Tane and Kadka. "You're the ones they call the Magebreakers?" Her voice trembled.

"We are." Tane had to force himself to meet her eyes, and he didn't correct her on the title. It felt more than a bit voyeuristic to be intruding on the grief of the senior senator of a great house. "I'm very sorry for your loss, Senator."

She didn't acknowledge his condolences, just looked back down at the toy dragon. "Sit."

They did, Tane and Kadka beside each other on an overly-cushioned couch across from the senator. Endo steered his chair in beside them.

Senator Stooke didn't wait for them to settle in. "Endo says you want to help find my Ulnod's killer."

"That's right," said Tane.

"I've heard of you," said the senator. Tane thought she was going to mention the rail accident, but instead, "My son was an admirer."

Tane glanced at Endo, who shook his head. "Not me. My brother. I've followed the rumors, but Ulnod… he devoured every story he could get out of the servants. He particularly liked the idea that you two had something to do with getting the University to accept non-magical students. He always felt a certain kinship for others without magic."

Tane and Kadka shared a look. *Spellfire, that's not what I wanted to hear. Indree wouldn't have had any reason to ask before, but if Ulnod was an admirer…* He'd come hoping to find that the message left with Byron Rosepetal's body was just unfortunate wording, but it was increasingly hard to believe. He gave a slight shake of his head to Kadka to keep her quiet. Better the Stookes not know about the connection, if they didn't already.

He didn't think they would take it well.

Senator Stooke was eyeing Kadka with suspicion. "The way Ulnod told it, you two have caused a great many problems for the constabulary."

Tane raised his hands, palm out, and took a placating tone. "Well, that's not quite—"

"He also said that you get results where they can't." The senator swallowed, and took a long, shaky breath. "I need you to find who killed him. *Please.*"

"We will," said Kadka. "Is what we do." She offered the woman a toothy smile that was, perhaps, meant to be comforting.

Umbla Stooke narrowed her eyes and pursed her lips in apparent distaste. When she spoke again, it was to Tane. "You'll take the case, then?"

Tane didn't much like the way she'd dismissed Kadka. "My partner speaks for both of us," he said firmly. "But we're going to need to know more. Anything you can tell us about Ulnod or the night it happened could be useful." He glanced at Endo. "Either of you. Things you saw or heard, even if they didn't seem important at the time."

"There was nothing," said Senator Stooke. "We didn't hear anything, didn't find him until… until the morning." She blinked away tears. "By the Astra, it should have been someone else!" The senator lifted the painted dragon from her lap. "This was his favorite, when he was a boy. Even then he had such imagination, such… grand dreams. He would talk about how… how he could make things better, if he was Lord Protector. And he might have been, after Lady Abena. All he wanted was to *help* people. Why would anyone…" Her voice choked off, and she started to sob, wiping angrily at the tears as they rolled down her cheeks.

Endo moved his chair to her side, and took her hand in his. "Mother, if you can't… I can take care of this."

Senator Stooke looked uncertainly at her son, and then nodded. "Yes, I… You'll have to excuse me. Endo will tell you whatever you want to know." She stood to her full height, just over three feet and smoothed her dress with great dignity. "Consider yourselves hired. Find justice for my son, and you will be rewarded. I promise you that." And then she strode from the room to be alone with her grief.

Endo wheeled his chair around to face them. "Please, forgive her for any offense she might have caused," he said with an apologetic glance at Kadka. "She's taking this very hard. Ulnod was always her favorite." He glanced down at his hands. "My brother had a way with people. He would have known how to comfort her better than I do."

"There's nothing anyone can say," Tane said. He was no stranger to grief. "Trust me. When you lose someone close to you, it takes time to make sense of the world again."

"Is good you do this, though," said Kadka. "Take burden from her."

Endo gave them a shallow, sad smile. "Thank you," he said. "But this is about my brother, not me. Before we get started, can I offer you anything? Tea?"

"Anything… stronger?" Kadka asked with a raised eyebrow.

"Oh, I… I'm not sure what we…" Endo stammered.

"Tea is fine," Tane said, and elbowed Kadka again. "We're working."

She flashed him a shameless grin. "Yes. Hot water and leaves is fine."

Endo let out a small chuckle "Well, you can add as much sugar as you like. Just a moment." His eyes lost focus, and not long after Tane heard a sound from the hall outside, the squeal of wheels rolling across wood.

I thought he said they didn't have any servants here. The door swung open, and a small rolling table pushed in, with a fine porcelain tea set and tray atop it. It seemed to be moving under its own power—no one was pushing it.

And then Tane saw the automatons, the brass spiders Endo called 'crawlers'. Several of them scuttled along the floor, pushing the tea table; two more sat atop the surface, setting cups on small plates. These ones appeared to lack the daze-wands the others had used to attack Tane and Kadka—instead, they had surprisingly dextrous three-pronged pincers at the end of each arm. Their eye-like lenses glowed silver-blue, brightening and dimming as the brass iris behind modulated focus.

"So they're not just for security," Tane said as the crawlers rolled the table up to him and Kadka.

"Oh my, no," Endo said, and looked appalled at the thought. "They're *meant* for this, not stopping intruders. I made them to help with tasks that I have a hard time with from the chair. Extra hands."

One of the crawlers took the teapot in its pincers; another held a cup in place, then pushed it toward Tane when it was full. He accepted it, and smiled as the crawler that had poured the tea prodded a small cream pitcher and a bowl of sugar toward him. After he'd added his cream and sugar, they rolled the table on toward Kadka, who was watching with abject fascination.

"Is almost like they live," she said with delight as the little automatons filled her cup. "Best magic I see yet." She paused, and then, "Except maybe airship." She even accepted the tea, which Tane had never seen her drink before—though her interest in the crawlers couldn't entirely mask the scowl of distaste when she took a sip.

"They're amazing, Endo," Tane agreed. "I've never seen anything like them. You said I could look at the spells?" It wasn't what he'd come for, but he couldn't contain his curiosity. Even without any magic of his own, Tane considered himself as well-versed as any mage in the theory behind it, and this was an incredible advance in a field most artificers treated like story-book fantasy.

"Oh, yes. Of course." Endo's eyes went unfocused again, and one of the crawlers hopped from the tea table onto the couch, and crawled toward Tane.

Tane flinched slightly at the approach—it hadn't been very long since he'd been attacked by these things—but hesitantly put out his hand to pick it up. When he did, a hatch on its back opened with a click, and the crawler's eight segmented legs ceased moving and fell limp. Inside the hatch sat three tightly rolled scrolls perhaps as thick as a child's clenched fist, each held firmly in a pair of copper end-caps.

Tane reached for the first scroll, and then paused. "Can I…?"

Endo nodded. "It's safe to remove. They go dormant when the panel opens."

Tane carefully removed the scroll and unfurled the first foot or so of glyphs. As he'd suspected, it was incredibly dense. Rolled as tightly as it was, it had to hold thousands of glyphs in the *lingua magica*, every one of them utterly necessary to animate such an intricate au-tomaton. For spells this complex, glyphs engraved in metal were impractical—surface area became a very real restriction. It was little wonder that it didn't all fit on a single scroll.

"It's… very thorough," Tane said, reading through line after line of instructions in the *lingua*. The first foot of the scroll just dealt with activation and basic mobility, and even that was incredibly complicated.

Kadka leaned over to look. "Nonsense to me. You can make sense of this, Carver?"

"Some," Tane said. "But the way some of these commands are nested inside each other… I can barely follow it." The spells were sufficiently detailed to allow Endo's creations to navigate unfamiliar terrain without guidance, and Tane kept getting lost in complicated conditional loops. "The broad strokes, I think I understand. They see through the lens, and the rest of it is outlining how they react."

"More or less," said Endo. "Although that 'rest of it' is the hardest part. I've given them enough to move on their own and react to a range of situations, but it's impossible to cover it all. They still work best when I'm directing them."

"But that has to be easier with the basic functions already laid out," Tane said. "Outlining every motion you want them to make would get tedious." That was the fatal flaw of any automaton he'd ever seen: they required too much direct oversight to be practical. He had to respect Endo's magecraft—the attention to detail in these crawlers was far beyond the slipshod work he was used to. Most mages took their power for granted, and lacked the patience for precision.

"Yes, exactly!" Endo beamed broadly. "They don't need to be fully autonomous, as long as they have the framework to respond to commands in a useful way."

Kadka laughed. "Sounds just like you, Carver. Like Indree says. I never hear anyone else so happy to talk magic nonsense."

"It's *interesting*," Tane objected with feigned indignation. "Not my fault you and Indree lack the discerning intellect to see that." He rolled up the scroll, slotted it back into place, and looked back to Endo. "It would take me weeks to begin to grasp what you've managed here, Endo.

It's brilliant work." He shut the hatch, and the crawler's legs came to life once more. When he set it down on the couch, it skittered quickly back to the tea table with the others. "You certainly live up to your reputation."

"So do you, Mister Carver!" Endo enthused.

The honorific sounded odd, from someone so near his own age. "It's Tane. Please."

"Tane." Endo repeated it nervously, as if Tane might take offense to the familiar address even after insisting on it. "It's just hard to believe you don't have any mag—" He cut himself off, and his cheeks flushed. "That's rude, isn't it?"

Tane shrugged. "It's true. And being born with mage-craft doesn't have much to do with being *good* at it, in my experience."

Kadka grinned. "Carver thinks mages are stupid. Is mostly true, with ones we fight so far."

"I think *some* mages are… careless," Tane clarified, shooting Kadka a glare.

"It's fine," Endo said quickly. "I'm not offended. I knew something about your stance already. Ulnod was fascinated by your dissertation. I… can understand how you feel." Consciously or not, he rubbed one of his short-ened legs with one hand. "Your father was the conductor of the train we were on, is that right?"

"What does that matter?" Long-smouldering resent-ment flared to life again, and Tane's hand fell to the watch in his waist pocket. "It wasn't his fault, he didn't cast—"

Endo raised both hands, his eyes wide. "I didn't mean—"

Tane barreled onward angrily. "—the spells. He couldn't have known. No one ever *taught* him, and he wasn't allowed to—"

"Carver." Kadka put a hand on his shoulder, and he snapped his head in her direction, glaring. "Is fine. Look." She gestured at Endo; the young man was all but disap-pearing into his chair, his instinctive gnomish camouflage casting tones of brass and wood across his body.

Astra, what am I doing? He was just asking a question. Tane took a long breath. "I'm sorry. That was... uncalled for."

"No, no, it's my fault!" Endo insisted, his natural color gradually returning. "I was insensitive, I shouldn't have—"

Tane shook his head. "You didn't do anything wrong, it's just a sore point. You didn't know."

"I promise I wasn't trying to accuse anyone," Endo said. "I only meant that... we both lost something important in the accident. I'm not surprised it shaped your views on magic. It did the same for me. Maybe... we could talk more sometime?" He blushed, and lowered his eyes. "If you want to, I mean. I don't meet many people who understand what I'm trying to do with my automatons."

Endo's earnestness was hard to refuse, and his work *was* fascinating, but Tane wasn't sure he was ready to talk any more about that particular day with this particular man. Too much history. "Maybe," he said. "But we've strayed from the matter at hand. Right now we should really focus on the case."

"Oh. Of course." There might have been a note of disappointment in Endo's voice, but he bobbed his head agreeably. "Please, ask me anything."

"Well," said Tane, "let's start with the obvious. Is there anyone who might have wanted your brother dead?"

Endo's eyes widened. "Oh, I... I don't think so. Ulnod got along with everyone he met. Do you really think this could have been personal? I thought... there was another murder, wasn't there? Byron Rosepetal?"

"You know about that already?" *Indree won't like that.*

"Only that it happened. Should I not? Mother... tends to get information promptly."

"I suppose it couldn't stay hidden long," Tane said with a shrug. "But even with another victim, we can't rule anything out yet. If there's anything at all about your brother, any grudge you can think of, it gives us a place to start."

"There is one thing…" Endo hesitated, but when no one interrupted him, he went on. "Ulnod had no magic, and he was rather outspoken about non-magical rights in the Senate. Like Mother said, he might have been Lord Protector one day. Someone might have… there are people who resent that only those without magecraft can hold the office." He was clearly reluctant to offer a name.

"Endo, we're not going to start wildly accusing anyone," said Tane. "But if we don't have all the information, we're not going to get very far."

Endo sighed. "I shouldn't… It's only speculation. I just thought, there are a few senators who have been arguing for removing the restriction on the Protector's office."

"Who?" Tane asked, leaning forward in his seat. It had been a while since he'd read the political coverage in the Gazette.

"Rulik Deepweld," Endo said. "There are others who support him, but he leads the pro-magical movement in the senate."

The Deepwelds were an old and powerful dwarven house—it was hard to imagine any of them resorting to murder. "Both your manor and the Rosepetals' would have been inaccessible by anyone without permission to pass your wards," said Tane. "Has your family entertained Senator Deepweld as a guest?"

"Oh, yes. Several times. Others from his house, as well."

"What about these houses you say are allied with them?"

"Most of them have been guests, too," said Endo. "House Uuthar, House Crysthammer, House Nieris… Mother does most of her politics over dinner."

"Can you get us a list of names? Anyone with access to your wards who might also have been able to enter the Rosepetal manor?"

"Of course," Endo said eagerly. "Whatever you need. Most of the names on the list will be at the Brass Citadel for tomorrow's Senate meeting. I can get you in, if that would help. I... have to represent our family. Mother is in no condition."

"That would be perfect," said Tane. "People will be wary when word of the murders gets out. Kadka and I may have trouble getting access."

"I'll see that you're allowed as my guests," Endo said. "Give me a moment, and I'll get that list for you." He spun the lever on the arm of his chair and wheeled himself out the door.

When they were alone, Tane turned to Kadka. "That's going to be our list of suspects. The only ones who could get into both manors. Doesn't explain why there's no Astral trace on the weapon, but it's a start. Although even if we get inside the Citadel, I'm not sure how you and I get a bunch of aristocrats to talk to us."

"Could ask Indree for help," Kadka said, a mischievous glint in her yellow eyes. "Is just what she wants, us asking senators if they murder anyone."

Tane snorted. "Yes, I'd love to spend the next week in a holding cell." He spread his hands. "She won't like it, but we have a client now. We're obligated."

"Could have refused." By Kadka's tone, she knew full well that hadn't been an option.

"No," said Tane. "You heard what the Stookes said. Ulnod was an 'admirer' of ours. The message at the other scene could have just been a strange turn of phrase, but this is too much to be a coincidence. We're part of this." He could still hear Elsa Rosepetal's voice. *My son is dead because of you.*

Kadka nodded. "If someone comes for us, we should find first."

"It might not be that simple," said Tane. "Whoever did this had to know we'd find these hints. That we'd feel some kind of responsibility." A deep breath, and then he gave voice to the suspicion that had been building in his gut for hours:

"I think the killer *wants* us on this case."

CHAPTER SEVEN

————

AUDLIAN'S CROSSING TEEMED with protestors.

The last time Kadka had been there, it had been late at night, and the bridge to the Brass Citadel had been empty. She'd come shortly after she arrived in Thaless to see the famed statues that lined the span, stone sculptures of past Protectors of the Realm. Most races were represented—from tiny sprites to towering ogren—but there were some exceptions. There were no goblins or kobolds among the Senate houses. And no orcs. No surprise there, but she noticed it even so. The statues grew older as the bridge neared the great brass dome of the Citadel. It was like walking through history in the wrong direction, towards the founding of the Audish Protectorate. There was something appealing about that, even if Kadka didn't know most of their names or what exactly they'd done with their time in office.

This afternoon, though, it was hard to concentrate on anything but the crowd, so thick that Kadka couldn't see through to the Aud River flowing by below. Most were goblins and kobolds—races with no voice in the Senate and little magecraft in their blood—but people of all sizes and kinds swarmed behind the rope cordons on both sides. Some must have been there for days, or weeks—their clothes were wrinkled and filthy, and they'd set up small tents to sleep in. Here and there, groups crowded around portable artifact stoves, heating food or staying warm. A great many men and women wore the sign of the Silver Dawn: a twilight-blue armband emblazoned with a rising silver sun.

Mageblades were posted all along the bridge to keep the crowd behind their cordons and out of the main thoroughfare, but their presence didn't stop the protestors from voicing their displeasure. Cries of "*Equal representation in the Senate!*" and "*Rights for the magicless!*" and the like were most common, but they were answered by an "*Audland for the magical!*" now and again, which led to small shoving matches among the protestors. Kadka watched one lanky goblin woman lean over the cordon to scream "*Give goblins a voice!*" up at an ogren Mageblade's face. The big warrior just pushed her back with one arm, apparently unrattled. A few times someone even recognized them and called out "*Magebreakers!*" loud enough to make Carver flinch at Kadka's side—he'd been jumpy since leaving the Stooke house last night.

"So angry," Kadka said. "Is funny. I go through worse places to come to Protectorate, and don't see people yelling in streets like this."

"You mean like Belgrier?" Carver asked. "Makes sense. Speaking against the Kaiser isn't exactly encouraged over there."

"Not just that," Kadka said. This had been on her mind of late. A lot of what the Silver Dawn said—or shouted—made sense to her. "Is not like this when I first come here. Maybe letting non-magicals in University makes them see other things that need fixing. Hard to see their home so close to right, but not there yet."

"Maybe," said Carver. "I wonder what *he* would think." He jutted his chin ahead at the small square at the end of the bridge—the Founder's Plaza—where a single statue stood apart from the rest. A tall, handsome elven man, looking down the road as if to judge all those who approached the Brass Citadel. He stood straight and proud, one hand over his heart and the other resting on the hilt of a sword at his hip.

Kadka knew this one. The bridge was named for him. The first Protector of the Realm, a hero of the Mage War. Audlian. She couldn't remember his first name— something particularly elvish-sounding. One of the only elvish Protectors, Carver had told her once. "He is one who makes rule that Protector must not have magic, yes?" she asked.

"He was," Carver said. "Illuvar Audlian. He made that law despite knowing it meant his people would rarely hold the office. They say he did it to appease the nations of the Continent, show them there wouldn't be another Mage Emperor. But I think he also understood the value of putting power in the hands of people who weren't born with too much of it. Imagine having armies at your beck and call *and* the Astra at your fingertips. It would be easy to forget you weren't some kind of god."

"So he would support protestors, you think?" Kadka liked the idea. She'd come to Audland looking for magic, and she'd found it, but sometimes she didn't feel a great deal more welcome here than she had on the Continent. It was nice to believe that the founder of the nation might have been on her side.

Carver shrugged. "I don't really know. I like to think he'd approve of giving a voice to people who don't have one. But then, he also helped create the same Senate that hasn't raised a goblin or kobold house to power since… ever. They can petition for it, but granting seats to a new house is ultimately done by vote in the Senate. Hard to blame people who aren't represented already for feeling powerless."

That was less heartening.

They reached the Founder's Plaza and circled around the statue of Illuvar Audlian toward the gates just behind. The rope cordons looped wide around the statue on either side and ending at the tall fence that surrounded the lush green grounds. Here, nearest the gates, the press of protestors was at its heaviest—there were no tents or amenities, just people crowded against one another, shouting at the great brass building ahead. And they were even louder than the men and women further back. "*No more non-magical deaths!*" came from one side, answered by "*They got what they deserved!*" from the other. Here the fights that broke out involved fists and feet, not just shoving—Kadka watched with interest as the Mageblades intervened in a particularly bad scuffle. It seemed everyone knew about the murders, which was confirmed when she heard someone shout "*Beware the Emperor's Mask!*"

Carver jumped at that, and then tried to look like he hadn't. "The Emperor's Mask," he snorted. "Of course they've already given him a name. Apparently the word is out."

Kadka just nodded, unsurprised. News, she had found, traveled very quickly in a world of divination magic and instantaneous sendings. Very unlike the orc homeland of Sverna, where a message was only as fast as the messenger carrying it.

Beyond the gates, the Brass Citadel sat on its small isle, a huge metallic dome looming against the clear blue sky with the waters of the Aud forking around it on both sides. This was the seat of Audish power—the Lady Protector's residence spanned several of the upper floors, and the offices and meeting chambers of the Senate took up the lower ones. The building was sheathed in brass to protect the important people working within from outside magics. Kadka knew these things only by reputation, of course. She'd never set foot inside.

The gates were easily fifteen feet high, and a pair of Mageblades in gleaming brass cuirasses stood guard outside. Through the bars, Kadka could see dozens of others patrolling the grounds and standing guard at other doors. They weren't taking any chances with security, not with a murderer hunting senators.

As they neared, one of the Mageblades—an elven man with silver hair—looked Kadka up and down. "Protesters stay behind the cordon."

Kadka clenched her fists. One look at her and he'd decided she couldn't possible have business at the Citadel. Orcs were one of the lesser races to him. And not *just* to him.

"Not here to protest," she said.

Carver stepped in front of her. "We were invited to see the Senate in session. Tane Carver and Kadka. Endo Stooke said he would leave word."

The other Mageblade, a stoutly built human woman, pulled a scroll from behind her back and looked it over. "I've got their names here, Caelis."

The elven man—Caelis—frowned. "The Magebreakers. I remember." Carver scowled at that, which made Kadka grin. He *hated* the name, but she rather liked it. "But…" Caelis flicked a finger at Kadka. "Not many orcs with citizenship. We'll have to check that. Can't let a noncitizen in, can we, Anna?"

The woman named Anna pursed her lips a moment and shook her head. "Too dangerous."

"You can't be serious," Carver protested. "We have an invitation! Our names are on your list!"

Anna shrugged. "Security. Rule is, we can't let noncitizens in without special dispensation from a senator or the Lady Protector. Senator's son doesn't count." Her eyes lost focus for an instant. "Checking her name. Kadka, was it? Is that all?"

"Of Clan Nadivek," Kadka said. She was a head taller than either of the guards, but just then she felt very small. She already knew what they'd find.

She lived in Audland and worked there, but she was no citizen. For a woman with orcish blood born outside the nation's borders, that kind of acceptance wasn't easy to come by.

"That's nonsense!" Carver declared indignantly. "The Stookes' junior senator is dead. Endo is representing the family in the Senate. Call it emergency succession if you have to, but by any reasonable standard of what constitutes a senator, he absolutely 'counts'."

"Rules are rules," Caelis said smugly. "We have to be strict about it, with this Emperor's Mask lunatic running around."

But Carver wasn't done. "You'd never have even *blinked* if Kadka wasn't—"

Kadka took him by the shoulder. "Is fine, Carver." She drew him to one side against the cordon while the Mageblades checked on her citizenship. He resisted, but came along when she tightened her grip.

"We both know why they're doing this," said Carver. "Since when are *you* the one convincing me to back down?"

"Is not your battle, Carver." She shrugged. "If this is rule… Does no good to argue." She appreciated the effort, but she'd seen this attitude enough times before to know there was no changing it. "Just makes them keep you out too."

"Maybe, but I don't—"

"Excuse me." The voice came from beyond the cordon to Kadka's right. It was a goblin woman, hunched and potbellied and thin-limbed, with green-brown skin and stringy black hair. On her right arm, she wore the silver-on-blue sunrise of the Silver Dawn. "You're the Mage-breakers? I heard you talking to the guards."

"Yes," Kadka said. "You need help?"

"In a way," the goblin said in a thick, nasal voice. "I'm Gurtle Hruve. Someone who wants to speak with you sent me."

"What does the Silver Dawn want with us?" Carver raised an eyebrow, immediately suspicious. "How did you even know we'd be here?"

Gurtle laid a finger alongside her protruding nose. "We have our ways. But I'm not here for you. Only her." She looked to Kadka. "If she'll come with me."

"What does this someone want?" Kadka wasn't sure what to make of that—people didn't often seek her out.

"To talk," said Gurtle. "In exchange, he'll give you some information that you'll want to have."

"Why only her?" Carver asked.

"Because she might listen. It's one thing to be born magicless, and another to be a kobold, or a goblin. Or an orc. When you barely have a chance at magic in the first place, people look at you different. " Gurtle didn't look away from Kadka. "Will you come?"

Kadka glanced at Carver and shrugged. "Won't let me in Citadel anyway. Maybe learn something if I go." She hadn't much wanted to watch politicians debate, and she *was* curious about the Silver Dawn.

"I don't like it," said Carver, shaking his head. "We have no idea where he wants to take you, and in case you've forgotten, there's a certain someone out there with a keen interest in us."

Gurtle's beady eyes widened. "The Emperor's Mask, you mean?"

Carver sighed. "Has *everyone* heard about that already?"

"You surprised?" Gurtle asked. "Senators murdered, a masked killer challenging the Magebreakers. That kind of story spreads fast. But you're in no danger from the Silver Dawn. We don't wear masks." She turned to Kadka once more. "And like I said, if you agree to talk to the man who sent me, he's got something very interesting to tell you."

"Who is this man?" Carver demanded. "One of your leaders? Do you *have* leaders?" Kadka was curious about that too—the Silver Dawn protesters weren't without some loose organization, but no one seemed to know much about their leadership.

Still, Gurtle spoke to Kadka, though Carver was making more noise. "I can't say more here. It's your choice. Trust me, or don't."

Carver scowled. "Why should we—"

"I will go," Kadka interrupted.

"What?" Carver shot an alarmed look in her direction. "Kadka, think this through."

"Have," said Kadka. "Don't think murderer walks up to us in daylight with people everywhere. And I am not so easy to ambush." She grinned. "Maybe this Mask tries, and I solve case before you are done watching senators argue."

Carver's fingers dipped into his pocket to rub his watch case, and then he sighed. "I suppose if your mind is made up, I can't stop you." He smiled slightly. "This must be how Indree feels most of the time. Just… be careful. We don't know what we're up against yet."

"No promises," Kadka said, and grinned wider at Carver's answering groan. She turned to Gurtle. "Lead. I will follow."

Gurtle ducked under the cordon. From behind Kadka, the elven Mageblade at the gate yelled, "Hey! Protestors stay behind the—"

"We're just leaving, brassback!" Gurtle shouted back in a tone far less polite than she'd used with Kadka. She started back down Audlian's Crossing away from the Citadel, and glanced over her shoulder. "Quick, before they decide to make an example."

Kadka followed her back across the bridge into the Citadel District, full of foreign embassies and offices for aides to the Senate houses. Humans and elves and ogren and gnomes strode along the streets with purpose, moving between important meetings and the like, and they all wore crisp, formal clothes. Not that she cared greatly, but Kadka's roughspun shirt and tattered suspenders didn't exactly fit in.

"Is not far?" she asked, trying to get a sense of where they were going.

"No," Gurtle answered. "This way." She turned off the busy street into a narrow alley.

There was no one in sight, but Kadka's ears were keen. She heard movement around the next corner. Maybe it was nothing, just someone taking a shortcut. But then, she *was* being led down a blind alley by a stranger.

Maybe Carver had been right after all.

"Why here? Office on street too expensive?" Ahead, the sound of footsteps ceased. Walking out of earshot, or going still to hide?

"We aren't always too welcome around the Citadel," Gurtle said without looking back. "Better to keep out of sight."

"Ah. Makes sense." And it did. Some. But still, Kadka's hand went to the small of her back, where she had a knife hidden under her shirt.

She could hear breathing around the corner as they drew near. Very faint, but unmistakable. Whoever had been moving there hadn't gone away.

Someone was waiting for her.

And she was ready.

Grinning wide, she followed Gurtle around the corner.

CHAPTER EIGHT

———

TANE'S FOOTSTEPS ECHOED along wide corridors as he followed an aide to the Senate chambers. The interior of the Brass Citadel was all broad white halls and elegantly framed artwork. It didn't feel quite right. He'd never been inside before, but he'd assumed—however impractically—that it would be coated in brass inside as well as out.

"Through here, Mister Carver," said the aide—a dwarven woman working for House Stooke. She pushed open a large door at the end of the corridor and held it for him as he passed through.

He found himself in a crowded gallery looking down over the Senate floor. Men and women in clothes much more expensive than his surrounded him, engaged in conversation on a variety of political topics and sipping drinks from fine crystal glasses. He recognized some, senators and diplomats and ambassadors, people with power and influence beyond what he could imagine—and more than a few whose names were on the list Endo had given him.

People with access to both murder scenes.

Several turned to look as he entered, and Tane felt the hair on the back of his neck stand up. *The most powerful people in the Protectorate and any one of them could be the Mask. Maybe I'm doing exactly what I'm expected to do by coming here.* Knowing the killer had intended to draw him and Kadka into the investigation made every action feel like part of someone else's plan. It wasn't a feeling he liked.

"Mister—um, Tane!" Endo's chair emerged from behind a gaggle of well-dressed elves standing to one side of the door. The young gnome raised a hand in greeting, and then glanced about curiously. "Where is Miss Kadka?"

"Following another lead," Tane said. "She… sends her regrets." *Astra, I wish she was here.* Not just for his sake—he'd felt better when he could watch her back as much as the other way around.

"Oh, it's no trouble," Endo said.

"Listen, Endo…" Tane hesitated before he went on. But it seemed everyone had already heard about the Emperor's Mask taunting the Magebreakers—there was no point trying to hide it. "There's something you should know. The killer left a message at the Rosepetal manor—"

"For the Magebreakers." Endo said. "I… heard about it."

"I'm sorry I didn't say anything last night."

Endo shook his head. "No, no. I didn't tell Mother either. She hasn't left the house, so I don't think she knows. She wouldn't take it very well."

That wasn't the reaction Tane had expected. "You aren't angry?"

"The Mask killed my brother, Tane." A shadow passed over Endo's face, and he ducked his head. "I… I just want him stopped. And I trust you and Miss Kadka to do it."

Tane wasn't so certain, but he knew what it was like to lose someone, and to need some kind of answer for it. He'd spent years chasing one of his own. "I promise you," he said, "we'll do everything we can."

"I know you will," said Endo. A moment's silence, and then, "It's going to be a little while. Do you want to have a look at the floor?" He wheeled his chair around and led Tane toward the edge of the balcony.

Below, several rows of long curved tables sat in a half-circle facing the Lady Protector's chair at the front of the room. A table for each of the twelve great houses of the Senate, and two seats at each table, for the senior and junior representatives of the house. The sizes varied wildly, from massive reinforced thrones for the ogren to tiny sprite chairs that sat atop their table rather than before it. A handful of aides hurried about distributing papers and testing voice-casting artifacts—palm-sized concave dishes before each seat, made of copper-lined brass at the end of adjustable stalks. The chairs were still empty. The Senate wouldn't convene for a quarter hour still.

"Not much to see yet, is there?" Tane said.

"That depends on what you're looking for." A deep, powerful voice from behind. Tane turned to see a dark-haired dwarven man standing behind him, with long black mustaches over a beard streaked with grey. He stood some four and a half feet tall, and he was broad-shouldered beneath his fine black topcoat.

Endo turned his chair around to look. "Senator Deepweld," he said timidly. "This is Tane—"

"I know who he is." The senator thrust a thick-fingered hand out for Tane to shake, but he didn't smile. "Tane Carver, Magebreaker. I'm Rulik Deepweld."

That was the top name on Endo's list, the man Tane had come to see above the rest. Rulik Deepweld was both the head of House Deepweld and its senior senator, known for his strong pro-magical leanings. *And maybe an insane murderer.* But Tane looked him in the eye and shook his hand firmly. "A pleasure, Senator Deepweld."

Deepweld grunted. "Is it? I know why you're here. Digging around after this 'Mask' in all the wrong places." He glanced around, as if looking for someone. "I see you had the good sense not to bring the other one, at least. This isn't the place."

Tane blinked. "The… other one? You mean Kadka?"

Deepweld waved a hand dismissively. "Yes, yes. The orc."

Before Tane could muster an answer, a grey-haired elven woman approached. "Try not to let Rulik offend you too badly, Mister Carver. He's impossible to talk to otherwise." She wore long blue robes with little other adornment; her hair was long and unbound, flowing around gracefully pointed ears and falling down her back. It was a look that might have seemed plain on someone else, but on her it presented as simple elegance.

"Daalia," Deepweld said with a curt nod.

"Senator Audlian." Endo bowed his head in greeting.

This was Daalia Audlian, then—one of the most revered figures in Audish politics. House Audlian had been founded by Illuvar Audlian, the first Protector of the Realm, and Daalia had sat at its head for centuries. She'd retired as senior senator in favor of her younger cousin Saelis some years ago, but even retired senators retained their title.

She was also another name on Endo's list.

"It's an honor to meet you, senator," Tane said.

"Oh, the honor is mine," said Daalia. "You and your partner are becoming quite famous of late. Particularly among the working class. I heard them shouting about you on my way in." She turned to Endo. "I'm very sorry about your brother, Endo. Ulnod was well loved by everyone who knew him. A constant voice of compassion in a Senate often too preoccupied with politics."

Deepweld let out another grunt. "Ah. Yes. Naive, but… well-meaning. Condolences."

"Th… thank you both," Endo said, his voice trembling. "That's very kind." He ducked his head—hiding tears, and not well.

"Now, forgive me for eavesdropping, but I heard you speaking of the Mask," said Senator Audlian, and Tane got the impression that she was changing the subject for

Endo's sake as much as anything. "Is that why you're here, Mister Carver? Investigating?"

"Kadka and I have been asked to look into it by the Stooke family," Tane confirmed.

"Well, I'm very curious to know what you've found," she said. "My nephew Faelir has no magic—the first elvish candidate for Protector of the Realm in several centuries. As you can imagine, this situation is of grave concern to our house. We've already increased our security substantially." That was probably an understatement—House Audlian was the oldest of the Senate houses, and their wealth could buy every sword in Thaless if they felt the need. They might be a tempting target for the Mask, but also perhaps the most difficult.

"We're still in early stages," Tane said cautiously. Senator Audlian seemed a kind woman, and her house's ambition for Faelir Audlian was common knowledge. But that didn't clear her name. *Eliminating the competition is as likely a motive as pro-magical fervor.* "Just looking into leads."

"The wrong leads," Deepweld said. "That's what I was saying."

"If you have any insight, senator, I'm happy to be enlightened," said Tane.

"You're here looking at us because of the wards. Obvious enough. Probably at me more than most. Non-magicals get killed, look at the one fighting for magical advancement. Well, I might think the restrictions on the Protector's office are outdated, but I want to change them the right way. None of this sneaking around murdering people. No honor in that. And besides, my grandson Dernor hasn't got a lick of magic himself. I want this killer found as much as anyone. But there's not a person in the Senate who would sink so low, whether I agree with them on the floor or not. You're wasting time here."

Some of that was surprisingly astute. Moreso than Tane had expected, given the man's gruff demeanor so far. "We're not focusing on anyone in particular yet," he lied.

"But you seem to have given this some thought. Where would you be looking, if not here?" The more he could get out of Deepweld—either to prove his guilt or to rule him out—the better.

"You want someone who sneaks around in the shadows? Look at the protestors out there." Deepweld gestured vaguely in the direction Tane had come from, although there were no outside windows here—any gap in the brass dome would be vulnerable to magical assault. "Those Silver Dawn fanatics."

That caught Tane's attention. *Kadka.* He fought a sudden urge to march right out of the Citadel and find her. But he had no idea where she was, and she'd proven time and again that she could take care of herself. "Why do you say that?"

"What do we know about them?" Deepweld said, spreading his hands. "They rise up out of nowhere, nobody knows who's in charge, and then this starts happening? They're behind it, I promise you."

Daalia chuckled. "A man of the people, as always. Don't let Rulik's paranoia lead you too far astray, Mister Carver."

But Tane couldn't ignore the possibility. The Silver Dawn had Kadka, and if they were dangerous… "How do you think they would they have done it?" he asked. "Like you said, we have a list of people who could have bypassed the wards. The families didn't share any staff. How would a member of the Silver Dawn have gotten in?"

"You're assuming it was one man," said Deepweld. "Easy enough to have agents in both manors. Maybe a few. The lower classes eat up that Silver Dawn nonsense."

That was a fair point. The Mask's voice had been magically distorted, and there hadn't been any Astral residue on the murder weapon. Nothing to prove a single person had committed both murders. Something about it didn't feel quite right, though—the taunting hints for him and Kadka had the feel of a personal vendetta. He needed more than speculation. "Do you have any—"

A chime from below interrupted him, and Tane looked down over the railing to see a number of senators taking their seats. The Senate was being called to session. Flanked by two Mageblades, Lady Abena strode down the central aisle toward her seat at the front of the room. As if she could feel him watching, she glanced up at the gallery, and their eyes met. She quirked an eyebrow upward before moving on. *Oh good. There's no way Indree doesn't hear about this. She'll love what a low profile I'm keeping.*

"Time for you two to go," Senator Audlian said to Endo and Deepweld. "I'll keep Mister Carver company."

Endo swallowed nervously. "Wish me luck."

"You'll do fine, Endo," Tane said. Endo gave him an uncertain smile as he wheeled his chair around toward the door.

Deepweld didn't follow right away—he was still looking at Tane. "If you need more convincing, visit me at home this evening, after dinner. I'll leave word at the gate." He moved to follow Endo, but paused beside Tane's shoulder. "And you watch those Silver Dawn types. Or you'll wind up dead too."

———

Kadka saw movement to her left as soon as she turned the corner, and she drew her knife. A red-scaled kobold was advancing on her, just over five feet tall with a pair of small, useless wings, wearing nothing but a breechcloth. Kobolds weren't much for clothes—they preferred to rely on their scales.

She spun to one side, wrapped an arm around his neck, shoved her knife against his back. "Why do you sneak—"

Before she finished, the kobold craned his head around and exhaled a lick of golden flame right into her face. Not much, but the surprise and the heat were enough to make her release him and stumble back.

She'd heard that some kobolds could do that. A gift from their draconic ancestors, it was said. She grinned as she closed with him once more. "Should thank you. Dragon fire is something I always want to see." If it came from dragon blood, even a small flame was impressive to Kadka's mind.

Suddenly, someone gripped her wrist from behind and twisted, digging strong fingers between the tendons at the base of her hand. Her grip failed, and her knife fell to the ground. Keen as her ears were, she hadn't even heard the second attacker coming. She tried to wrench her hand free, and couldn't. Whoever it was, they were stronger than her.

Instead, she twirled into her attacker's grip, wrapping her trapped arm around her body. She made a blade of her free hand, jabbed it stiff-fingered at the attacker's throat. He leaned aside, grabbed that hand as well. And now she was looking right into his face, tangled up in his arms.

An orc.

Yellow-gold eyes glinted under a head of black fur-like hair, shaved on both sides to leave a shaggy crescent that curved from his forehead to the back of his neck. His nose was flat and broad, his lower jaw thick and jutting. The sharp tusks Kadka lacked protruded from his lower lip, and the fur on the backs of his arms was far thicker and fuller than hers. Not half-blooded like her, then, but a full orc, several inches taller and considerably more muscular than she was.

"Peash, shishter," he said. He had no trace of a Svernan accent, but Audish words weren't designed for orcish mouths—his tusks gave him a kind of sloppy lisp that sounded out of place alongside his rough voice. "You're in no danger from ush."

"*Deshkanek*," she spat into his face. She tried to kick at his groin, but he'd anticipated that—he stood with his hips turned so she couldn't get the angle. Most men, she could have pushed them off balance like that, but he was too heavy. He didn't budge when she threw her weight against him. "Let me go!"

He smiled, revealing a mouthful of sharp teeth. "That sheemsh ill-advished."

"You don't have to fight us," Gurtle said—she'd stayed out of the fight, but now she approached again. "This is just for security. We can't bring you in armed."

"Should have asked, then," Kadka growled. "This? *Poskan* trick."

"Can't take any chances," Gurtle said with a shrug. "Seskis, check her for weapons."

The red-scaled kobold nodded and moved in close. "Sorry about the fire," he said, hissing his 's' sounds slightly. "Or you're welcome, I suppose. I respect your work, I really wasn't trying to hurt you."

Kadka struggled as he patted her down, but she couldn't free herself from the orc's grasp. Her knives were removed, one by one—the one in her boot, the one strapped to her calf, the small blades up her sleeves. The longer one from her back that she'd dropped was retrieved as well, and Seskis tucked it with the rest into a small sack.

"You'll get them back after," Gurtle said. "Vladak, bring her."

The orc didn't hesitate, just started moving, dragging Kadka with him. She didn't resist further—better to bide her time, wait for an opportunity.

A few yards away, they stopped by a round brass plate set into the alley floor. Seskis and Gurtle lifted it from its mooring and slid it aside. Below, a hole opened into the space beneath the street, with a ladder just below the edge. Access to the sewers, Kadka assumed—she and Carver had used them on a previous case, to access the tunnel Tonke Dookle had been forced to dig below the Bank of Audland.

Carver. He was going to be so smug when he heard about this. It was almost enough to make her consider staying with her kidnappers.

Gurtle and Seskis went down the ladder first, and then Vladak lowered Kadka into the hole, supporting her while she found the rungs. "Don't try to eshcape," he said. "They're waiting for you below, and I'm coming down right after."

Kadka said nothing, just slid quickly down the ladder.

This was her chance. Vladak was stronger than her, but she could get by the others.

At the bottom, she faked left and then spun right, slipping by Seskis along the side of the tunnel. He grabbed her arm, but she pulled free, and then she was running. There was no water—or worse—underfoot, she noticed. Not the sewers, but made of the same brick with metal support beams. She could hear, distantly, a deep, hollow whoosh of moving air. Something large moving at high speed. The discs, then. Subterranean platforms of ancryst propelled by magic that carried passengers quickly between city districts. They had to be near, which meant these were the maintenance tunnels that went wherever the discs did.

Footfalls sounded from behind, some of them grow-ing closer too quickly. That had to be Vladak. She was nearly around the next bend when a hand grabbed her shirt from behind and held tight. She jerked to a sudden halt, choking at the sudden constriction around her neck. In a moment, Vladak had her firmly by the arms again. She cursed his speed and strength under her breath—it brought back memories of her training in Sverna, over-powered and outmatched by full-blooded orcs.

"I told you not to run," he said, not unkindly. "You could get losht down here."

Gurtle caught up, panting. "The blindfold. Can't let her try that again."

The kobold called Seskis produced a thick black length of cloth, stepped past the lanky goblin woman, and wrapped the blindfold around Kadka's head. Her world went black.

"What is this?" Kadka demanded. "Where do you take me? What can't I see?"

"Can't risk you leading anyone back to where we're going." Gurtle's voice, high and nasal. "Come on."

Vladak forced her into motion, and she couldn't break his grip. They traveled for perhaps a quarter hour, twisting and turning beneath the streets of Thaless, but Kadka had a strong sense of direction—even blind, she thought she'd tracked the turns well enough, bearing west toward Rosepetal Park and the Gryphon's Roost. When she escaped, she'd have to find her way back alone.

At one point, they paused briefly, and she heard her captors moving something. Metal scraping on brick, like when they'd opened the hatch above. Vladak ducked her head below something and then they were moving once more. After about the same length of time again, she heard a door opening. They passed through, and came to a stop. This time, they didn't resume their march. This was their destination, wherever it was.

"Kadka of Clan Nadivek." A rich, powerful voice that didn't belong to any of her three kidnappers. "I'm very sorry that this is how we had to meet. My associates are very protective of me. Please, Vladak, let her go."

The heavy grip on Kadka's arms abated. Immediately, she tore the blindfold from her eyes.

She stood in a large, surprisingly comfortable-looking room. The walls were brick and metal—she was still in the tunnels—but this place had been made livable. Well-spaced magelight lamps lit the space in silver-blue. A cot sat in one corner, a desk in another, and a few pieces of worn but comfortable looking furniture circled a sitting area to one side. The place had been decorated with keepsakes and art pieces. Someone lived here.

Probably the kobold standing in front of her.

At more than six feet, he was taller than any of his kind she'd ever met, with scales of shimmering silver that she'd never seen before either. His slitted reptilian eyes were a sapphire blue so vibrant they almost seemed to give off their own light. Nothing covered his lean, muscular body but a leather breechcloth about his hips, and Kadka couldn't help but appreciate his impressive chest and shoulders. Silver ridges ran from the top of his head to the tip of his tail, which was more than the stubby thing common to most kobolds—thick and tapered, it stretched long enough to reach the floor behind him.

But most impressive of all were his wings.

Kadka had seen kobolds like Seskis before, with wings as useless and vestigial as their short tails. These were something very different. Folded behind the man's back, their central joints jutted a foot above his head and their tips reached midway down his calves. They flexed and flared as he moved, revealing shimmering silver membrane. He looked like he might take flight at any moment. Like the dragon blood his people boasted of might actually flow strong in his veins.

"Who are you?" Kadka asked. It came out tamer than she'd meant it; she was more than a little bit distracted by his appearance. "Where is this?"

"My name is Iskar Estiss," the big kobold said in that deep, strong voice. "I am… a guiding hand behind the Silver Dawn. And this is a safe place. These tunnels were used during the digging of the main disc lines, but most of them have been long closed and forgotten. We have found them quite useful."

"Not so safe for me," Kadka said. She glanced over her shoulder. Vladak, Seskis, and Gurtle had taken position behind her, blocking the door.

"This may be hard to believe, but you are in no danger," said Iskar. "I hope you will stay and hear me out, but if you wish, you may go." He gestured with a clawed hand at the door and the three figures guarding it. "My friends will take you out of here. Without the blindfold, this time."

"Iskar, no," Gurtle protested. "If she tells anyone, she could put you in danger."

"I have had to move before, and I will again," Iskar said calmly. "But we are not in the business of taking our brothers and sisters hostage. The choice is yours, Kadka. Stay and listen, or go freely and in peace."

And Kadka found herself saying, "I will stay." There was something about this man—the strength in his voice, the calm surety of his words. Despite everything, she wanted to trust him.

And he wasn't hard on the eyes, either. Kadka *had* always been fascinated by dragons, after all.

Iskar's reptilian snout opened in something like a smile, revealing sharp dragon-fangs. "I'm glad. I have great respect for you. I would like for us to be friends."

"Friends don't cover eyes and take to secret rooms," Kadka said, and then quirked an eyebrow suggestively. "Except maybe *very* good friends."

Iskar looked at her a moment, blinking, and then let out a deep, pleasant laugh. "And yet it hardly seems to have shaken you at all. You are an impressive woman, Kadka of Clan Nadivek."

It was very hard not to like this man, and not only because of the way he looked. "And you are very pretty, dragon-man. But maybe we flirt after you tell me why you want me here."

He laughed again. "You offer a compelling case for haste. Very well, let me explain. What do you know of the Silver Dawn?"

"Why don't you say what I *should* know?"

"We believe that a new age is dawning. A time of cooperation and equality. The changes at the University were only the beginning. So much more can be done for the less fortunate in Audish society. The non-magical, races with no voice in the Senate. I believe you could serve as a great symbol for our movement. You and your partner are seen as champions of a sort to many people like us. Helping those who cannot find help elsewhere. As I said, many see the University's new admission policy as the spark that lit the fire, and there are whispers that you had a hand in it."

"That was Carver, mostly," Kadka said. "Why bring only me? Why not him?"

"Mister Carver seems a fine man, but I believe you feel our plight more keenly. He is human, and certain privileges come with that. But you will have experienced the scorn some have for… what they call the lesser races. And it will mean more to those who have experienced the same to see you standing for them."

Kadka *had* experienced the things he was talking about—the guards at the Citadel gates were still fresh in her mind. She raised an eyebrow. "You want me to fight for you?"

Iskar shook his head vehemently. "No. That is the last thing I want. The Silver Dawn is a peaceful organization. This nation was founded on great ideals, and I believe it is past time they were realized, but to use violence would betray those same ideals. What I would have you do is stand beside us. Speak to those who will listen."

"Is not even my nation." That was what she'd always told herself, the way she'd learned to let it go when people looked down at her. It was easier to shrug it off when it wasn't her fight. "I am no citizen. No one will hear me."

"Yet you live and work within the same borders as we do," Iskar said. "Does that not make these problems yours as much as mine? I think you would be surprised what your voice could mean."

That all seemed like a lot of responsibility to Kadka. "Why not you? Why hide here, if speaking is so useful?"

Iskar shook his head. "As I said, I am a guiding hand, nothing more. My name is not known the way yours is, outside. It would mean little."

"How long do you live down here that no one knows? Not many kobolds look like you."

"It has been… quite some time," Iskar admitted. "The Silver Dawn has existed in other forms, before this one. And there are those who would like very much for it to end—hence the secrecy. But I do not believe those people can stop what is happening now. Change is coming. Will you be part of it?"

Kadka hesitated. Part of her wanted to say yes, if it could mean an end to the insults and scornful looks she'd learned to let bounce off her hide. But she had other commitments, and she'd only just met this man, however much she liked him. "Need to think," she said.

Iskar smiled. "That is all I ask. As I said, you will not be blindfolded on your way out, but I will not always be in this location." He pressed a large silver coin into her hand; it was marked with a sunburst. "If you want to speak further, leave this in the window of your office. Someone will come for you." He paused, and then, "I very much hope to see you again, Kadka."

"Not the first man who says that," she said with a grin, tucking the coin into her pocket. "We will see. But you still owe something. Gurtle says you have information if I hear what you say. What is it?"

"Is that what she said?" Iskar glanced at Gurtle and shook his head with a fond laugh. "How very like her. I'm afraid she misled you to get you down here. We do have information, but she was meant to share it as a sign of faith. I had hoped you could bring it to the proper authorities."

"The other one was looking down his nose at me!" Gurtle protested. "He was going to convince her not to come. I needed something."

"Doesn't matter now," Kadka said. Maybe it was even for the best—she was glad she'd spoken to Iskar, all things considered. "Just tell me."

Iskar nodded. "It concerns this Mask who has been killing non-magicals—a man we very much wish to see brought to justice. Any follower of the Mage Emperor's teachings is an enemy of ours." His long dragon-snout dropped, and sorrow dimmed his bright blue eyes. "And

Ulnod Stooke was an ally, in contact with our agents. His work in the Senate could have changed a great deal, if he'd lived."

Kadka's ears perked at that. "Stooke was one of you? His family said nothing."

"Perhaps they didn't know," said Iskar. "Involvement with the Dawn is not… politically expedient. Most wouldn't approve."

"I am sorry," Kadka said. "Was good man, it sounds like."

"He was," Iskar said sadly. "I hope we can be of help in finding his killer. As I said before, we use these tunnels to travel unseen, among other things, and we have… many eyes throughout the city. Of late, we have not been the only ones down here. Particularly these last few days."

Kadka cocked her head. "Who else?"

"I'm not certain. Figures in dark clothing, always hooded. One was seen traveling sealed areas of the tunnels below the Gryphon's Roost," Iskar said. "Quiet and stealthy enough to evade our eyes at several points, which is saying something. Given the location, I suspect it may have been the Mask."

That was something. Maybe even enough to mitigate Carver's I-told-you-so's when she found her way back to him. "Where?"

"That is the most interesting part," said Iskar. "He left the tunnels somewhere on the grounds of the Deepweld manor."

CHAPTER NINE

———

"HOUSE STOOKE DEMANDS action." Endo's voice sounded as if it was right next to Tane's ear, even in the gallery; the little gnome leaned forward in his chair to speak into the dish of the voice-caster on the table before him. "Something has to be done before this killer takes another victim." He delivered the words timidly, as if they belonged to someone else. His mother, presumably. "My brother"—a hitch in his voice, there—"deserves justice. And we can't stop at this crime. We need to make sure that something like this never happens again."

It had been perhaps an hour of preliminaries before Lady Abena had opened the floor, and of course the first issue raised had been the Mask. Another hour of arguing back and forth about who was to blame and what was to be done before Endo had plucked up the courage to say what his family had sent him to say. Tane hadn't realized just how slowly things moved in the halls of the Senate until now—and the weight in his stomach grew heavier with every minute. All he wanted was to go see if Kadka was waiting for him outside, but he'd never be allowed back in while the Senate was in session. *She'd laugh if she knew I was this nervous. She's probably fine, and if she is in trouble, she can protect herself better than I can.* Even so, his fingers circled the brass watch case in his waist pocket over and over again, and Deepweld's warning about the Silver Dawn echoed in his ears.

"Before I reopen the floor, let me again offer my sincere condolences to House Stooke and House Rosepetal," Lady Abena said. "Ulnod and Byron were good men, and we all mourn their loss."

A murmur of sympathetic agreement passed through the chamber. Elsa Rosepetal barely acknowledged it; alone at House Rosepetal's table, she slouched in her doll-sized chair and didn't look up. Endo just inclined his head, having apparently exhausted his desire to speak before the crowd.

After a moment of silence, Rulik Deepweld stood from his chair, and Lady Abena acknowledged him with a gesture. He adjusted the dish of his voice-caster to the proper height and spoke into it. "Mister Stooke makes the same point that I've been arguing for weeks," he said. "We must take action! We need to change the outdated laws that make the weakest members of our families targets for fanatics like this so-called 'Emperor's Mask'. Audland's greatest strength is our magic—it's time to let our leaders wield it!"

A round of applause there, from more tables than Tane liked. And it wasn't just the emphatically pro-magical houses. Nieris and Crysthammer and Thiel he'd expected, but House Uuthar and House Rosepetal were generally known to be moderate voices in the Senate, and they were clapping with the rest. *Elsa Rosepetal I can understand—she just lost a son. But Uuthar?* While it was perhaps a stereotype, ogren tended towards careful deliberation, not this sort of knee-jerk reaction.

One of Uuthar's senators stood next, a massive, flaxen-haired ogren woman who could only be Noana Uuthar, head of the house. Another name on Endo's list. "House Uuthar supports House Deepweld in this. These laws were one thing after the Mage War, but it has been centuries. How long must we show the world our bellies for a mistake made generations ago?"

That was surprising, even after she'd applauded for Deepweld. Endo *had* mentioned the house as one of Deepweld's allies, but Tane hadn't imagined this level of support.

"How long have they been working together?" he asked, turning to Daalia Audlian, who had remained beside him in the gallery these past hours.

"A month or more now," Senator Audlian answered. "A number of houses felt the need to choose sides after the airship treaty, but I wouldn't have guessed Lady Noana would lean so heavily pro-magical. She was always a moderate in my time on the floor. Now she follows Rulik's lead religiously. They must have come to some agreement between their houses."

Or been thrown together by a greater cause. If the Knights of the Emperor were out there, he had no way of knowing how high their reach extended. Sudden changes in stance among the great houses could well be a sign of the order consolidating its power. And if they took enough of the Senate, things could get very dire very quickly for the non-magical, Mask or no. *Don't jump to conclusions, Carver. It could just be the usual politics.* But that nagging fear was hard to ignore. Especially when he didn't know where Kadka was.

Next to speak was Saelis Audlian—Daalia's cousin, who had replaced her as senior senator for the house. "No one has more reason to wish for a change to these rules than the elven houses," he said. "But my ancestor, Illuvar Audlian, put the restrictions on the office of Protector in place for reasons beyond appeasing the Continent. If we allow a mage to command our armies and control our relations with foreign governments, another Mage Emperor is inevitable. That is too much power for one person to wield."

Another round of applause, this time from Audlian's allies in the equality movement—the humans of Thesson and Jasani, the dwarves of Steelhand and the sprites of Springbloom. But some who normally leaned that way were silent. Endo was too flustered to sound for House Stooke, and many of the moderates had already backed Deepweld.

"Easy to say when your son is magicless," Deepweld retorted without waiting for Lady Abena's acknowledgement. "A chance at the Protector's seat at last. I suppose you'd rather keep away competition than keep him safe!"

"By the Astra, what an ass," Daalia muttered under her breath at Tane's side.

The younger elf beside Saelis rose to his feet, scowling. That had to be Faelir, House Audlian's junior senator. The son in question, famed for the quirk of birth that had left him without magic in an elven house. "Don't use me as ammunition for your idiocy, Deepweld! House Audlian has always taken this position, even when we had no hope to hold the Protector's seat! We are no hypocrites!"

"Your house will be singing a different tune if the Mask comes for you next," Deepweld said. "For that matter, what does the Stooke boy say?" He jabbed a finger at Endo. "Your brother died because he had no magic. Made him a target. If removing these restrictions could have saved him, isn't that worth it?"

All eyes turned to Endo, who shrank in his chair. Flickers of illusory camouflage ran over his shortened legs, but he kept it largely under control. "I... I'm not sure..."

"Speak up!" Deepweld insisted. "You asked for action, so tell us. What would you choose?"

Tane bristled at that. *He just lost his brother. Leave him be.* Whether he was a killer or not, Rulik Deepweld most certainly *was* an ass.

"If... if it would have saved Ulnod..." Endo hung his head. "I would give anything for that."

Half the floor rose to their feet then, shouting over each other to be heard, but Tane just watched Endo, hunched sadly in his chair. *Oh Endo. That was not the right thing to say to this room.*

Finally, Lady Abena touched something on the arm of her chair, and the voices were silenced. Or rather, diminished—she'd deactivated their voice casters. She stood. "Enough. If we cannot behave like adults, I am forced to suspend this session. For now, the constabulary will decide how to proceed regarding the Mask. We will reconvene when I return from the Continent, and I expect that cooler heads will prevail."

The chamber quickly began to empty. Apparently many of the senators were as eager to leave as Tane was.

"It's been a pleasure, Senator Audlian," Tane said, and offered her a quick bow. "Excuse me."

"So eager to be rid of me?" she said with a slight smile.

"Of course not, but I have work to—"

She raised a hand. "I understand. Go. For Audland's sake, I hope your investigation bears fruit."

Tane was on his way before she finished speaking. He pushed his way out of the gallery, and strode quickly down the hall. *Astra, let Kadka be waiting.* When he reached the stairs down to the ground floor, he took them two at a time, and then hurried for the exit.

"Tane!"

Tane swiveled his head to see Endo wheeling his chair out of a crowd of senators exiting the Senate hall. Reluctantly, he slowed as the little gnome caught up.

"Are you angry with me?" Endo asked quietly, rolling alongside Tane. "I know you care about non-magical rights, and what I said in there… I didn't mean it. Or… I don't think I did. Everyone was looking, and he asked about Ulnod, and—"

"I'm not angry." Strangely enough, Tane found himself wanting to offer some kind of comfort. He *had* been angry at Endo once, a long time ago, but it was hard to hold onto that now, watching him go through a very familiar pain. "He asked you if you would have saved your brother if you could. Of course you said yes. There was a time I probably would have said the same if someone asked me about my parents."

Endo looked up at him with a glimmer of hope in his eyes. "Does it get… easier?"

"Eventually," said Tane. He wasn't used to talking about this sober, but he had to offer something. "Or at least you get used to it being hard."

"It was like that after…" Endo glanced down at his legs. "You know. I didn't think I'd have to go through something like that again. All of this is just… Mother can't even leave the house anymore, and that only leaves me, but… it's too much. You saw what happened in there. I'm not cut out for the Senate."

He was probably right—politics was no place for someone as sheltered and earnest as Endo. But Tane didn't think that would be a very useful thing to say just then. "Deepweld was looking for any opening he could get. It wasn't your fault."

"Wasn't it? If they use my family as an excuse to change the law…"

"If you hadn't taken the bait, he'd have found another way."

They reached the exit, and a pair of Mageblades pushed the doors open for them. The well-manicured Citadel grounds waited outside, rich and green and opulent, but Tane only had eyes for the gates. He walked a bit faster, and Endo accelerated to keep pace.

"Maybe you're right," Endo said doubtfully. "Was it useful, at least? Did you see any… clues, or leads, or… whatever you call them?"

"I spoke to some of the people on your list," said Tane. "They had some interesting things to say." He wasn't sure he had much to go on, really, but he wasn't about to say that to a client. *Deepweld* did *use the situation to his advantage, though. Could he have arranged it that way?*

The gates were before them now, and the guards let them through along with a small group of others. Tane raced through ahead of the rest, sweeping his gaze over the Founder's Plaza.

"Carver." There she was, leaning against the base of Audlian's statue.

"Kadka!" He slowed his step, tried not to let his relief show too obviously—she'd only laugh.

She laughed anyway. "Happy to see me, Carver?"

"Overjoyed. Have you been waiting long?"

"Not so long," Kadka said, and nodded a greeting at Endo as he maneuvered his chair alongside them.

"The Silver Dawn," said Tane. "What did they want? Where did they take you?"

"Tunnels around the discs," Kadka said. "Put blindfold on me, and—"

Tane blinked. "They *blindfolded* you? I *told* you—"

"Wait until story is done, Carver. Didn't go how you think." Kadka quickly summed up the ordeal.

By the time she finished, Endo was staring at her wide-eyed. "Ulnod was working with the Silver Dawn?"

Kadka shrugged. "That is what they say."

"He never... I didn't know." Endo swallowed and looked down at his hands.

Tane didn't know what to make of it, especially after Deepweld's dire warnings. *Not exactly confidence inspiring behavior. But they did let her go.* "You think it's true?" he asked Kadka. "Can this Iskar be trusted?"

"I think so," said Kadka. "I like him." She grinned. "Very pretty."

Tane couldn't help but chuckle. "We *might* need more than that. What about the information we were promised?"

"Was saving it for last," Kadka said. "Says his people saw cloaked man in tunnels last night. Under Deepweld manor."

"Deepweld again." Tane wasn't certain he trusted the

Silver Dawn's information, or this Iskar Estiss, but if they were right, it was certainly suspicious. No one had been killed at the Deepweld manor last night, which suggested that the Mask might have had another reason to be there. "Was he sure about the location?"

She shrugged. "Seemed sure enough. Is important?"

"Maybe. Deepweld was happy to use the murders to advance his cause in the Senate—could be a motive." And then it occurred to Tane that there was something else. "And he was*very* eager to point me at the Silver Dawn. Which, if he's the Mask, or pulling the Mask's strings, and he knew Iskar's people had seen something…"

"Turn enemies on each other," Kadka said. "Clever. Think he talks to us, or do we try to follow him?"

"As it happens," said Tane, "he invited me to his home this evening."

———

"Mister Carver. Hoped you'd come." Deepweld sat in a high-backed chair behind the desk in his study, holding a glass of some amber-colored spirits in his hand. Tane noticed his eyes flicker to Kadka as a human footman ushered the two of them into the room. "And your… friend." The disapproval in his tone was unmistakable. "Well, sit. Dwarven whiskey?" He lifted his glass by way of example.

"Yes," Kadka said immediately.

Tane shot her a sidelong glance that she ignored. Dulling their wits probably wasn't the best idea while talking to a man who might have murdered two people, or arranged to have it done—and who might have drawn them into the investigation on purpose. Which was a thought that very much made Tane *want* a drink. *But then… maybe it's best to put him at ease. Don't want him to get suspicious, do we?* Finally, he just shrugged. "Why not?"

Deepweld gestured to his footman as Tane and Kadka sat, and a moment later a pair of drinks were set in front of them.

"We both know why you're here, so no point wasting time," said Deepweld. "I told you those Silver Dawn fanatics are behind the murders. You want to know more." He took a long swallow of his drink.

Tane didn't disabuse him of the notion—if Deepweld thought they were only there to ask about the Silver Dawn, he might let his guard down. "You said to come if I needed more convincing." He took a sip of his own drink, and barely kept himself from coughing it back up. Apparently Dwarves liked their whiskey to burn even more than the cheap stuff Tane kept in his office. Beside him, Kadka tossed back a gulp that rivalled Deepweld's without flinching. *Show-off.*

Deepweld was watching Kadka finish her drink with slightly more respect than before, but he turned back to Tane and nodded. "Ask your questions, then."

"Well, first of all I'm not certain what the motive would be," Tane said. "The Silver Dawn champions non-magical rights, and the victims have been magicless."

Deepweld snorted. "You think that matters? The victims come from Senate houses. To people like that, we're all the same. Part of the establishment. This way they win twice over—hurt us and get sympathy for their cause."

Not for the first time, Tane had to admit there was some sense to what Deepweld was saying. *He's thought his argument through, I'll give him that. And he makes it with conviction.* Whether he was lying about the murders or not, Tane was certain of one thing: the man really didn't care for the Silver Dawn.

"Do you talk to any of them?" Kadka asked. "Just people from Porthaven, Greenstone, mostly. Only want fair laws."

Deepweld waved a hand dismissively. "Of course you think so. Rights for the orcish, is it? Well, I'm not saying they're all killers. Only takes a few going too far, and we all know self-control is in short supply among those sorts."

Something flashed in Kadka's eyes—Tane knew that look. She was going to argue. It wasn't like her. Or rather, it was *very* like her to make her opinion known about a great many things, but usually she let prejudice like Deepweld's roll off her back. Hadn't she been the one telling him it was a waste of breath, earlier?

"Let me ask you something else," Tane interceded quickly. "You mentioned your grandson earlier. He has no magic?"

"Dernor," said Deepweld, and his face softened slightly. "Not a bit of it, Astra help him."

"Which makes him a possible Protector of the Realm, one day, out of a fairly narrow field of candidates. I wonder, why are you so eager to change the law to increase the competition?"

Deepweld's eyes narrowed. "I love my grandson," he said. "Magic or no. But it's a larger question. We've spent too long trying to look weak to the nations of the Continent for a sin centuries gone. Audland needs to embrace its strengths. I don't want to take away anyone's chances— I want to open them up. My way, Dernor could still be Lord Protector, but so could someone born with magecraft." He paused to take another long swallow of his whiskey, and then abruptly stood. "Follow me."

Tane shared a glance with Kadka, and they both rose to follow Deepweld out of the room. They'd discussed creating an opportunity to look around the manor, but this was easier than any of the ploys they'd considered.

Deepweld led them back through the manor to the enormous foyer. All along the way, guards kept watch, and at the front door a pair of Mageblades stood at attention— part of a detail assigned by the Lady Protector. While the Mask was at large, those with non-magical sons and daughters to protect were taking every precaution.

From the foyer, they climbed a grand marble staircase and turned right at the second floor landing, down a long hall. Finally, Deepweld stopped outside a door bearing an image painted in a simple, exaggerated style like something from a children's book. It depicted a scene of an armored dwarven hero fighting a huge serpent, deep underground with gems glittering in the cave walls all around.

"Dernor's room," said Deepweld. "The boy loves the old dwarven tales. He's five years old, Mister Carver. As they are, the laws around the Protector's office make children like him targets from birth, without any magic to protect themselves. I don't want him growing up like that." He turned the handle, pushed the door open slowly to cut down the noise. "Look at him. He's too young to have to worry about madmen like this Mask coming after—" His voice cut off as he looked inside the room.

Silhouetted in the dark against the open window, a huge figure in black robes loomed over a dwarven child sleeping soundly in his bed. In its hand, Tane could see the shadow of something long and sharp. As the door swung open, the figure looked toward the movement.

Dim silver-blue light spilled from the eyeslits of a brass mask, emblazoned down the center with the Mage Emperor's staff and crown.

CHAPTER TEN

THE MASK RAISED a hand, and the brass spike clasped within glinted in the light from the hall. Carver and Deepweld stood frozen in shock.

Kadka had no such problem.

She crossed the room in a sprint, lowered her shoulder, and struck the Mask hard in the side just as the spike swept down. It was like running into a lamp post—the dark figure was near nine feet tall, solidly built, unyielding as iron. Pain exploded down her arm as her bones jarred against one another, and she stumbled back. Spots swam in front of her eyes.

But the impact sent the spike wide. It missed the sleeping boy's head by an inch, plunged through the pillow into the mattress beneath. Dernor blinked open his eyes, rubbed his face—already bearing a light fuzz that would one day be a thick dwarven beard—and saw the giant shadow above him.

He shrieked, the way only a child could.

The spike lifted again, swept down.

But Carver was already there, finally spurred into motion. He grabbed Dernor in his arms and rolled aside as the crowned staff bit into the bed again. This time Kadka heard it hit the frame, lodge deep in the wood.

She drew her long knife from behind her back, slashed at the Mask's belly. The figure abandoned the crowned staff-spike in the bed to block her blow with the back of its wrist. Metal struck metal beneath the black cloth robe. Some kind of armored gauntlets. How had an armored giant crossed the grounds and entered the manor without being seen or heard? That had to be magic.

Carver stumbled past Kadka with the boy, and she moved to block the Mask from following.

"Guards! The Mask!" Deepweld's voice, from behind, and then he began to chant in the language of magic. Further back, footsteps sounded in the hall, drawing nearer—guards and Mageblades answering the call.

"Get down, orc!" Deepweld shouted, and then uttered a final word of magic.

Kadka ducked, and a wave of silver force passed close overhead, stirring her hair. It struck the robed figure full across the torso.

The Mask took a single step backward, and moved no further. One hand rose; a glyph glowed silver-blue in the dark, the same color as the light behind those eyeslits.

"What in the—" Deepweld didn't get the rest of the sentence out.

A wave of force threw Kadka against the wall, and blasted Deepweld out of the doorway. Toys scattered and tumbled across the room. The air burst from Kadka's lungs, and she hit the floor hard. Pushing herself to her feet, she saw a black silhouette stepping out through the big open window.

She couldn't let the Mask escape. They might not get another chance like this. Forcing shaky legs into motion, she leapt at the figure's retreating back.

A huge hand swept through the air and struck her with impossible strength. She slammed into the wall behind her in almost the same spot as before. He was too strong. Or maybe she just wasn't strong enough. Again.

The Mask was out the window before she could get her feet back under her.

"*Poska!*" she shouted. "If you are so strong, come back and fight!" She staggered to the window, leaned out. The Mask had dropped to the ground below—two floors down—and landed upright on both feet. Three steps across the dark grounds, and then the figure began to blur and shift before Kadka's eyes. She could see plainly at night, but somehow the Mask was fading into the dark even so.

"Where is he? We can't let him get away!" Carver's voice, just behind her.

He arrived at the windowsill beside her just in time to see the Mask disappear.

———

"It had to be an ogren," Tane said. "Too big for anything else, and too strong."

They stood in the foyer of the Deepweld manor; the bluecaps had just arrived, joining the Mageblades already at the scene. Indree—in full uniform—was debriefing Tane and Kadka, and she'd brought a dozen others. She'd ordered them to search the grounds as soon as they arrived, but Tane didn't think they'd find anything more than they had at the other scenes. *Spellfire, we had the Mask right in front of us. How can we have so little to show for it?*

Indree took his observations down in a small notebook, and turned to Kadka. "You got the closest, Kadka. Did you notice anything else?"

"Was strong, like Carver says. Armored some, on arms at least, but quiet. Solid, like wall. Barely moves from Deepweld's spell. And has own magic, too. Throws me with it."

"So we *are* looking for a mage." Indree scribbled something down.

"We don't know that," said Tane. "Probably true, given the pro-magical rhetoric, but we never heard any spells being cast directly."

Kadka nodded. "No words, just wave of magic."

"It was an artifact," Tane clarified. "In the palm of the hand. I saw the glyph glow. Which makes sense—if you need to move quietly, you can't go around muttering in the *lingua*. Better to rely on artifice."

"Were there other spells?" asked Indree. "Beyond the force wave? I need to know what we're dealing with."

"Moves too quiet for that size, and in armor," Kadka said. "Comes in second floor window. Nothing there to climb. Had to be magic. And at the end, disappears in front of me."

"Invisibility?" Indree frowned. "Not possible."

"I think it was an active illusion," said Tane. "With the black robe, in the dark… it would have been easier to blend in. Probably used it to get in unseen too. But to fool Kadka's night vision, it must have been perfect. Which makes no sense. Only an ogren has that kind of size and strength, but only a gnome can camouflage that well in motion. And even if someone *could* replicate the effect with an artifact, it would burn through the gems powering it faster than most people could afford."

"Well someone managed it, however it was done." Indree wrote something else down and looked at it for a long moment, prodding her cheek with her tongue. "I wish you'd called me sooner. We might have ended this here, or at least learned more. Why didn't you use the locket I gave you?"

"There wasn't time," Tane said. "It happened fast, and afterwards the Mageblades were already here and the bluecaps had been called in."

"You could have told me what you were do-ing *before* you came across the actual murderer," said Indree. "And Lady Abena tells me you were in the Citadel while the Senate was in session. You two are drawing too much attention to yourselves. I might be able to keep Chief Durren off you for a while, but if the Mask has an interest in you already, this isn't helping."

"I know." The thought had occurred to Tane more than once, and he didn't much like it. "But we weren't the targets here, as far as I can tell."

Kadka nodded. "Tries to stab Dernor through the head first, like the others. Even after I attack, only tries again. Hardly notices me at all." She dipped her head there, and her voice was unusually subdued. "Everything after Carver took boy away was just defense, covering escape."

"But you *did* save the boy." Indree gave Tane a look he couldn't read. "I suppose I can't fault your methods too much if they put you in the position to do that. And thanks to your Silver Dawn source we know to put constables on the old maintenance tunnels, although I don't think half the ways in and out are even on our maps anymore."

"We can probably cross Deepweld off the suspect list, too," said Tane. "If the Mask *was* here last night, it was probably for reconnaissance. Trying to find a way around the increased security in the Roost."

"At least the patrols were good for *something* then." Indree couldn't keep the frustration from her voice. "Not enough to stop the attempt, but a night off is more than we got between the first two murders."

Tane was about to answer when the outside door opened behind her, and he saw the last person he wanted to see.

"You two!" Chief Durren shouted, jabbing a finger toward Tane and Kadka. His face was bright red. "Every time, right at the scene of the crime!" He tromped across the foyer to stand beside Indree. "Inspector Lovial, I want these two taken—"

"Durren." Deepweld's voice, from the landing above. He leaned over the rail. Dernor wasn't with him—he'd taken the boy somewhere out of the way while the bluecaps went over the manor. "These two saved my grandson's life. You aren't taking them anywhere."

The red in Durren's cheeks paled abruptly. "Oh, Senator Deepweld. I didn't... of course not, if you vouch for them. I only want to be as thorough as possible in finding whoever attacked young Dernor. When I heard what had happened, I came right away. Perhaps we could talk elsewhere?"

Deepweld was descending to the foyer now. "About how this Mask is going to be found before he acts again? Yes, I think we damned well should." At the bottom of the stairs, he turned toward his study, and glanced impatiently over his shoulder at Durren. "Well? Are you coming?"

"One moment, Your Honor," Durren said. "Inspector Lovial, I'm leaving the scene to you." *As if Lady Abena left him a choice.* "Don't disappoint me. I expect this to be done right." And then, with a final glare at Tane and Kadka, he followed Deepweld down the hall.

Kadka watched him go with a frown. "How do you stand him? Is not man who should lead anything."

"No. But he knows how to play politics with the Senate houses." Indree sighed. "And he isn't happy that a case this big has been taken out of his hands. He'd have me off it if not for Lady Abena. I'm not sure I'm going to have a career left when this is over."

Tane knew how important her work was to her—and that associating with him hadn't made things any easier. "Ree, I—"

She shook her head. "No time to feel sorry for myself now. We have work to do. Come on, I need to see the scene." Moving with purpose, she started up the stairs.

Dernor's room was still in shambles from the fight. The wall was dented and broken where Kadka had struck it twice, toys were strewn everywhere, and feathers and padding from the twice-stabbed bed drifted across the floor.

An elven bluecap stood beside the bed, and another, a sprite woman, perched on his shoulder.

"Find anything?" Indree asked.

The elven man shook his head. "No, inspector. Just like the other scenes. The spike is clean, no Astral signature that we can find. Arlene was about to give it another go."

"Don't bother," Indree said. For a brief moment her eyes went out of focus, and then she shook her head. "Nothing. And I doubt we'll find anything more on the grounds either." Again, that hint of frustration crept into her voice. "It's like no one was ever here. Nobody should be able to evade so many spells without leaving a trace."

"There's one trace," said Tane, his eyes on the crowned staff jabbed through the mattress into the bedframe. "And we haven't checked it yet."

"Ah, yes. More insane rantings. This should be a treat." Indree pulled a handkerchief from her pocket to cover her hand, then reached out and twisted the crown around the head of the staff.

Just like at the Rosepetal scene, glyphs flared blue all around the crown, and then the Mask was in front of them, staring with glowing blue eyeslits through a brass plate engraved with the Mage Emperor's sigil. Only an illusion, but somehow it seemed far more menacing to Tane now that he'd seen it in person.

"*You cannot stop me, Magebreakers.*"

Kadka cocked an eyebrow. "Not so subtle this time."

But the Mask had more to say. And the next words froze Tane's heart in his chest.

"*A new age of the magical is nigh. My victims die to herald the Emperor's coming, and there will be more. Bow your heads, or join them.*"

CHAPTER ELEVEN

———

THE NEXT DAY found Tane and Kadka back in the Gryphon's Roost, this time without a bluecap escort. Walking down the immaculately maintained tree-lined street, Tane felt like his every move was being watched— like powerful people were staring at him through the curtains of every carriage that rolled past. And there was no shortage of those. The people who lived here didn't walk—they were driven in opulent vehicles, horse-drawn or ancryst-powered. Especially with a killer on the loose. The Roost was largely empty of foot traffic, save for him and Kadka.

And the Mageblades. Dozens of them patrolled in pairs up and down every street at Lady Abena's order, on watch for any sign of another attack. *Didn't do anything to stop the Mask getting into the Deepweld manor, though.*

"You see this Uuthar woman in Senate," Kadka said as they walked. "Could be her, you think? Ogren killer... seems strange."

"I wasn't trying to throw Indree off the trail, if that's what you mean," said Tane. "After last night, I'm perfectly happy to let the bluecaps deal with the Mask." He'd caught Indree up on their investigation the previous evening;

they'd arranged to meet this morning at the Uuthar manor. "Noana Uuthar was on Endo's list, along with others from her house. Apparently she's been acting strangely the last month. Siding with pro-magical partisans where she wouldn't have before. And the person we saw last night… the size points to ogren."

"So why attack Deepweld's family? He is on same side in Senate, you said."

"I don't know. Sometimes converts are the most zealous believers—maybe she thinks all non-magicals who could be named Protector of the Realm one day need to die. Maybe she's with the Knights of the Emperor, and their agenda trumps a Senate vote. Or maybe she's not involved at all, and we're looking in the wrong place."

"You still worry about Silver Dawn," Kadka said. It wasn't a question. "What Deepweld said."

"The man is a bigot, but… he wasn't wrong about the possibility. The Silver Dawn is popular with the lower classes—it wouldn't be hard for them to win over a servant or two in some of these manors. And the lack of Astral trace at any of the scenes *could* mean another half-orc is involved. I can't think where we're more likely to find one than among the Silver Dawn."

Kadka frowned. She was uncomfortable with the idea, he could tell. Whatever this Iskar fellow she'd met had said to her, it had made a strong impression.

"You already said, too big for half-orc," she said. "And Silver Dawn speaks for non-magicals. Why use Mage Emperor's symbols? Why kill people with no magic? Why Stooke, if he was ally?"

"The size does hurt the half-orc theory," Tane admitted. "But we also saw the Mask use active illusion to disappear like only a gnome can, so I'm not ready to rule anything out. As for the rest of it, we only have the Silver Dawn's word that Ulnod was one of them. And like Deepweld said, if they wanted to create sympathy for their cause, inventing a pro-magical murderer is a way to do it. Or…"

"Or what? Say it, Carver."

"What if the Knights of the Emperor are pulling the strings? They might have infiltrated the organization." *Spellfire, that sounds crazy.* The past few days, Tane saw the hand of the Knights everywhere, no matter how far-fetched. *Except… crazy doesn't have to mean wrong. Not when we're dealing with a giant killer in a metal mask who can walk through wards and leave no trace.*

Kadka shook her head. "No. Makes no sense. Why send us to Deepweld then? If they are behind Mask, why put us in place to stop him?"

"Because the Mask has been playing with us from the start! Sending us messages, trying to draw us into this. If the Knights of the Emperor are pulling the strings, maybe they sent us there because they *wanted* us there. Because we beat them once, and they can't let that stand. We've been challenged now, and people are going to hear about it. Every murder we can't stop discredits us a little bit more. Iskar told you that we were becoming a symbol for the cause, but maybe it's a symbol his masters want erased."

"Is not like that," Kadka said stubbornly. "You read people, Carver, but I was there, not you."

They were nearing the Uuthar estate now, an opulent gated manor like so many others on Riverview Avenue— home to the eldest and wealthiest of the Senate houses. Further down at the end of the road, Tane could see the massive Audlian estate, guarded by a veritable army. Daalia Audlian had certainly meant it when she'd talked about increasing security.

"I know you liked him, Kadka," Tane said, "but right now—"

"Is not just because I *like* him," Kadka said, narrowing her eyes. "Was way he talks. Like he believes in… better things."

Tane raised his hands. "Alright. But we can't ignore any possibility right now."

"Including Uuthar woman. As much points at her as Iskar and Silver Dawn."

"Believe me, I haven't forgotten. That's why we're going to talk to her. For all I know, it's her and the Silver Dawn and the entire Senate. It feels like everyone we talk to could be a secret killer." Tane's fingertips found his watch-case and traveled over the familiar dents. "We need to end this, and the only way I know to make that happen is to follow every lead."

Kadka cocked her head at him, and the annoyance faded from her eyes. "Is not our fault just because Mask uses our name, Carver. Is not *your* fault. You know this, yes?"

"I know," he said. "But that doesn't make me feel any better about it."

As they reached the Uuthar estate, a blue coach bearing the emblem of the constabulary—a golden shield emblazoned with a rearing gryphon—drew up outside the gate, and Indree climbed out. She was dressed in plain clothes rather than her uniform, presumably to spare the family embarrassment. Not a courtesy the bluecaps ever offered in the poorer districts.

Indree raised a hand in greeting. "Tane, Kadka. Good timing. Come on."

The guards gave them no trouble at the gate. They were expected. A towering ogren footman led them across the grounds—not to the manor entrance, but around the side of the house, toward the rear gardens.

"Remember, you're just here to observe," Indree said, glancing pointedly at Tane. "Senator Uuthar is speaking to us as a courtesy. I asked you here because you're good at seeing lies, and I can't start casting truth-spells on senators without stronger evidence than we have. But I don't want you saying anything. Either of you."

"Understood," said Tane. "I won't say a word." *Unless I have to.* He trusted Indree to ask the right questions, but it

wasn't her the Mask kept leaving messages for on top of
dead bodies.

Around the back of the manor, the grounds opened
up into a vast well-maintained garden, divided into sections by manicured hedges. At the far end, the grounds
sloped down toward the Aud river, and a high wall separated the estate from the bank. In a gazebo at the garden's
center, Noana Uuthar reclined in a huge chair with an
open book in her hand. The footman led them to her, and
she looked up as they approached.

The footman bowed and introduced them. "Constable Inspector Indree Lovial and company, Your Honor."

Senator Uuthar remained in her chair—even sitting,
only Kadka matched her height—and her perfect features
broke into a gentle smile. "Welcome, all of you." She was
impossibly lovely, like all ogren—near nine-feet tall with
golden hair and cheekbones that could have been carved
from marble. Tane felt himself flush as she turned her eyes
to him. "And I can only presume these are the ones they
call Magebreakers? How interesting. What *have* you come
to ask me about, Inspector Lovial?"

"I'm very sorry I have to do this, senator, but I need
to ask where you were when the Mask was seen at
Deepweld manor last night, as well as the nights of the
murders." Indree handed a slip of paper to Senator
Uuthar. "We'll need to talk to these others too."

Uuthar looked over the list with solemn gravity. "My
husband and my nephew." Her nephew Aigan was the
junior senator and heir to the house—Noana and Oden
Uuthar had no children of their own. The great curse of
the ogren was that they rarely carried to term, and when
they did, one in three were born mindless, brutish ogres
who had to be sequestered in a remote sanctuary at the
south end of the isle. "Everyone in House Uuthar with
standing invitations to all three crime scenes. Are we being
accused of something?" Her voice didn't fluctuate in the
slightest, but Tane could have sworn he saw her eyes flick

over Indree's shoulder toward the manor house. *What is she looking at?* It was hard to follow her eyeline accurately given their difference in height, and there wasn't much there. Some windows, another covered patio, a cellar door set into the foundation.

"Not at all, Your Honor," Indree said. "Again, I'm sorry, but we do need to be thorough. Every name we check off the list narrows it down. If you can all account for your movements, we'll be on our way."

"We were here, of course. Oden and Aigan are brunching with guests in town, but I can tell you that we were together all three nights. The incidents were all late in the evening, weren't they? We would have been settled in the lounge by then." Again, the senator's eyes moved. Just for an instant, and she covered it well, but Tane was certain now—she was looking at the cellar door. And she was nervous, for some reason. *What does she have in there?*

"We'll need to verify that with your staff," Indree said. "Do you mind if we speak to them now?"

For the briefest moment, Noana Uuthar's perfect facade faltered. "Right now? I…" She regained her composure almost instantly. "Now isn't a good time. We're renovating a number of rooms in the house. But I know just who you'll need to talk to. What if I send them to Stooketon Yard?"

Tane caught Indree's eye, and raised a brow. She nodded. She'd noticed it too.

"That is very generous, Your Honor," Indree said. "But I had hoped to have a look around the house and grounds as well. Just to be thorough, of course."

"I don't think that will be necessary, Inspector," Senator Uuthar said firmly. "I'm sure Chief Constable Durren would agree. I will send the appropriate staff to the Yard. Now please, excuse me." She hefted her book, and smiled again—it was as lovely as before, but this time Tane could see the insincerity behind it. "I had just reached a rather exciting chapter."

Polite, but a dismissal all the same. They were ushered back around the house and off the grounds without delay.

Tane waited until they reached Indree's coach, away from the guardsmen at the gate, and then he said, "She was hiding something. She didn't want you poking around the house, and she kept glancing at the cellar door."

"The cellar?" Indree frowned. "I didn't catch that. But she certainly was quick to get rid of us when I suggested looking around the grounds."

"Which means is just what we should do, yes?" Kadka said. "Why leave?"

"Because I need a warrant to search her property without her permission," said Indree. "And Durren isn't going to be happy when I ask for one. Not for a senator's estate." She sighed. "I hate this case, I really do."

"We both know that's going to take too long," Tane said. "By the time you have your warrant, she'll have hidden whatever it is she needs to hide. Spellfire, Ree, someone else could be dead by then!"

"What else can I do, Tane?" Indree demanded. "I'm bound by the law. I'll try to make Durren see reason—he'll at least understand that more murders look bad for him. Until then, I don't want you two doing anything stupid."

Tane held up his hands in surrender. "Couldn't if we wanted to. Our invitation was temporary. There's no way we're getting back in through the estate's wards."

Indree fixed him with a long look, and then nodded. "True, I suppose. Do you two need a ride?"

Tane shook his head. "No, you should get straight back to the Yard and get started on that warrant. We'll take the discs."

Indree just nodded and climbed up to her seat. "I'll let you know when I have something." She motioned to the driver, and then they were away.

Tane turned to Kadka as soon as Indree was out of earshot. "She'll never get it in time. Come on."

"I know this look." A grin spread across Kadka's face. "You have plan. What is it?"

"To get back in through the estate's wards. But we're going to need help."

CHAPTER TWELVE

———

"MY FRIENDS! WHAT a wonderful treat to see you again!" Bastian Dewglen fluttered up to meet them on iridescent butterfly wings. He was dressed, as ever, in an impeccably tailored green suit and matching masquerade mask. Behind him, a massive warehouse workshop was filled with cluttered tables, and a small army was hard at work assembling artifacts out of brass and copper and gold and precious gems. Here and there, pincered brass arms attached to the tables performed simple tasks like sorting charms and artifacts into different crates—automation in its most basic, limited form. Even when there was nothing in front of them, they continued their grab-and-move motion in an endless pantomime.

"Bastian," Tane said with a smile. The round-bellied little sprite might have been a criminal, but his enthusiasm was hard to resist. "You've grown your operation, I see." Bastian's previous shop had been destroyed by men working for Chancellor Nieris—the new location was easily three times the size.

Bastian sighed mournfully and placed a hand over his heart. "It was all I could do, in memory of the friends lost in that barbaric attack. We cannot let such evils press us down, Mister Carver! We must hold our heads high and show them the strength of the Audish spirit!" He flew by Tane to perch on Kadka's shoulder. "My dearest Kadka, you understand what I mean, don't you? Your irrepressible spirit is a great part of what I admire so about you."

Kadka laughed, tilting her head to look at him. "Still say too many words for what you mean, little man. But I understand."

Bastian beamed at her. "I knew you would!" His smile quickly fell into a frown. "But there do seem to be more evils than usual haunting our streets of late. A terrible thing, this Emperor's Mask business. I suppose that's what brings you here?"

Tane raised an eyebrow. "What have you heard?"

"It is all over Thaless that this Mask has challenged the Magebreakers," Bastian said. "A grave mistake, and one I have no doubt that he will soon regret! But is it true?"

All over Thaless. Wonderful. Well, no point lying, I suppose. "More or less. And don't call us Magebreakers."

Bastian pouted his lower lip. "It seems a shame to waste such a wonderfully vivid title, but if you insist. In any event, I am delighted to know you are on the case! The Mask *must* be stopped. Anyone who fancies the rise of another Mage Emperor is a traitor to everything Audland represents. Magic for the magical? Pah! Magic is for everyone!" He punched a little hand into his palm as punctuation, his round cheeks flushed with passion. "My friends, your dedication to our nation's interests never ceases to amaze me. I know that you will get the better of this madman in short order. But let us speak of happier things! I understand you have brought a very interesting guest to see me."

"Endo Stooke," said Tane. "You've heard of him too, I take it."

"A young prodigy!" Bastian exclaimed by way of confirmation. "So little of his artifice work reaches the public, but I make a point of knowing the most talented names in the field. What I've heard of his progress with automation is astounding!"

"So… can we bring him in?" Tane asked.

"Ah," said Bastian. "That little issue. I *am* sorry my friends had to hold him outside, but you know, the young son of a Senate house doesn't come to my little shop every day. Normally there are channels for that, and of course my usual policy of acquiring a divination focus is out of the question. Are you quite certain he can be trusted to keep a secret?"

"I believe so," said Tane. "We were hired to investigate Ulnod Stooke's murder. Endo just wants justice for his brother. He won't do anything to jeopardize the investigation. And right now, we're at a dead end without his help. And yours."

"Well that won't do at all! Let us not delay another instant! If you trust him, I trust him!" Bastian clapped his hands together and motioned to the men waiting at the door. "Bring him in!"

Bastian's men escorted Endo in through the door. Wheeling in his chair, Endo surveyed the huge workshop with wide eyes.

"I didn't think it would be so big," he said as he drew up alongside Tane and Kadka.

Bastian hopped down from Kadka's shoulder in a flutter of wings to alight on the arm of Endo's chair. "Endo Stooke. My deepest condolences for your loss. A true tragedy." He extended a tiny hand, and Endo hesitantly took it between his thumb and finger. Bastian shook vigourously. "Bastian Dewglen at your service, and let me say that even in these dark times, it is an honor to meet you! I have followed your artifice work where I could—particularly your work in automation. I've dabbled myself"—he gestured towards the brass arms working away behind him—"but only for the most repetitive tasks. I understand you have a great mind for it!"

Endo flushed and ducked his head. "Thank you, but I'm not sure about that."

"Nonsense!" Bastian gestured at the chair beneath his feet. "This is your work, no? Such elegance!" He took flight once more, surveying the spells etched into brass and copper. "The efficiency is astounding." Hovering by the wheels, he jabbed a finger excitedly at a section of glyphs and looked back at Tane. "Have you seen this?"

Tane stepped closer and knelt to look. The glyphs etched around the circumference of the wheels detailed spells of motion and guidance. "That's interesting. The way the steering and the momentum spells are integrated…"

"I could never have arranged it so elegantly!" Bastian said. "The way one plays into the other, eliminating redundancies! Expensive to power even so, I imagine—my clientele prefers a better cost to effect—but to make such a thing function all day without an ancryst engine… Bravo, Mister Stooke!"

"Well, I had a lot of free time to work on it," Endo said, leaning over the side of his chair to look at them. The blush was fading from his cheeks, and there was a spark of excitement in his eye. "If you find that interesting, you might like the levitation spells underneath. They're not perfect yet, but—"

"Maybe you three talk about this later," Kadka said from behind, and Tane glanced back to see her watching them with a sharp-toothed grin. "Could go all night, I think. But is not why we are here."

"Right." Tane stood and brushed off his knees. "Bastian, we need something illegal fast."

Bastian landed on the arm of Endo's chair once more. "Well, you have my attention! Perhaps it's best if we speak in my office."

Bastian took flight and beckoned for them to follow, then led them through the warehouse to a room in the back corner. Inside, several comfortable chairs sat before a pedestal with a sprite-sized desk atop it. A countertop ran around the edge of the room with a number of small work stations set upon its surface, most bearing artifacts in various stages of construction.

Bastian landed atop the pedestal and rested his round body in the tiny chair behind his desk. "Please, sit," he said. "Tell me more."

"We have to bypass some powerful wards," Tane explained, lowering himself into a chair. Beside him, Kadka did the same, and Endo rolled his chair between theirs. "Probably best if I don't say where, but Endo has a standing invite. The problem is, he can't get where we need to get without being noticed. So I need a mimic vial."

"Ah," said Bastian. "So that is why I've been given the pleasure of meeting young Mister Stooke." He smiled at Endo. "I am glad to have had the opportunity, but a hair or fingernail would have sufficed. You hardly needed to trouble yourself coming here."

"I wanted to," said Endo. "I... didn't feel comfortable, after what happened to my brother... I couldn't give a focus to a stranger without seeing with my own eyes what happened to it." He rubbed the back of his neck awkwardly. "I'm sorry. I don't mean to offend."

"No offense taken whatsoever!" Bastian exclaimed. "I do hate the label, but I am what some might call a criminal, after all! No, you were wise to consider the dangers. Perhaps you would like to put your focus into the vial yourself? I won't lay a hand on it, and once our mutual friends have taken it from here, I expect I shall never see it again. Does that ease your mind?"

Endo was silent a moment, and then nodded. "I... suppose it does."

"Well then, to business!" said Bastian. "I have the vials, of course. But there is a complication. They are only useful for confusing detection spells, not breaking wards." He turned to Tane. "If you want to replace your Astral signature with his, you of all people must know it won't work, Mister Carver. The vial will only overlay a second signature on top of yours. A masking spell won't help—it might stop a spell from identifying you specifically, but not from sensing an Astral link at all. And any worthwhile ward will have been set to lock out such conflicts. It's been tried a hundred different ways."

"That won't be a problem," said Tane, and tipped his head toward Kadka.

She grinned. "Don't need to mask anything. We have me."

A smile of understanding spread across Bastian's face. "Of course! Oh, well done, my friends! Brilliant! It couldn't work for anyone else, but with your natural invisibility to the Astra... the ward will detect a sentient creature with Mister Stooke's signature, and nothing else! Wait here!" In a flurry of wings, he flew out of the room, and Tane heard him rummaging around outside. A moment later, he reappeared, holding a brooch-sized cylindrical artifact in both hands. "I'll have to make some modifications, of course." He moved to an empty worktable at the edge of the room and set down the vial.

Tane stood to observe; Kadka and Endo followed. The mimic vial was a small glass tube in a copper sleeve, with glyphs etched around the outside. Whatever divination focus was put in the vial would give off the semblance of its owner's Astral signature to detection spells and the like. They were quite illegal—usually used, as Bastian had mentioned, to confuse divinations or raise false alerts from detection spells. No one had ever managed to use one to get through a ward, though.

But there's a first time for everything.

Bastian took a small scrap of copper in hand, uttered a spell in the *lingua*, and began pulling and shaping the metal in his hands into a thin, sharp point, like a sewing needle. "This is the easiest way to bind it to you," he said to Kadka. Another spell uttered, and Bastian fused the needle to the copper case of the vial. Then, with an incredibly tiny etching tool, he began scribing glyphs too small for Tane to read along the narrow length. "Stick the needle into your flesh, and the copper will direct the decoy signature inward. The shoulder, I should think, where it won't do much damage. The spells will hold it in place until you remove it yourself. It won't be pleasant, but I suspect you can handle that if anyone can." Finally, he hefted the vial in his hands and fluttered down to the arm of Endo's chair. "There we are. If you would be so kind as to provide the focus, Mister Stooke?"

Endo took the vial, and—after a short hesitation—plucked a hair from his head with a wince. "I've... never done something like this before," he said, looking up at Tane. "Illegal, I mean. Are you sure... is this going to help find the person who killed Ulnod?"

"I wouldn't ask you to do it if I thought otherwise," Tane said. "Noana Uuthar is hiding something, and we need to know what it is."

"Then..." Endo took a deep breath and slipped the hair into the vial, then sealed it again and offered it to Kadka. "Here. Take it."

She did, offering him a toothy smile in return that was as gentle as Tane had ever seen her manage. "No one will know you helped us. Is right thing, to find Mask before he kills again."

"I know," said Endo. "Please, just... stop him."

"Soon," Kadka said. But for an instant, Tane thought he saw a flicker of doubt in her eyes. No more than he'd been feeling himself, but it was worse, somehow, coming from her.

"We'll get him, Endo," he said. *I hope.*

Bastian's relentless enthusiasm, at least, was undimmed. "You've put your trust in the right place, Mister Stooke! These two will not disappoint you." He raised a finger. "There is one more thing, however. The vial will not work forever. Once the needle is inserted, whatever Astral energy is left in that hair will be drained quickly to cast Mister Stooke's signature. But you needn't worry so long as you get inside within a few minutes—wards only function on entry. There may still be detection spells, but we both know those are of no consequence to our dear Kadka." He gazed at her wistfully behind his extravagant mask. "Ah, if only I could convince you to turn those gifts to my service. We would make such a beautiful team."

"Keep dreaming, little man," Kadka said with a fond grin. "One day, maybe I get desperate. But not now." She glanced down at the mimic vial in her hand, and then up at Tane. "Come, Carver. We have crime to do."

CHAPTER THIRTEEN

———

"IS BROKEN HERE," said Kadka, peering up at the ten foot wall around the Uuthar estate. "I can climb." After leaving Bastian's, she and Carver had waited for the cover of dark to sneak along the banks of the Aud, careful to stay out of sight. It wouldn't look good if the Mageblade patrols found a half-orc creeping around the Roost at night.

Here, where the estate walls butted up against the river, a number of bricks were loose or broken—enough to work as handholds. As Carver was so fond of noting, people who relied on wards and magic tended to let the old fashioned methods fall by the wayside.

"Alright," whispered Carver, peering nervously over his shoulder. "Wait until you hear me shouting before you go. I'll make sure the guards are distracted."

"Go, then." Kadka shooed Carver away. The plan was the plan—there was no purpose going over it for the tenth time.

He scurried away down the river, keeping low so that the walls of the estates along the bank hid him from sight. Kadka leaned back against the bricks to wait. She *hated* waiting. She'd learned to do it well enough in her youth, hunting prey in the Svernan tundra, but never patiently, and the time she'd spent guarding doors at the University hadn't made her like it any better.

Finally, after a quarter hour, she heard shouting from the far side of the estate. Her orcish ears had no trouble recognizing Carver's voice: "I demand to see Senator Uuthar! I have questions she hasn't answered, and I won't be denied!"

As good a signal as any. Kadka took the mimic vial from her trouser pocket, careful not to prick her hand on the needle, and then, without hesitation, jabbed it into her shoulder.

It stung, but not unbearably. A sudden warmth passed through her body, and she grinned wide. Magic never got old.

Carver shouted again, far across the grounds: "The Magebreakers won't rest until our questions are answered!" That must have been hard for him—he hated that name. She could picture vividly the way he'd have cringed as he said it.

No time to enjoy the thought. She had to get in before the vial's magic ran out.

Kadka turned, and started climbing.

Carver was still yelling as she peeked her head over the wall. She'd picked an isolated spot in one corner of the grounds, and there were no lights here. Her keen night vision picked out two guards beside a small gate to the riverbank halfway across the garden, and no one else. The rest must have already gone towards the noise. No Mageblades inside the walls either—according to Carver, House Uuthar lacked any notable magicless members to protect from the Mask.

The way was clear. Now all she could do was hope Bastian's device worked, and that she hadn't already run out of time. She took a breath and heaved herself over, preparing to smash her face against an invisible wall. It wouldn't be the first time.

Instead, she felt the tingle on her skin that she always felt passing through a ward. The white fur on the backs of her hands rose slightly, and then she was through. She dropped down on the other side of the wall, landing in a quiet crouch.

She was inside the Uuthar estate.

For a moment, she didn't move, just hunkered at the foot of the wall and surveyed her surroundings. She was alone; there were no guards nearby. The garden was wide, but not without cover—tall hedges divided it into sections. So long as she kept quiet, making it to the cellar would be easy enough. And not even *that* quiet, with Carver bellowing at the gates.

Ignoring the slight but persistent pain of the needle in her shoulder, she crept across the grounds, staying in the shadow of hedges where she could and placing her feet gently with each step. The pliant grass muffled most of the sound, but if she went too quickly, it would crunch underfoot. Moving silently was something else she'd learned hunting in Sverna when she was young. The white elk of the orcish homeland were more alert than most anyone in Audland.

As far as she could tell, no one had seen her by the time she reached the manor. The cellar was set into the ground against the back wall, a short distance to the left of a magelit patio overlooking the garden. The silver-blue glow reached far enough that she'd have to be careful getting closer. She could move without sound, and for whatever reason she was invisible to most magic, but she couldn't stop herself from casting a shadow.

There was a fairly clear sightline down the center of the garden, a cobbled path from the patio at the back of the house to the small gate opening onto the river. If either of the gate guards saw movement against the light, it would be a problem. The cellar was far enough to the side that it might be out of sight, and she hoped the gazebo in the middle of the garden would provide some cover, open-sided as it was, but she couldn't be certain.

Kadka went ahead anyway. Who needed certainty, really?

She was all too aware of her shadow against the grass as she closed the distance, but it was faint, blending into a hundred other darknesses. Drawing alongside the cellar doors, she stopped, glanced down the central path. The gate was hidden behind a hedge at this angle, but just barely; she could see the arm of one of the guards peeking around the edge.

The doors were standard cellar fare, a pair of thick wooden slabs in a stone setting, large enough for an ogren to pass through easily. Less common was the iron chain that joined the handles together, fastened with a heavy lock. Hardly enough to raise eyebrows—the Uuthars had a right to security on their own property—but intuition told Kadka that they were hiding something beyond preserves or old furniture.

She gripped the chain where it looped through the handles and pulled. It jangled slightly and held fast. Kadka looked over her shoulder to see if the sound had been noted; the bit of the guard's arm she could see didn't move.

Carver was still arguing with the guards at the front gate. She could hear him, distantly, although the shouting had hit something of a lull. A lull that wouldn't last, if she knew him. She gripped the chain again, and waited.

It didn't take long. "You can't send me away! I'll raise a formal complaint! I have a right to…"

Masked by his ranting, Kadka braced her feet against the stone setting, wrapped the chain tight in both fists, and yanked violently. The metal didn't break, but wood buckled and bent. Which was just what she'd been hoping for. Thaless was a city of magic—the prevalence of wards meant that even when someone bothered with a lock, they rarely thought about the strength of the door itself. Another pull, and one of the handles broke free in a burst of splinters.

Again, she looked to the far gate. Still no movement.

With one quick motion, she cast both doors open. They always creaked louder the slower you tried to open them, she'd found. Behind them, a stone stairway descended beneath the manor. She'd expected darkness, but there was a light at the bottom of the stairs, faint and silver.

Kadka stepped through the doors.

Something resisted.

There was nothing there under her foot, but she couldn't lower it any further. A ward. Either the magic of the vial had run out, or Endo's invitation wasn't enough to enter. Probably both.

There was definitely something down there, though. Which meant she had to get in.

How would Carver do it? He knew about tricking wards. Always a flaw, he liked to say. Maybe Endo couldn't get in, but someone had to be allowed. And Kadka thought she knew who. She glanced at her shoulder, where the small vial jabbed into her flesh, and an idea started to form.

The handle she'd yanked from the door lay on the ground at her feet, a heavy iron thing large enough for ogren hands. She picked it up; it had a solid heft to it. Aiming for a spot on the side wall near the back, she hurled the handle in a high arc over the hedges. It hit the wall with a loud clang and clattered to the ground.

"What was that?" One of the guards at the riverside gate, far away but loud enough for orc ears.

"Better have a look," his partner answered.

Across the grounds, the arm poking out beyond the hedge disappeared.

Kadka made for the path down the center of the garden. When she rounded the hedge that had blocked her sight before, both guards were gone, off to investigate the noise. That was lucky—she'd worried one might stay at the gate. Probably one *should* have stayed, but she couldn't blame them. She'd spent all night guarding a door before, and after a few hours, any distraction was welcome.

The gazebo was her target. She made for it in long, loping strides, covering ground as quickly as she could without giving away her presence. Stepping onto the marble base of the structure, she ducked low to take cover behind the furniture, and crossed to the huge chair Noana Uuthar had been sitting in when they'd visited earlier. She didn't have much hope of finding what she needed, but sometimes luck provided.

This time, it did. She had to climb halfway into the massive seat just to get a look, but against the back cushion, her keen night-eyes found a long strand of flaxen hair. Kadka plucked it up between two fingers.

She could hear the footsteps of the guards returning to their posts, and she was in clear sight of the gate now. Had to move quickly. She stole back up the path and ducked out of sight behind the hedge. No shouts from behind. Good. They hadn't seen her.

Her back against the hedge, Kadka grabbed the vial jutting from her shoulder and pulled it free. It hurt as much coming out as it had going in—not unbearable, but annoying. She unscrewed the cap and fished out a single dark strand of Endo's hair. She didn't need it anymore; it had probably lost power by now anyway. In it's place, she inserted the long blonde hair she'd taken from Noana Uuthar's chair. Then, bracing herself, she jabbed the needle back into her arm.

Magic never got old, but that particular part of it was becoming tiresome. She preferred the kind without needles.

The same strange warmth as before passed through her. Which meant it was working, she hoped.

She crossed to the cellar, and stepped over the threshold once more. This time, her foot touched the steps without interference.

"...one of those Magebreakers. They were here earlier. Don't know what he was so riled about." A man's voice from around the corner of the house, and footsteps moving in her direction.

"Persistent, I'll give him that," a woman's voice replied. "Well, he's in the Mageblades' hands now."

So the Mageblades had interceded to stop Carver's distraction. And as soon as the returning patrol rounded the corner, they'd see her.

Kadka moved quickly down the steps, and the tingle of a ward ran over her skin as she passed through. She drew the doors closed behind her. How she was going to get back *out* now, she had no idea, but at least she'd made it in unseen.

She descended toward the light at the bottom of the stairs, slipping one hand behind her back to grasp the hilt of the knife hidden there. If this was the Mask's lair, she was going to be ready. As ready as she could be, against an opponent who had barely seemed to notice her the last time they'd fought.

But it wasn't the lair of a murderer she found at the bottom of the stairs.

She was in a child's bedroom.

Except the child must have been a giant. Or an ogren.

A massive bed sat on one side of the room, and on a table beside it was the source of the dim magelight: a porcelain night-lamp shaped like a crescent moon. The bed was empty, the sheets left in messy disarray. Whoever slept there, they weren't anywhere in sight. To her right, a closed door led to another room. A privy of some kind, Kadka hoped, for the sake of whoever lived down here. Glyphs were carved in places high on the ceiling—relating to wards, she assumed. She recognized the upper half-circle within a circle glyph Carver had explained to her the other day, the one than meant 'all things sentient'.

Toys were scattered everywhere, just like in Dernor Deepweld's room, but the little dwarf boy would barely have been able to lift these. A ship, and a knight, and a dragon, and several others, all carved from wood, all near the size of Kadka's torso. Most were broken and battered and bent, and several had been torn clean in two. Whoever had done that, they were incredibly strong. Kadka remembered Carver saying that the Uuthars had no children, and Noana had only talked about a grown nephew, so whose bedroom was this?

Beside the bed was a chest of drawers. That seemed as good a place as any to start looking. Kadka picked her way across the room through the ruined playthings and pulled open the top drawer. Simple clothing, nothing of interest. She shifted the top layer aside, and metal glinted in the dim light. The edge of something, wrapped in black cloth.

Kadka pulled the object free, unwrapped it. The cloth covering it wasn't just cloth, it was a long black robe.

And inside was a brass mask with narrow eyeslits, emblazoned with the Mage Emperor's sigil.

"*Deshka*," Kadka swore under her breath.

Footfalls from across the room. *Heavy* ones.

Kadka whirled. The door at the side of the room swung open.

It was the furthest thing from a child she could imagine. At a glance, the figure in the door was muscular enough to win a wrestling match with a manticore, and ugly enough to lose a beauty contest. He stood close to ten feet tall, broad-shouldered and barrel-chested, with a heavy gut and arms as thick around as ancryst cannons. His face was hideous and misshapen, one eye larger and higher than the other under a thick, single eyebrow that stretched across his bulging forehead. His nose was turned up like a pig's snout, and a wide mouth drooped at one side above at least four chins of folded fat.

An ogre.

Kadka had never seen one, but she'd heard the stories. One in three ogren children were born so monstrous and savage that they had to be kept in a remote sanctuary somewhere on the island. People said that they were as ugly as their parents were beautiful, and now she knew that was true—although statuesque ogren beauty had never been much to Kadka's taste anyway. More importantly, ogres were supposed to be far stronger than even their pure-born kindred, which was saying something. This one certainly looked it.

And he was between her and the way out.

She transferred the brass mask to her left hand and drew her knife, although she had a feeling it wouldn't bother this creature much more than the needle in her arm bothered her.

For a moment he just looked at her, blinking those dull, lopsided eyes. And then he growled, his lip pulling back to reveal an incomplete set of crooked teeth.

The ogre lowered his head and charged.

CHAPTER FOURTEEN

―――――

BROKEN TOYS FLEW aside as the ogre trampled towards her—and not slowly, despite his size.

Kadka leapt to the side, but a broken toy ship caught her leg before she could fully clear the ogre's path. A massive arm clipped her in the side, threw her and the ship hard against the wall. The mimic vial struck first, jarring the needle, and a sharp pain tore through her shoulder.

The ogre was already turning for her again, and the strength of even that glancing blow told her he was an opponent she couldn't fight. Another one. She clutched the brass mask tight in her hand. Her priority had to be getting out alive so she could show it to Carver and Indree, and she had a clear path to the stairs now. She shoved the toy ship aside and ran.

She wasn't fast enough. The ogre outpaced her on huge legs, wrapped meaty hands around her waist from behind. He lifted her from her feet like she weighed nothing at all. Kadka twisted to face the ogre; he roared full in her face, throwing spittle and hot breath against her cheeks. Those massive arms raised her high overhead, as if he meant to dash her against the floor.

She slashed backhanded at his wrist, drew blood. The ogre squealed in shocked dismay, released her with that hand, and brought the wound to his mouth to suck at it. The other hand around her waist loosened, and she squirmed free, dropping several feet to the floor.

The stairs were only an arm's length away, and Kadka scrabbled towards them, started climbing. Another roar, and thumping footsteps. He was following.

She was nearly at the doors when a massive weight struck her from behind, knocked the breath from her. An iron grip wrapped tight around her body. The force carried her up the last few steps, slammed her against the doors with concussive force. They flew open. Kadka could see stars above, swimming in her blurred vision. The mask flew from her hand to land in the grass. Her feet didn't join it there. She was trapped, held aloft by a giant arm.

The ogre had tackled them both through the doors, but his attention wasn't on her now. Instead, he swivelled his head from side to side, and made a strangled noise of confusion deep in his throat.

He wasn't used to the world outside his cellar. Something had to have been keeping him in. The wards. He probably couldn't leave unless he was with one of his keepers. Jailers? Kadka wasn't sure.

But whatever they were, Noana Uuthar was one of them. Kadka looked to the vial jabbed into her shoulder as understanding dawned. A red stain was growing on her shirt where the needle had torn flesh, but just then the pain didn't matter.

What mattered was that *she* had let this thing free.

"What in the Astra?" A woman's voice, one of the guards Kadka had heard earlier. A dwarven woman. She approached with her human partner, and there were more closing in on all sides, weapons drawn. "Don't move!"

The ogre moved. He looked left, then right, saw guards surrounding him. With one hand, he lifted Kadka like she was a toy.

And then he *threw* her.

She flew through the air, crashed against the dwarven woman and her partner, and all three of them fell to the ground in a heap. Kadka heard the ogre moving again, grabbed the woman under her, and rolled to the side just as a huge foot stomped down the grass where they'd been. Craning her neck, Kadka watched the ogre go; he crashed around the corner of the house and out of sight. Toward the front gate.

Toward the street. There were people out there. Guards, Mageblades, maybe others.

Carver.

And it was her fault this thing was loose.

Kadka pushed herself up, snatched the mask from where it had fallen, and staggered after the ogre, her head still spinning from the impact.

"Stop!" an ogren guard commanded, moving to pursue. "Who are you?"

Kadka just kept going, faster with every step as her head cleared. "Not first problem, now," she said, and pointed in the direction the ogre had gone. "*He* is."

As if to prove her point, a startled cry came from the other side of the manor, and then a loud, angry roar.

The guards were following her now, either to stop her or pursue the ogre. It didn't matter which, really.

Kadka led them toward the sound.

————

Tane struggled against the Mageblade's grip, putting on a show. Anything to keep attention on him instead of what Kadka was doing. The dwarven man holding his arm just squeezed tighter. "You need to calm down, sir."

"Calm down? I'm being manhandled by—"

A loud crash interrupted him, and then shouting from deep in the estate. Tane snapped his head toward the sound. *Kadka, what did you do?*

The second Mageblade, a blue-scaled kobold, motioned to his partner. "Could be the Mask. We need to get in there now."

The dwarf nodded and released Tane's arm. "Sir, we need you to get to a safe distance." He and his partner approached the gates. Tane followed two steps behind.

Something was moving around the side of the house. A massive shadow emerged into the glow of the magelights along the manor's front steps. Something as tall as an ogren but broader at the shoulder, with a hunched head, a huge gut, and massive arms. Several guards approached the shape, and a pair of Mageblades already on the grounds left their posts at the door to get closer.

Several cries, an angry roar, a sweep of a giant arm, and guards went flying. The thing never stopped moving; it seemed to be headed for the gates, and closing fast.

And then Tane understood what Noana Uuthar had been hiding. An ogre. They were meant to be sent to the sanctuary at the south end of the island at birth, where they could live safely without putting anyone in danger.

Apparently the Uuthars had taken exception to that policy.

The ogre showed no sign of slowing as it neared the gate, just lowered its head and dropped a shoulder.

It's going to go right through. "Get out of the way!" Tane shouted, and leapt to one side. The gate guards heeded his warning, scrambling to either side. The Mageblades didn't.

They began to chant in the *lingua*, a coordinated duet of arcane words, and both raised their hands at the same moment. A sheet of silver-blue shielding rose across the gap in the wall where the gate sat.

The ogre collided with the gate, and it was iron that buckled, not flesh. Metal squealed and broke, and the doors crashed open. The Mageblade's shield fared better; with a great silver flash, it arrested the ogre's momentum.

But the two Mageblades flinched back, as if struck by a physical blow. They set their feet as the ogre took three steps back and hurled himself at the shield again.

It didn't hold. Another silver flash and the sheet of energy evaporated. The ogre swept the Mageblades aside with one arm as it crashed through, hurling both men to the cobblestones several yards away.

And then it was free, loping away down the street.

Free, and strong enough to break a shield cast by two trained combat mages.

Spellfire, that thing could tear the city to pieces. We're going to need more than a few Mageblades.

Tane dug in his left pocket and came out with the sending locket Indree had given him. He squeezed it tight in his hand.

And instant later, a familiar pressure grew in his ears, and he heard Indree's voice. *"Tane, what's wrong? Did you find something?"*

"You could say that. There's an ogre loose in the Gryphon's Roost."

"What? How is that even possible?"

"Carver! Is no time to stand around! Come!" Kadka yelled as she came sprinting through the broken gates. She jabbed a finger after the ogre; another Mageblade patrol was moving to stop it now. Tane didn't like their chances.

"Kadka, there's nothing we can—"

She tossed him something that glinted in the silver-blue magelight of the street lamps. He caught it. A brass mask, bearing the Mage Emperor's sigil.

"Found this in cellar with him," she said.

That, Tane couldn't let pass. "Let's go."

Kadka started after the ogre once more, and Tane chased behind, tucking the mask into his belt.

"Tane!" Indree's voice again. *"What in the Astra is happening?"*

"I told you, Ree. An ogre. You have to get people here to contain this thing fast, and a lot of them. There aren't enough

Mageblades." Tane fumbled in his pockets as he ran, badly outpaced by Kadka. He'd bought several charms from Bastian, but he wasn't sure which of them would be of use now. Certainly not the shield, if two Mageblades couldn't hold one against the ogre's strength.

Indree didn't waste any more time. "*Where?*"

"*We're on Riverview, beside the Aud. Coming up on the intersection with Audlian's Way.*"

"*I can have a squad there in a few minutes. Just tell me if it moves. And stay out of its way.*"

"*Will do,*" Tane lied.

Ahead, two Mageblades were trying to bind the ogre with magic. Silver-blue cords wrapped around its wrists. It heaved against them once, and again, and then the Astral bindings broke. With a backwards sweep of its hand, the ogre threw a brass-armored elf against the wall of the adjacent estate. The other Mageblade, a human woman, fired her ancryst pistol, chanting in the *lingua* as she did. The ball struck true, and the ogre howled in pain, but didn't stop. It was on her before she could finish her spell, grabbing the hand holding the pistol. The ogre lifted her by one arm and squeezed; the woman screamed as pistol and bone broke.

Kadka was behind the ogre now, and she leapt onto its back, wrapped both arms around its neck. Surprised, it dropped the Mageblade, who fell clasping her ruined hand. Keeping her grip with one arm, Kadka raised her knife and plunged it into the ogre's shoulder. It let out a bellow and shook its massive body like a dog just out of the water, whipping Kadka back and forth like a rag doll. Her grip failed, and she flew free, landed hard on the ground.

The ogre tromped after her.

Closing the distance at last, Tane stepped in front of Kadka and raised his fist. "Close your eyes!" he shouted, and then he closed his, and crushed the charm clasped in his palm.

A flash of light burned pink through his eyelids. The ogre roared in shock. Tane opened his eyes to see it stumbling back, turning away. And then it ran, covering distance quickly on massive, muscular legs.

Kadka climbed to her feet, didn't even take a moment to steady herself before giving chase again. As she moved by, Tane saw a look of fierce determination in her eyes, very different from the grin she usually wore when she fought.

Tane pulled another charm from his left pocket, and the charmglobe from the right—a palm-sized brass sphere that could activate a charm on a short delay. Fumbling with the globe's clasp, he ran after Kadka once more.

The street was blocked just ahead—a bulky ancryst-powered carriage lumbered to a stop on huge brass wheels as the ogre approached. Through the front window, Tane could see an elegantly dressed man and woman staring wide-eyed at the giant bearing down on them.

It's going to kill them. Even if it didn't mean to, it had to move the carriage to get by, and it wasn't going to do that gently.

Tane pushed his charm into place, snapped the charmglobe closed, wound the key just a fraction of a turn. With all his strength, he hurled it overhand, and hoped his aim and his timing were good.

The globe flew over the ogre's head, bounced once on the blocky snout of the ancryst carriage, and then burst open. A wave of silver blue energy rippled outward in an expanding circle. The man and woman in the carriage ducked down in their seats as the repulsion charm cracked their window, rocked their vehicle backwards a half-turn of those big wheels. The ogre staggered back several steps, shielding itself with both arms.

Which gave Kadka time to catch up. She ducked around the ogre, put herself between it and the carriage.

Tane skidded to a halt just behind. "What now?" he called to her, praying that she had some kind of plan.

Kadka just raised her knife. "Now we try not to die," she said.

The ogre stomped toward her, growling. Tane scooped up a piece of cobblestone that had broken under a heavy foot. None of his other charms were going to be much use, and he had to do something. He drew back his hand to throw.

He didn't have to. As the ogre lifted a huge arm to strike, a silver-blue manacle materialized around its wrist, and then another further up, and then more, all the way to the shoulder. The magical bindings wrenched the creature back. More shackles materialized on the ogre's other arm, and around its ankles and knees. A dozen men and women in blue uniforms and caps spilled around the halted ancryst carriage, chanting in the *lingua magica*.

Indree's squad had found them.

Thank the Astra. Tane let the rock fall from his hand. *They can handle this.*

And then the ogre moved.

Roaring in anger, straining every muscle in its body, it moved. Against all that Astral power, it took one step, and then another. With slow inevitability, it advanced on the bluecaps. A silver-blue shackle around its bicep shattered, and it picked up speed. Almost as one, the bluecaps drew a dozen ancryst pistols and readied to fire.

"No! Don't hurt him!"

Tane swiveled to see Noana Uuthar running up the street, a look of sheer terror on her face.

"He doesn't know what he's doing!" she shouted. "Please, you have to let me handle this!" She darted past Tane to put herself in the bluecaps' line of fire, towering over even the tallest by half their height again—there were no ogren among them.

"Step aside, Senator Uuthar," ordered a dwarven man standing at the front of the bluecap line. None of them lowered their pistols.

The senator didn't answer, just turned her back on them to face the ogre. "Be still, Odeth. Mother is here." Her eyes fell to the bleeding wounds left in the ogre's shoulder by blade and pistol. "Oh, my dear child, what have they done to you?"

The ogre slowed at the sight of her, recognition lighting its dull eyes. She laid a gentle hand against its cheek. *His* cheek, Tane supposed, although he hadn't thought of the creature in those terms until that moment.

And then Noana Uuthar started to sing. It was soft and lovely, a lullaby by the melody, except the words were in the *lingua magica*. The ogre's lopsided eyes slowly closed. His great ugly head dropped to his chest, and his huge shoulders slumped. He fell to his knees, and then collapsed to the ground in a heap, snoring loudly.

"You see?" Senator Uuthar said, turning to the dwarven bluecap who'd spoken before. "You don't have to hurt him."

The dwarf motioned the others forward—apparently he was in charge. "Secure it," he said, and the bluecaps started to do just that, moving to surround the ogre and renewing their shackling spells. "Senator, I'm going to need an explanation."

"Please," Uuthar begged, tears glinting in her eyes. Even kneeling, she was taller than the bluecaps surrounding her, but in that moment, she looked very small. "Don't take him. You have to understand, we tried for so long for a child. When Odeth came, I… I couldn't bear to give him up to the sanctuary. You can't take him from me."

"I'm sorry, Your Honor, but it's the law," the dwarf said, not unsympathetically. "We have to take it—him—in. People have been hurt."

"It wasn't his fault," Uuthar said, but there wasn't much fight in her voice. She knew what had to happen. "He doesn't understand. He was just afraid."

"That doesn't explain this," said Tane, and drew the brass mask from his belt.

The dwarven bluecap went pale under his beard. "Is that…"

"This is what the Emperor's Mask wears," said Tane, and pointed at the ogre. "And it was in his room."

Senator Uuthar looked at the mask, blinked, and then met Tane's eyes with fear in hers. "I've never seen that before in my life."

"Well, you'll have to convince Inspector Lovial of that," the dwarf said. "You're coming with us."

"You don't understand," the senator said urgently. "I didn't put it there, and Odeth couldn't have. Which means it must have been *him*."

CHAPTER FIFTEEN

———

"SHE'S CLAIMING THAT she was framed by the *actual* Mask," said Indree. "It's not a very strong case. Our diviners confirm that she's hiding something, but she won't say more."

Tane and Kadka sat in the holding chamber at Stooketon Yard, a small room with benches along the walls where prisoners were kept awaiting processing and questioning. They'd just come out of initial questioning themselves, though there would likely be more after Noana Uuthar's interview was complete.

"So you think it's her?" Tane wasn't so sure. He'd seen the look in the senator's eyes when he'd shown her the mask, and it had been deeper than just fear that she'd been caught. He *wanted* to believe the case was done, but he had to know for certain.

Indree raised an eyebrow. "Do you *care* what I think? I told you not to do anything, and instead you let loose an ogre and chased it across the city."

"Was my fault," said Kadka, with an unmistakable note of self-reproach. "Only meant to look. Should have stopped him from escape. Stupid."

"You didn't know what you were walking into," Tane

objected. "It was my idea to go in to begin with. And we *did* find what she was hiding, to be fair."

"I'm happy to blame you both," Indree said, glaring at the two of them. And then her shoulders fell. "It doesn't really matter now. I'm the head investigator in name only at this point. Chief Durren has a likely suspect, and as far as he's concerned, if he brings down the Mask before Lady Abena returns, she can't very well punish him for pushing me aside while she was away. He's leading the charge against Senator Uuthar."

"You *don't* think she did it." Tane knew that tone in her voice—she had doubts. "You think he's focusing his attention in the wrong place."

Indree shrugged. "We know she didn't kill anyone, at least not directly. We've questioned her staff, and her alibi holds. The current theory is that she had the ogre do it. He's got the size and strength you talked about, and wouldn't need magic if it was all artifacts."

"I don't know if that's a much stronger case," said Tane. "Doesn't it seem a bit convenient? After all this, the Mask just keeps his costume in his top drawer? And dear little Odeth didn't particularly strike me as the silent assassin type."

Kadka nodded. "When I fight Mask, was different than ogre. Both are strong, but ogre is more like wild animal. No control."

"Exactly," said Tane. "Would *you* send an ogre to do anything that requires the kind of finesse we've seen from the Mask?"

"*I* wouldn't, but I'm told she demonstrated some power over him." Indree didn't sound particularly convinced. "Simple minds can be dominated by magic. It's not impossible." She sighed. "The truth is, there are a lot of questions I'd like to ask Senator Uuthar, but Durren isn't letting me in on the interrogation."

"How does *he* think she did it?" Tane asked. "Controlling her son through sendings, fine. It's possible. But how did she get him through all the wards and detections?"

"It's not actually an awful theory," said Indree. "Ogres have a very simplistic Astral link. Similar to wild animals, like Kadka says. And even the strongest Astral wards tend to allow for that kind of limited sentience, or we'd have dead birds sliding down wards all over Thaless. It's not quite enough to allow an ogre by default, but Noana Uuthar was a frequent guest at every house the Mask targeted. She could have accessed the wards at any time, altered the animal exemptions just enough to admit her son. An adjustment that small would be nearly impossible to detect, unless someone was looking for it. We're going over the spells again now, and there are some indications of tampering."

"It's… plausible," Tane admitted. "But—"

"But nothing. Your opinion isn't needed here, Carver." Chief Durren strode into the holding chamber from the corridor that led to the interview rooms. "You've been lucky a few times, but we're building a real case here. Which you don't know a thing about."

"Did you get anything more from her, then, sir?" Indree asked.

Durren frowned. "What more do you want, Lovial? The diviners say she's lying, and she had the mask. You just explained how she had the means."

"So is no, then?" Kadka said with a mocking grin. "Can't make her say more, after this long?"

Durren didn't respond, just scowled and looked to Indree. "Get rid of these two. We don't need anything more from them. You two can consider yourselves lucky I don't want to muddy the senator's arrest, or I'd be charging you both for breaking onto her property."

"Wait," said Tane. "You talked about means, but what about motive? Why would she have killed those people? She was acting suspiciously, I'll grant you, but I probably would too if I had a secret ogre in my basement. Wanting to keep her son close doesn't make her a killer."

"You're asking me... *You* were the ones sneaking around her estate! Suddenly you can't think of a word to say against her?" Durren's cheeks flushed red. "You want a motive, fine. Jealousy. She had to hide her son while so many houses groom their non-magical offspring as future Protectors of the Realm. She couldn't take it anymore."

"I don't think—" Tane began.

"I don't care what you think," Durren snapped. "Lovial, I need to notify the Lady Protector of my findings. I want these two gone when I come back. And see that Senator Uuthar is put in a holding cell until I'm ready to speak to her again." He crossed the room and let the door slam behind him.

"I need to talk to the senator," Tane said as soon as Chief Durren was gone.

"What?" Indree shook her head. "No. Even if I wanted to, I can't put you in an interview room with her. There are guards on the doors, and they'll have orders from the chief. If Durren hears I tried, I'll be in an even worse position than I already am. Besides, you've done quite enough. He was right about one thing—you're lucky you haven't been arrested already."

"If there's even a chance she didn't do it, we're risking the real Mask going free," said Tane. "Your diviners say she's hiding something, and I think I can get her to talk. If there's something else there, Kadka and I can still act on it, even if you can't. Don't try to tell me this story about the ogre feels right to you. I know you better than that."

Indree looked at him for a long moment, and then she said, "I've got my orders. She needs to be moved to a holding cell." She strode away toward the interview rooms.

Kadka got to her feet, stretched out her neck and shoulders. "Is time to go then, yes? If we can't see—"

Tane held up a finger. "Give her a minute."

Indree emerged from the corridor, leading Senator Uuthar and a pair of ogren constables. Just common sense, that—if Uuthar decided to resist, no one else was going to be able to stop her. Walking at the head of a nine-foot-tall procession, Indree looked no taller than a gnome.

She led the senator to a bench near Tane and Kadka. "Wait here a moment. We have a private cell for you. I need to make sure it's ready. I'm sure I can trust you to behave— I'd rather not have to cuff you." Then, turning to the pair of ogren bluecaps, "On the door, just in case. I'll be back shortly." Indree gave Tane a pointed look, and then strode down the opposite corridor toward the holding cells. The ogren constables followed her orders, taking guard positions over the chamber's only exit to the outside.

Which left Tane sitting beside Noana Uuthar, largely unsupervised.

He leaned closer and kept his voice low. "Senator Uuthar. I wanted to ask you something. Indulge me?" Kadka moved to stand between them and the guards, lending some degree of privacy.

The senator turned her head slightly to look down at him with sad, tired eyes. "You have questions? So do I. Why would you do this to my family? They took my son from me, Mister Carver." The way she said it, it didn't matter that her son was an ogre, or that she'd broken the law—just that Tane and Kadka had broken her family apart.

Tane swallowed and forced himself to look her in the eye. "I'm sorry, senator. That wasn't our intent. But we didn't put that mask there, and if you can't explain where it came from, you have bigger problems than being separated. If they think he's killed people, they're going to do a lot worse than just sending Odeth to the sanctuary. They know you're hiding something. If it can help him, you have to tell me what it is."

She shook her head. Again, that fear in her eyes. "No. I can't. He'll… it's too dangerous."

"They'll execute your son, senator. If you haven't noticed, no one else is very inclined to believe your innocence, or his." *Spellfire, this is low. It had better work.*

She didn't say anything for a time, just hung her head in defeat. And then, "Very well." A deep breath before she went on, in a barely-there whisper. "Some weeks ago, I received an anonymous message from a person or persons who knew about Odeth."

"What sort of message?" Tane asked. "Do you still have it?"

The senator shook her head. "No. It was a letter without originating address, charmed to incinerate itself shortly after I read it. It contained instructions to support certain pro-magical proposals in the Senate. To protect my son, I did as I was told. Each week further instructions came, and I had no choice but to follow them as well. I didn't know who was behind it until today, but..." Her hands trembled in her lap. "It had to be the Mask. Who else could have put those things in Odeth's room? And if he could do that... Mister Carver, he can get into my home. My family isn't safe. If I talk to the constabulary..."

"Senator, if you would come with me." Indree was back. Sooner than Tane had hoped, but he knew she'd given him what time she could. She motioned to the ogren constables, who approached to escort Senator Uuthar to her cell.

"Please," Noana Uuthar whispered urgently. "I'm telling you the truth. I can't speak freely to anyone else. You two have to stop him."

CHAPTER SIXTEEN

———

"YOU BELIEVE HER," said Kadka, leaning back in her chair with her feet on Tane's desk.

"I think I do," Tane answered "I wish I didn't. It would be easier if this ended with her."

He knelt beside the bottom cabinet in the desk, where he kept the apparatus that operated his office wards. A flip of a switch and it was active, draining power from gems he could scarcely afford. But it was worth the cost, given the circumstances. His office wasn't much—a cheap single room at 17 Tilford Street in Porthaven with a folding screen at the back that hid the mattress he slept on—but it was all he had. The Mask wasn't sneaking onto this list of exemptions. While they were up, Tane's wards allowed only himself, Kadka, and Indree to enter.

"Is something about sad mothers with you. Always works." Kadka didn't grin her customary sharp-toothed grin. She'd been curiously reserved since the incident at the Uuthar estate, Tane had noticed.

"It's not that," he said. "It was the way she acted. She was genuinely afraid."

"Could have been faking."

"I have a feeling that she wasn't." Tane lowered himself into his desk chair, pulled a near-empty bottle of cheap whiskey from the top drawer along with two glasses, and filled one for himself. He gestured to the other and raised an eyebrow at Kadka; she held up a hand to decline. *That's... unusual.* "It's all too easy, is the problem," he said, taking a sip of his drink. "We happen upon the Mask at the Deepweld manor just in time for a heroic rescue. The size of the attacker leads us to the Uuthars, and their strange activity in the senate. We find extremely incriminating evidence sitting in a top drawer. The Mask is caught, everyone goes home happy. Including all the extra guards and security."

Kadka frowned. "You think all this is part of plan?"

"Imagine that somehow the Mask, or whoever the Mask is working for"—Tane didn't say *Knights of the Emperor* aloud, but he knew Kadka would get the implication—"found out about Odeth. They knew they were going to need a scapegoat after the first few murders, a way to lower defenses. So they blackmail the Uuthars into acting suspiciously in the Senate. They let us get a glimpse of someone too big to be anything but an ogren. They lead us to Odeth and plant evidence for us to find—we know the Mask can get through wards to do that. They give us a story, and it's easy to believe, because the Uuthars already look guilty for keeping an ogre in secret to begin with. Then all the Mask has to do is lie low for a few days, let everyone think the threat is gone before going after another victim."

"We need to know who blackmails Uuthar, then," said Kadka. "But letters all burned, she says. We have nothing."

"We're more or less back where we started," Tane agreed. "We have the list of people allowed through the wards on all three manors, which just gives us a dozen important families we don't have easy access to, and no place to start. But there are still a few links we haven't fully explored. The Knights of the Emperor, for one." He sighed, swished the whiskey around in his cup, and took a sip. "I think I have to try to talk to Nieris. There's a chance he knew something about this."

Kadka cocked her head. "*Can* he talk? Mind is burned out by wraith, I thought."

"The Astra-riven are still alive, just… empty. Sometimes they respond to certain triggers that meant something to them before. Like a reflex."

Kadka nodded. "He is at family estate in country. We have to take rail to get there. Is alright for you?"

Tane touched the battered watch case in his pocket and took another swallow of his drink. He hated riding the ancryst rail. "I'll manage. It's a few hours by rail and a day or more by carriage. We can't afford the time. But I'm going alone. There's something else I need you to do."

Kadka didn't say anything, just waited. There was a resignation to the way she looked at him—she knew what was coming. And he knew she wouldn't like it. He gulped the rest of his whiskey to steel himself.

"The Silver Dawn," he said. "This Iskar. You said he gave you a way to contact him. You should arrange a meeting. Ideally somewhere safe with lots of witnesses."

"You still think they are part of this." Kadka said flatly. She took her feet off his desk, leaned forward in her chair. "Told you, I trust him. Didn't feel like liar."

"Kadka, he's the one who sent us to the Deepweld manor. If we were meant to see the Mask, that means someone *knew* we'd be there. We need more than just a feeling."

"Do we?" Something flashed behind Kadka's yellow eyes. Anger? He couldn't remember ever seeing her truly angry. "Always you believe people or don't on feelings. Like Uuthar today. Why does my feeling not matter?"

Spellfire, I know Iskar made an impression on her, but where did the rest of this come from? "It matters, but right now we need to follow every possible lead. We don't have anything else left. And you have to admit, it's strange that this man keeps himself hidden underground when a kobold like you described could make a huge difference for his people. A sign of the dragon heritage they always claim. Why doesn't he show himself? I don't like it."

"You don't understand, Carver," said Kadka. "What is like, being goblin, or kobold here. Or orc. People Silver Dawn stands for."

"That's not fair," Tane protested. "People with no magic don't exactly have it easy in Thaless. I've spent my whole life fighting that."

She shook her head. "Is different. No one *sees* you have no magic, not like they see fangs, scales, skin. Maybe Iskar hides because is *dangerous* to stand out. Makes people angry to see things outside what they know. Just want to see what they *expect*. Greedy kobolds, sneaky goblins, scary orcs. Like me. Just muscle. There to fight, not think." She scowled, shook her head. "But every time since we start this case, I am not strong enough. I can't fight Mask, can't stop ogre. Can't even get away when they take me in tunnels. If I am not more than muscle, I am nothing."

So that's it. I should have seen it sooner. "Kadka, that's not… I don't see you that way. I couldn't do this without you. We're partners. Friends."

Kadka shoved her chair back as she stood. "Then why not *trust* me? I say Iskar is not part of this. You trust me, you trust him. Simple."

Tane spread his hands. "It's not that easy. If we don't do something, people are going to keep dying, and our name is going to be the excuse at every scene. We *have* to find the Mask, and I don't know where else to look!" He took a deep breath, poured himself another finger of whiskey and tossed it back. *Shouting isn't going to help. She'll see reason. She just needs a peace offering.* "Look, I *do* trust you. If you say Iskar is clean, he probably is. Which means his people really did see the Mask that night, and they might see him again. That's as good as anything else we have. It's worth asking a few questions."

"Fine. I will ask, because maybe they see something useful. Is not just you who wants Mask found." Kadka fixed him with a fierce yellow-eyed glare. "But I am not stupid, Carver. You say that part to make me go, not because you believe. Every day I watch you trick people with words. You call me partner, but think I won't see when you use same tricks on me? You are no partner." She stalked to the door, threw it open. "And maybe not friend I think you are, either."

Before Tane could say anything more, the door swung closed behind her.

CHAPTER SEVENTEEN

KADKA GAVE CARVER ample time to leave for the ancryst rail before returning to the office the next morning. She wasn't in the mood to see him again.

The door to 17 Tilford Street looked much like the others in the long joined brickfront that took up this section of road, all painted in flaking green with a pair of high-set square windows. The only thing that made this one stand out was the small plaque centered beneath the windows, stenciled with the words 'Consulting and Investigation'. A space had been left above for a name that they hadn't yet chosen—Carver refused to entertain the idea of running with 'Magebreakers'.

She tried the door; it was locked. Didn't mean he was gone yet. Carver insisted on using traditional locks in addition to wards for security, a practice he often complained had been forgotten in Thaless. She couldn't hear him moving around inside, though, and she had sharp ears. She fished her key from her pocket and let herself in.

There was no sign of Carver. She crossed the room to peek behind the folding screen that hid his mattress. He wasn't there. Good. She wasn't done being angry with him, even if she only half understood why. Why she'd felt the need to defend a man she hardly knew, why it mattered so much to her that she be right. She'd been outmatched and outmuscled a few times these past days, and she didn't like how useless it made her feel, but that wasn't the whole of it.

She'd spent so long ignoring the way people in Thaless looked at her, because that was just how things were. Because she was an outsider, and it wasn't her fight. And then Iskar had told her that she could do something to change it. Not with fists or knives or bared teeth, but with her voice. She wasn't sure if she was up to that, or what she'd say if she was, or if she even *wanted* to be. But the idea lingered. If she could do something about it, then maybe it *was* her fight, citizen or no.

And she didn't like running from a fight.

She reached into her pocket and fished out the heavy silver coin Iskar had given her, marked with a rising sun. He'd said to put it in the window, and someone would come. The office had a single small window that looked out onto the street, and Kadka wedged the coin into one corner so it could be seen from outside. Then she sat herself down behind the desk, put her feet up, and waited.

It was near two hours before anything happened, and the wait was excrutiating. Kadka was lounging in her chair, picking her fingernails with her knife and seriously considering practicing her aim on the magelight lamp on Carver's desk when she heard footsteps outside. Then, the slight rustle of something being dropped in the letter box, and a tap on the door. She kicked back her chair, let it clatter to the ground as she lunged for the door to yank it open.

No one. They were already gone.

She looked inside the letter box. A small piece of folded paper rested at the bottom, and she pulled it out and unfolded it. Nothing but a single sentence, hastily scrawled. *Right out the door, again at the first alley.*

No way to know it wasn't a trap. But that was Carver's thinking—he'd wanted her to pick the meeting place, and his warnings had gotten into her head. If the

Silver Dawn wanted to hurt her, they could have done it last time. She slipped the knife back into her belt and stepped out the door, locking it behind her.

The alley mentioned in the letter wasn't far up the street, and no one paid her any mind when she turned in. Alleyways could be dangerous in Porthaven, but even so, everyone cut through them to save travel time. A large figure leaned against the wall, and stood straight as she approached. Taller than her, broad shouldered, grey-skinned. Vladak, the orc. He smiled around sharp tusks as she approached.

"Shishter," he said in that deep , rumbling lisp. "It'sh good to shee you again."

"You are one who leaves note?" Kadka asked. "Why not just knock? An orc in Thaless is noticed, sneaking or no."

"It washn't me," Vladak said. "Gurtle dropped it off and went the other way. Mishdirection, you know. You ready to come with me? Ishkar shaysh I shouldn't push it, if you don't want to."

"No blindfolds?"

"No blindfoldsh."

Kadka nodded. "Then I will follow."

Vladak led her a short distance through narrow alleys, and Kadka took care to mind the route for later. Eventually, between two long brick warehouses, he knelt and heaved aside a round metal plate set into the ground, just like the one they'd taken her down before. She went down first, and he pulled the cover back into place behind them with one muscular arm.

It was dark, but they both had orcish eyes, and here and there old magelights still glowed, oases of silver-blue light against the black. Kadka knew from listening to Carver that the lights wouldn't have lasted so long without Astral power—she guessed they were still connected to the main disc lines. Vladak led her past sealed hatchways and broken ladders, until they came to what looked like a dead end. An old hatch was set into the wall, but it had been welded shut all the way around.

"Maybe you take a wrong turn," Kadka said, grinning.

"Don't be sho hashty, shishter." Vladak took the hatch wheel in both hands and turned it. The door didn't open—it couldn't—but Kadka heard a grating noise, and followed her ears to a spot low on the wall to the right, where a brick jutted an inch out from the others. She didn't think it had been like that before. Vladak pushed it back in with his foot.

When he did, a section of brick parted from the wall beside him and swung open, revealing a hole scarcely over three feet high. They'd taken her through a secret way before, too, a section of metal in one of the tunnel walls that slid aside. She'd been blindfolded going in, but she'd seen it on the way out.

"Is not how these were built," Kadka said. "Does Silver Dawn add the secret passages?"

Vladak shrugged his big shoulders. "Before my time. Before the Shilver Dawn too, I think, but Ishkar shaysh other vershionsh exishted before ush." He didn't say more, just bent down and crawled through the hole.

Kadka followed, and then straightened up on the other side to look around. They were in a much larger tunnel, round and lined with glyph-etched copper plates on all sides—where they hadn't fallen away from the wall, at least. The tunnel was sealed off with a great brass plate at the near end, a few feet to Kadka's left, and with a crumble of rock and dirt at the far end, some hundred feet down. It didn't look like it had collapsed, though—more like it had never been finished at all. Recessed into the ceiling, enough magelights still survived to cast the tunnel in faint silver-blue. Along the bottom of the circular passage, a flat wooden floor had been erected, and desks and chairs and worktables sat all along it, most showing signs of recent use. A large meeting table sat in the approximate center of the tunnel, surrounded in an array of mismatched chairs.

"This is real disc tunnel," Kadka said, pointing at the copper plates along the curved wall. The discs were platforms of ancryst levitated by a magical field conducted through copper on all sides—Carver had explained it to her once. There was no other reason for a tunnel like this to exist. "Why seal it like this?"

A deep, pleasant voice answered her. "The artifice that created the discs became obsolete with the invention of the ancryst engine. Plans for a more extensive network of tunnels were abandoned, and in a few places where construction had begun, they were sealed away." Iskar rose from a worn armchair at a desk halfway down the tunnel. He'd been hidden by the high back until he stood. "Kadka. I'm so glad you reached out. I had hoped to see you again." He was as pretty as she remembered, silver scales glittering in the magelight, great wings flaring as he rose and then folding at his back.

As he drew near, Carver's warnings came to her again, unbidden. She was outnumbered now. She glanced over her shoulder at Vladak, standing by the hidden door they'd entered through. It was closed now, only seamless brick showing through where one of the copper panels had fallen away from the wall. Closed, and even if it had been open, she already knew that Vladak could stop her. She might take him by surprise, but the odds weren't in her favor. She hated how hard it was to put that wariness aside. It felt like admitting Carver had been right.

When she turned back to Iskar, his luminous sapphire eyes were fixed on Vladak too. Had he noticed her looking?

"Vladak, if you would give us the room?" Iskar said.

"Is fine. He can stay." Kadka wanted to believe in Iskar and the Silver Dawn. She couldn't let Carver's suspicions control her.

"No," Iskar said firmly. "We should speak as equals, and we cannot do that while I have you at a disadvantage. And besides that, Vladak and his friends are some of our busier agents. I'm sure he has things to do."

Vladak grunted. "You sure, Ishkar? I can shtay."

Iskar nodded. "Absolutely sure. Give the others my regards—we'll speak again soon."

Vladak didn't argue, just looked to Kadka. "Hear him out, shishter. It meant shomething to a lot of ush, how you shtopped Nierish. You could change thingsh for people like ush." And then he turned, fiddled with the wall for a moment, pushed in a few places. The passage swung open again. He crawled through, and a moment later the way closed behind him.

"Well," said Iskar, his dragon's snout opening in a fanged smile. "To what do I owe this pleasure?"

"Maybe I can't resist pretty dragon men." Kadka glanced down at his bare, scaled chest and quirked an eyebrow.

He chuckled. "I almost wish it was as simple as that, but somehow I doubt it. Have you given more thought to working with us?"

Kadka shifted her feet uncomfortably. She didn't have an answer to that yet. "I am… not so good, speaking," she said. "Can't even make Carver trust you. No stranger will listen to me."

"Mister Carver is… a unique man. Perhaps not representative of the larger whole." Now Iskar turned the full force of those shining blue eyes on her, solemn and serious. "The people we deal with speak of you very highly, Kadka. A half-orc woman who prevents mages from taking advantage of those without magic. Who bested one of the most powerful mages in Thaless, rumor has it. That means something to the goblins and kobolds and orcs struggling to make a place for themselves in this city. Your name has weight."

"Maybe." She didn't know what to do with that; she wanted to believe it almost as much as she didn't. And then a question popped into her head, and she was asking it before she could stop herself. "Why not you? You say is dangerous, but a kobold like you would be hero with your people." Carver's distrust again. But she was curious to know the answer, she had to admit. "They always say they come from dragons. If they see you, people will believe it. Worth some danger, yes?"

"That is something I have been thinking about quite a bit since last we met. You asked me then about hiding too." Iskar bowed his head, and his wings flared slightly. "I do have my reasons, Kadka. I have been doing this for a long time, and I have found that it is better this way. Not just for myself. There are things I can't… it is more complicated than it may seem. But I understand that it is hardly fair to ask you to do something I will not. I won't push you. I believe your voice would make a great difference, but it is your decision to make."

Not what she'd been hoping for. His answer had a hole in the middle of it that Carver would never have let pass. But there had been something like sorrow in his voice. It didn't feel like a lie so much as something too painful to talk about. And she didn't think pressing the issue would get her anywhere.

"Is not why I came, anyway," she said. "We need help with Mask. Your people see him once. I need to know if they see him again, or anything else strange. Every place, every time."

"Of course," said Iskar. "As I told you before, there have been others in the tunnels recently, but I have seen nothing of note since we last spoke. What I can do is put word out for any of our agents with information to meet here. I should have something for you within the hour."

"How do you put out message so fast?" Kadka asked. "Sending? You have magic?" She'd assumed not, given the nature of the organization.

He shook his head. "Too few of us have magecraft to rely on sendings. But we have ways to spread word quickly. Signals and runners, artifacts where needed. We have cells pursuing our agenda all over the city—Vladak, Seskis, and Gurtle are one of many. If anyone has seen anything, they will be glad to share it. The Mask's message has to be stopped. Magic for the magical is a sentiment that cannot be allowed to thrive." He paused. "Perhaps… if you would like, you could stay and speak to some of us. See who we are, and how your presence could make a difference." He sounded a little bit uncertain now, almost shy; his tail flicked back and forth along the floor. "Only if you want to, of course. As I said, I don't intend to push, and we will help no matter what you decide."

Carver would *hate* that—letting herself be surrounded in Silver Dawn agents in a closed tunnel with a man who was quite obviously keeping secrets from her. But it wasn't Carver's choice to make. Secrets didn't concern Kadka. Everyone had pain in their past. Whatever Iskar's particular pain was, it wasn't her business, and something in the way he'd talked about it made her trust him more, not less. She understood wounds. It was the people who didn't seem to have any that worried her.

And he was just so *pretty*. Kadka always knew when someone returned her interest; that hint of nervousness when he'd asked her to stay was a dead giveaway.

She grinned. Maybe she was just being a fool for a pretty face, but it was so much more *fun* that way. "Since you ask nicely, I will stay. Send for these agents."

———

Tane breathed deep and clutched his watch case in one hand, trying to find calm as he watched the gentle hills of the Audish countryside roll by through the coach window. He could handle the discs—barely—to get around Thaless, but the ancryst rail was something else. His heart was still beating too quickly even now, a quarter hour after disembarking, and he knew by the wary looks the other passengers and the coach driver had given him that there wasn't much color left in his cheeks.

And he still had to take a train back to Thaless when he was done here.

Can't think about that. Right now I need to focus on how I'm going to get in to see Nieris. He'd hired the carriage to take him the rest of the way to House Nieris' country estate—it was a twenty minute ride from the rail station, and far longer by foot, so he'd grudgingly accepted the expense. They were nearly there, and he still didn't know how he was going to convince the family he'd disgraced to let him see the Astra-riven criminal son they were trying to hide from the world.

Not for the first time that morning, he was distracted by thoughts of Kadka. Without her, he would never have stopped Talain Nieris from destroying Audland's first airship—he would have died beside Lady Abena, falling out of the sky over Porthaven. And last night she'd walked out on him, called their friendship into question. He didn't have enough friends that he could afford to lose any, and especially not her. There was very little she could have done to help him get at Nieris, but after the way she'd left, he felt somehow less equipped to deal with the problem. Or any problem. Like he was alone again, the way he'd been for a long time before they'd met.

He hadn't been worth much in those days. He didn't want to go back.

But he also couldn't let the Mask get away, and he didn't know how else to move the investigation forward. The Silver Dawn was one of the few potential leads they had left. *Still, I should have handled it better. Shouldn't have tried to talk around what she was saying. All she wanted was for me to listen.*

The coach driver rapped on the wall, stirring Tane from his thoughts. He glanced out the window to see that they'd arrived. The coach was drawing up a hillside road shaded by large elms toward an ivy-covered manor house built in stately elven fashion. There were no guards—out here in the country, there was little need for them.

The carriage rolled to a stop, and Tane climbed out with a nod to the driver, a goblin man with a bushy mustache under his long nose.

"Wait here. This might not take long." He'd paid for the trip both ways—he was going to need a ride back when he was done.

He approached the doors. There was a glyphed copper panel at one side, and he laid his palm against it. A chime sounded inside the house. A moment later, the door opened, revealing an elven footman in black and violet Nieris livery.

"Who may I say is calling?" the man asked, standing with impeccable posture on the other side of the gate.

"Tane Carver."

The man's eyes widened. "…One moment." He closed the door once more, and Tane heard hurried footsteps on the other side.

A few minutes, and then the door opened a second time. Now a haughty-looking elven woman in a dress of fine violet silk stood beside the footman. Tane couldn't guess her age at all, other than that she was beyond childhood—she had the smooth, unlined face common to even the eldest of her kind. Her hair was raven black without a hint of grey, so perhaps younger than Talain.

"Tane Carver. You have nerve, coming here, I'll give you that. What do you want?"

"Talaesa Nieris, I take it." That was a guess, but an educated one—it was common knowledge that the ex-chancellor's youngest sister had been tasked by the family with caring for him, and there was a family resemblance there. "I need to talk to your brother."

She blinked in disbelief. "You want to… No. Of *course* you can't. No one can 'talk' to my brother after what you did to him. I'm going to give you thirty seconds to turn around and get back in that carriage before my men throw you off our property."

There was no finesse approach here—or at least Tane hadn't come up with one on the ride over. It was blunt force or nothing. "You don't want to do that. I know you've heard about the Emperor's Mask by now, even out here. I'm investigating the case, under the oversight of the constabulary and Lady Abena's office." Stretching the truth a great deal there, but it was close enough. "Your family can't afford to look like you aren't cooperating, after the airship incident. You *certainly* can't afford for one of the few people who knows the truth"—Tane tapped a finger against his chest—"to start confirming rumors. It's as simple as that. You give me ten minutes with your brother, or all your efforts to keep what happened quiet are over."

Talaesa said nothing for a long moment, just glared at him with overt hostility, and then, "Fine. It doesn't matter, does it? You're wasting your time. He hasn't said anything coherent since…" She trailed off, turned around, and marched away into the manor.

It took Tane a moment to realize he was supposed to follow. The footman didn't stop him when he stepped through the door, just fell in behind. Talaesa led the way down a hall of seemingly endless doors, and then outside again to a central garden courtyard. There, in a chair beside a small pool, sat a man whose face was burned into Tane's memory.

Talain Nieris looked the same, a fine-featured elven man with black hair greying slightly above pointed ears, the only visible sign of some three centuries of life. He was dressed impeccably, as always, in a black and violet suit that probably cost more than everything Tane owned put together. The only difference was that his bright blue eyes, once full of piercing intelligence, now stared emptily at nothing in particular. He didn't so much as look up when Talaesa drew near, and he showed no reaction to Tane's presence.

"Talk, if you like," said Talaesa. "It's pointless. He might respond, but it's always just… random babble."

Tane knelt in front of the chair, putting his face in the ex-chancellor's eyeline. "Chancellor Nieris. Do you remember me?"

Talaesa laughed bitterly at that, but said nothing.

Nor did her brother. He just stared ahead as if Tane wasn't there.

"You claimed to be with the Knights of the Emperor. I need to know if you've heard of someone called the Emperor's Mask."

"Mask," Nieris mumbled. There was no particular inflection to it. Just a word triggered by some fragment of a broken mind.

Tane wasn't sure if he was just repeating what he'd heard, but it was something. "Yes! The Mask. What does he want? What do you know?"

"Mask," Nieris said again. His hands trembled slightly, but there was nothing in his eyes. "Emperor is coming."

Talaesa made a small noise in her throat. "Talain? Do you understand what he's asking? Is that you?"

No answer.

"The Emperor, that's right," Tane said encouragingly. "The Mask says he heralds the coming of the Emperor. But who is it? Is there a plan beyond just killing people?"

"Kill," said Chancellor Nieris. A line of drool trickled down his chin. "Audlian."

Tane's heart seized in his chest, and he pushed himself abruptly to his feet. "Audlian? House Audlian? What about them?"

"Audlian," was the only response.

"Right," said Tane. "Whatever word gets you talking. Audlian. Mask. Emperor."

Nieris was silent.

Tane gripped him by the shoulder, shook him. "You have to have more than that! What about House Audlian?" But he had a feeling he already knew.

"That's enough!" Talaesa pulled Tane away by the arm and put herself between him and her brother. "Leave him alone!"

It didn't matter; Tane understood enough. "Spellfire, it makes sense. The first few were practice, or maybe just to get attention, but the real target... Faelir Audlian is the first magicless elf born to a great house in a hundred years. He could be their first Lord Protector since Illuvar Audlian. If he dies at the hands of the Mask, it's going to be chaos. And Durren is going to tell everyone the threat is gone. No one is going to be ready for it."

For a moment, before he remembered that she wasn't there, he half expected Kadka to answer. But no one did. Talaesa Nieris was ignoring him; she'd knelt before her brother and was murmuring to him in a soft voice, trying to prompt a response. There were tears on her cheeks. Tane couldn't help but feel a twinge of guilt over that— Talain had been a madman, but his sister's affection seemed genuine.

But there wasn't time to second guess his actions. The Mask wasn't going to wait, which meant Tane had a train to catch. He turned on his heel and marched back toward the manor's front door. As he walked, he dug the sending locket from his pocket, and squeezed it tight in his hand.

The pressure in his ears came on almost instantly, followed by Indree's voice. *"Tane? What is it?"*

"I'm coming into Stooketon Circle Station on the evening train. Meet me there. I know where the Mask is going to strike next."

CHAPTER EIGHTEEN

―――――

TANE STAGGERED OFF the train, trembling, and grabbed the railing on the far side of the platform to steady himself. The other passengers disembarking shot him worried looks, but he ignored them, just focused on catching his breath.

A pair of boots entered his downcast eyeline, stepping near. "Are you going to make it?" Indree's voice. She laid a hand on his shoulder. When he looked up, there was genuine concern in her eyes.

"I'm fine," said Tane. "You know me. I love trains."

"I didn't think anything could get you back on one. I remember trying to get you to come out to the country once, with Allaea and me. You were ready to tie yourself to your bed to get out of it."

"If it stops the Mask, it was worth it."

Indree smiled slightly. "You're a mystery, sometimes, Tane Carver. Just when I think you're the most irresponsible idiot I know, you surprise me." Her mouth turned downwards. "But we have a problem. Durren is convinced he has the Mask already, and Talain Nieris isn't exactly a reliable source these days."

It was only then that Tane recovered his wits enough

to notice that she'd come alone. "He wouldn't give you the constables we need? That Astra-riven moron! Someone needs to just throw him into the sea—he'd be about as useful as he is now." He took a breath, tried to gather himself. "What about the Mageblades?"

Indree shook her head. "Most of them have been re-called now that the case is supposedly solved. There's only a token patrol left. Lady Abena might listen if I could talk to her, but she's somewhere on the Continent by now. Getting her a message through proper channels would take days, and I'd need a focus to contact her by direct sending over that distance."

"So we're out of official strings to pull," said Tane. "Then we need to warn the Audlians ourselves. They can afford to bring in more guardsmen, at least."

"It's not that simple," said Indree. "You're forgetting something obvious."

"Well, you try thinking clearly when your brains are being rattled around by an ancryst-powered deathtrap," Tane said, more peevishly than he'd intended. "What did I miss?"

"More than one Audlian shows up on the list of people who had access to the murder scenes. Including Daalia herself. When you said 'Mask', Nieris might have given you the name of the killer, not the victim."

"Spellfire," Tane swore. "I didn't think…" He shook his head. "But the Audlians have always spoken against magical superiority. I could see them doing this to remove competition for Faelir, but not as Knights of the Emperor. And if they aren't with the Knights, why would Nieris know about it?"

"Believe me, it's not unusual for an elven house to have a fanatic or two for magical purity in the family tree. I would know." Indree was half-elven, and not everyone on her elven father's side approved of his marrying a human woman. Tane had comforted her after more than one awkward family gathering in their university days. "And that means we can't know which of them to trust. Trying to warn them could reveal us to the Mask, maybe even move up the timetable of the next killing."

Tane rubbed at the watch casing in his pocket, trying to think. "So… we need to watch the estate ourselves? But we don't have the people to do that, without the bluecaps or the Mageblades. Maybe Kadka can get the Silver Dawn to help." He still wasn't convinced they could be trusted, but he *did* trust Kadka, and there was no doing this without help. "Except… I don't know where she is, and without a divination focus you aren't going to be able to get a sending to her either."

"She'll be waiting at your office if she's found anything, won't she?"

Tane rubbed the back of his neck awkwardly. "I don't know. We… had an argument last night. She might not want to see me."

Indree rolled her eyes. "You really have a way with people, don't you? Well, we can check, at least."

"It's not enough" said Tane. "*Maybe* she's there, and *maybe* she can get the Silver Dawn on board, but that's a lot of maybes. And even then, we can't get onto the Audlian estate past their wards. Whether the Mask is coming or going, we're going to need a better view than we can get over the walls. I could try to rig something up with Bastian, but it's already getting dark—" And then it hit him. He could get exactly what he needed, already built. And nearby. "Follow me!" In a near-sprint, he raced down the stairs from the boarding platform and out of the station.

The sun was just beginning to set, and silver-blue magelamps blinked to life overhead as Tane raced through Stooketon. The Stooke's townhouse was only a few streets over from Stooketon Circle Station, but he was panting by the time he reached the door.

Indree was just a step behind him. "The Stookes?" she said, and he envied how easily she was breathing. "How can they help?"

"You'll... you'll see," he gasped, and pressed his thumb against the bell-glyph.

A moment later, Endo's voice issued from the mouth of the brass badger mounted on the door. "Who is it?"

"Endo, it's Tane. I need your help."

"Tane? Come in." The door swung open.

Tane led Indree in, and the door closed behind them. On the far side of the small entry hall, the lens mounted in the wall flared silver blue, moving to size them up.

"Constable Inspector Lovial," Endo said through the wall panel. "I... didn't expect you." They would have met when she'd come to investigate Ulnod's murder, Tane supposed. "You'll have to provide a focus to get through the wards." The small drawer below the lens popped out, and Indree plucked a hair and placed it in one of the small vials. A few short moments later, the inside door opened.

Endo was waiting in his chair on the other side, a pensive look on his face. "Is this about the Mask?"

"We know who the next target is," said Tane.

Endo frowned. "I'd heard... they're saying that the Uuthars were behind everything. That you and Miss Kadka helped to stop them."

Tane shook his head. "I think the Uuthars were a mislead. A way to lower the guard around the Gryphon's Roost." He explained the situation as quickly as he could, his theory about the Uuthars and his meeting with Nieris.

"I'd hoped you were here to collect your pay," Endo said. "I thought it was over." He sounded tired.

"It can be, if we catch the Mask at the Audlian estate," said Tane. "That's where we need your help."

Endo went pale. "Me? Surely the constabulary, or the Mageblades—"

Indree shook her head. "Not an option right now. They think Noana Uuthar and her son are to blame. We're on our own."

"But... if they can't help, what can *I* possibly do?" Endo asked.

"We need your crawlers," said Tane. "We don't have the men to watch over the Audlian estate, but a dozen or so crawlers could get it done. And they're not self-aware—they'll probably get through the wards."

Indree raised an eyebrow. "Crawlers?"

"Show her," said Tane.

Endo nodded, and furrowed his brow a moment in concentration. A moment later, a half-dozen spider-like crawlers skittered along the hall toward the entryway along the walls and ceiling.

Indree took a step back as they approached. "You said he was working with automatons, but I didn't real-ize... I've never seen anything like these." One of the crawlers stopped just above her, focusing on her face with its cyclopean silver-blue lens. She stared back, obviously impressed. "They could work."

Endo didn't look so sure. "I don't think I can be seen letting them loose on the estate of another Senate house. I want to help, but if it goes wrong... I'm the only one representing my family right now. I have to think about our reputation."

"We'll take care of that," said Tane. "All you have to do is supply them."

"Someone has to control them," Endo said uncertain-ly. "It takes an Astral bond to send commands and receive information. That means a mage."

"I can do it," said Indree. "Just show me how."

Endo nodded, slightly more confident now. "That won't take long—the automation spells handle most of it. But they're calibrated for household tasks and security, not spying. I need to prepare them. Can you wait a half hour or so?"

"We have at least that long," said Tane. "The Mask isn't going to start moving until full dark, and probably some time after, when the streets have cleared. That gives us time to check if Kadka's waiting at the office, after you've shown Indree whatever she needs to know. Can you have the crawlers delivered to us there?"

"I think I can arrange that," Endo said.

"Then let's get started," said Indree. "We don't have a lot of time. Tell me how to work these things."

———

It was already dark in the narrow streets of Porthaven by the time Tane and Indree reached his office. In the yellow light of a nearby oil-lamp, Tane fumbled for his key, but when he reached for the door handle, he found it unlocked.

"Kadka must be here," he said. There was no light in the window, but she could see in the dark—she didn't always bother turning on the lamp.

But when he opened the door, he only saw an empty room. He could make out the dim shadows of chairs on either side of the desk, but both were empty. That was strange. Kadka seldom remembered to lock up when she was inside—despite his nagging—but she always did when she left.

"Something's wrong," he said. *Could the Mask have… no, I left the ward up. No one gets through my wards.* But his heart pulsed wildly in his chest, and he found himself stepping over the threshold, looking for signs of struggle. "Kadka?"

The office was silent.

Indree grabbed him by the shoulder a few steps in and moved in front of him, her ancryst pistol in hand. "She's not here."

"She always locks up when she leaves," he said.

Indree nodded, and levelled her pistol at the folding screen near the back wall, where Tane's mattress was hidden. The only place to hide in the small room. She moved forward slowly, cautiously.

Tane only saw the figure when it detached itself from the darkness. Not behind the screen, but against the wall beside Indree, silent and invisible until it lunged. And in that moment he knew exactly who it was—he'd seen the Mask melt into the darkness once before.

"Indree! Left!"

She twisted, saw the movement. A huge black silhouette, some nine feet tall, head nearly scraping the ceiling. Indree fired, a silver flash against the dark. The light illuminated a brass mask with slits for eyes.

The ancryst ball struck the Mask full in the chest beneath black robes, rang against metal, and ricocheted harmlessly aside.

Indree had only uttered the first word of a shield spell when the Mask reached her. One huge fist clasped her shoulder. She crumpled to the ground bonelessly. Tane recognized the effect. *Like a daze-wand. Another artifact built into the glove.*

Every instinct told Tane to run, but he'd seen the Mask's speed. He wouldn't make it far. And he couldn't leave Indree. Instead he took stock of the distance, moved a half step forward, and crushed the shield charm in his pocket—the last of the charms he'd bought from Bastian.

He'd judged the radius perfectly. A dome of translucent silver flashed into being, centered on him, but perfectly separating Indree from the Mask along the edge.

Tane rushed to her side, started dragging her away from the Mask, towards the far side of the shield. For all the good that would do when the charm failed.

"Who *are* you?" he demanded. "What do you want? Why bring me and Kadka into this?"

The Mask made no sound, just lifted two fists and brought them down hard on the shield. It flared bright silver, and held. It wouldn't hold much longer. If brute strength couldn't break it, time would—the kind of charm Tane could afford didn't have the power to last more than sixty seconds. And when it went, he didn't have any others left.

Spellfire, there's no way out. We're going to die.

Except… Indree *wasn't* dead. She was breathing. She'd been dazed, not stabbed with a spike. And the Mask had taunted the Magebreakers, but never come after Tane and Kadka until now. *Maybe...*

Tane's desk was half inside the shield, and an open inkwell sat at one corner. He put his back against the wood, tried to look like he was backing away in fear. It wasn't a hard act to sell, in that moment. Behind his back, he palmed the inkwell, slipped it into his trouser pocket. His clothes had always been shabby; he didn't have much trouble tearing apart one of the pocket's seams with his finger, just enough to leave a small hole in the bottom corner.

Again, the Mask pounded against the shield. This time, the silver barrier flickered and failed—it hadn't had long left either way.

The Mask closed the distance, grasping for Tane with one armored hand. Tane upended the inkwell in his pocket, felt ink running down his leg.

A heavy hand closed around his arm, and his consciousness fell away.

CHAPTER NINETEEN

———

IT WAS EVENING when Kadka emerged from the abandoned maintenance tunnels, not long past dusk. The alley was deep in shadow—dark always fell hard over Porthaven's narrow streets. It wasn't a problem for her orcish eyes, but there were other things distracting her tonight.

Not what she'd learned about the Mask—there hadn't been much of that. A few possible half-glimpses that didn't add up to a discernable pattern. Worth following up considering how few other leads they had, but she didn't think it would come to anything.

No, what Kadka couldn't put out of her head was how many of the Silver Dawn's agents had looked at her like she *meant* something, beyond just muscle or intimidation. And not just the so-called "lesser races". There had been kobolds and goblins and another orc woman—full-blooded, like Vladak—but a number of humans and dwarves and gnomes had answered Iskar's call as well. There had even been an ogren, and a pair of enthusiastic sprites. All those people stepping up to fight against something that she'd simply tried to ignore since she'd come to Thaless, and they looked at her like she could do something about it that they couldn't. Maybe she wasn't a citizen, but it was getting harder not to see it as her fight.

Absorbed in her thoughts, she didn't notice the door until she reached for the handle.

It was already open.

Just a crack, but that was enough to raise her hackles and clear her mind. There was no chance Carver had forgotten, not with the Mask still out there. Kadka drew the long knife from behind her back and inched the door open with her foot, peeking into the darkness.

The office looked empty, and her night-vision didn't pick up any sign of movement. She pushed the door open the rest of the way and crept inside. A quick search found nobody hiding under the desk or behind the folding screen at the back, but a childhood spent learning to hunt in Sverna had taught Kadka to read tracks and signs.

And there were two signs here she couldn't ignore.

First, a splintered hole punched through the wooden folding screen—the size of an ancryst pistol-ball, she estimated—and second, a coin-sized pool of fluid at the foot of the desk that she feared at first was blood in the colorless tones of her dark-sight. Her nose quickly corrected her when she bent closer. Ink. Someone had fired an ancryst pistol, and Carver's inkwell had been spilled. The pistol shot might have come from an attacker, or from Indree if she'd been there—it wasn't out of place at the scene of a struggle. Kadka could account for it.

It was the ink that bothered her.

There wasn't enough of it, for one thing. If the inkwell had just been tipped off the desk, there should have been more. And where was the bottle? She crouched to look under the desk again, peeked behind the screen, checked every corner of the room. Nothing.

But there was another droplet of ink on the floor just inside the door. And that was when she knew.

Carver had been taken.

The ink hadn't been spilled by accident. Someone had come for him, and he'd somehow secreted the bottle on his person to leave a trail. It was a leap, but it was just the sort of thing he would have done. She was certain of it.

He'd been taken just when she hadn't been there to protect him. She *should* have been, but she hadn't. And a sick weight settled in Kadka's stomach when she realized just who was responsible for that.

No. She pushed the suspicion aside. Follow the trail first, and then she'd know more. She raced out the door, skidded to a halt in the street, looked both ways.

There. A spattering of dark ink stains leading up the right side of the road. Kadka followed.

Carver must have been carrying the inkwell in his pocket, letting the ink filter through the fabric of his clothes to keep it from draining all at once. Still, though, it wouldn't last forever. The trail didn't continue far up the road, and she worried the ink had run out too soon—or that whoever had taken Carver had noticed it. But a quick circle found the next dab on the ground to her right.

It led into the alley she'd met Vladak in earlier. Toward the abandoned maintenance tunnels. She hadn't noticed the ink spots on her way back, had been too distracted to notice much of anything. But there they were. And she didn't like what that suggested.

She followed the trail, a drop here and there leading her along nearly the same route Vladak had. Another splatter just before the metal plate that covered the access to the tunnels. She passed by, checked further down, hoping, but there was nothing. Kadka returned to the plate, knelt, and heaved it aside. A dark smear ran down one side of the ladder, ending just below the second rung.

This was the way, then. No doubting it now.

At the bottom of the ladder, the ink spots led her down the passage opposite the one she and Vladak had taken before, and she followed the trail through dark tunnels. Here and there she had to check down several passages before she found another droplet, and they were thinning out, getting further between. And then, after perhaps a quarter hour, she lost the trail altogether.

But not because the ink ran out.

There was a dark splatter on the floor in front of her, a clear sign that Carver had been taken this way. But it was a dead end. The passage terminated in a solid wall.

"*Deshka!*" she cursed, and slammed a fist against the brick. She didn't think they'd doubled back. Maybe, but she hadn't seen any signs in other directions. No, it had to be a secret way. Like the ones the Silver Dawn used. Kadka started prodding bricks at random, twisting bolts on the steel supports, but she had no idea where to start. And even if she got lucky here, there could well be other closed passages waiting ahead.

But there was someone who might know the way. And if he didn't have the answers she wanted...

Her fingers clenched around her knife, and she turned back the way she'd come.

Another thing she'd learned in the Svernan wilderness was an unerring sense of direction. She remembered the way Vladak had taken her easily enough, traced the route back to the hidden passage, turned the wheel on the sealed hatch, prodded the brick that popped out with her foot. The low door swung open, and Kadka ducked through into the great sealed disc tunnel.

Iskar was still inside, bent over some papers on a desk at the center of the tunnel, silver wings folded at his back. Alone, just like she'd left him. The others hadn't stayed, only come to report and meet Kadka and then gone on their way.

He looked up when she entered, and revealed draconian teeth in an open-snouted smile. "Kadka. What brings you—"

She crossed the distance in an instant, knife in hand. Grabbed him by the throat, lifted him from his seat.

"Carver is gone. Someone takes him into these tunnels, while I am with you. Where is he?"

Iskar didn't struggle, though the muscle beneath those silver scales might have been a match for her. He didn't even flinch, just looked at her steadily with those luminous blue eyes. "I don't know. I swear to you, I had nothing to do with it."

Kadka tightened her grip, pressed the point of her knife against his ribs. "Who else knows I will be gone? And you keep me here meeting people, longer than I mean to stay. Carver says I trust you too easily, and now he is gone, when I… I should have…"

"Mister Carver… must have had defenses on the office." Somehow, Iskar remained calm, though his voice wheezed through a half-closed throat. "Wards. How would… one of us get in? And why?"

That was true. Carver didn't always have the office wards up, but he'd been paranoid about the Mask of late—he wouldn't have made himself easy to take. But if the Knights of the Emperor *had* infiltrated the Silver Dawn… "Mask walks through wards before. Maybe Carver's too. Maybe you send him." She relaxed her fingers slightly to let Iskar answer.

"And let you go, after showing you the way to find me? I understand that you're worried for your friend, but think clearly about this. Would I have betrayed you and then waited here alone, unguarded? I don't know anything about the Mask, Kadka. I'm not the one you're looking for. But I *can* help you. I know these tunnels."

He was making sense. And she still *wanted* to trust him. Wanted to believe she hadn't been completely fooled by the man who had taken her friend. "I…" She released him, pulled back her blade. "I am sorry. Is only… I should be with him when Mask comes, not here. Say some things, before I go…" She swallowed, shook her head. "Shouldn't be last things I say to him. Please, help me. I will join Silver Dawn, do what you ask. Anything. Just help."

Iskar shook his head, and put a hand on her shoulder. "No bargains. Not while you fear for Mister Carver's life. That is not our way. If you join us, it will be your choice, made freely. Right now, just tell me what you need."

Kadka didn't waste time. She could thank him properly later. "Trail leads to dead end. Is secret door, I think, but I can't open."

"If there is a door down here, I know it," said Iskar, and started for the exit. "Come. Let us find your friend."

CHAPTER TWENTY

———

TANE WOKE WITH his head in Indree's lap. She was leaning over him, a look of concern on her face. The room behind her was hazy, and he blinked his eyes, trying to clear them. The floor was hard and cold against his back, and something thick and sticky was drying against his leg. For a terrifying moment he feared it was blood, and then he remembered the inkwell in his pocket.

"Tane? Thank the Astra, you're awake."

He sat up from her lap. His head spun, but he propped himself up on one arm and managed to keep from collapsing to the ground again. Glancing down, he saw the black stain down the outside of his right leg where the ink had drained. *Astra, I hope that gave Kadka something to work with.* "How long has it been?" he asked.

"I don't know," said Indree. "Long enough to get us… wherever we are. That gauntlet had a hundred times the kick of the average daze wand."

"Which wouldn't be cheap." Daze wands channeled pure Astral energy through the target's link to the Astra. They ran through gems quickly, and that was for just a few moments' incapacitation. "Apparently the Mask can afford to burn a lot of power." Something prickled at the back of

Tane's mind, there. Not quite clear yet, but enough to set a weight rolling in the pit of his stomach.

As his vision resolved, he saw that they were in a cell of some kind, bare brick and stone with a metal door. A sliding plate was mounted in the door at eye level. It was closed. There were no windows to the outside. They were prisoners, and he couldn't see a way out.

But they were still alive. That was something.

He got shakily to his feet. "We have to get out of here. The Mask could be going after Faelir Audlian already."

Indree stood too. "Believe it or not, I arrived at that conclusion without your help. But I don't see how."

"Do you know where we are?"

"I only woke up a few minutes before you did. All I've seen is the inside of this cell."

"What about magic? Can you do anything?"

Indree shook her head. "I tried. The cell is magically isolated, like the ones at Stooketon Yard. I'm cut off from the Astra."

Tane moved to the door, slid open the metal plate, and peered into the room beyond. It didn't reveal much—there were no particular distinguishing features to identify their location. To his right, a set of stairs led to an upper level, and across the room a plain wooden door went somewhere he couldn't guess. For all he knew, it was a storage closet.

"Hey!" he shouted through the small opening. "Can anyone hear me? We need help!"

"Do you really think it's going to be that easy?" Indree asked from just behind.

He shrugged. "Worth a try. Hey! Anybody!"

"Quiet in there!" A man's voice from just to the right of the door.

A figure stepped into view—average height, muscular, probably human, but his face was covered in a black cowl like an executioner's mask. He was dressed all in black too, with a badge at his breast. A gold crown and staff on a deep purple field. The sigil of the Knights of the Emperor. Tane had seen this before—the same outfit and badge Randolf Cranst and his followers had worn, men and women gathered by Chancellor Nieris in his plot to bring down the airship Hesliar. *So there are more of them. Nieris wasn't lying about that.*

"There's no point yelling," the man said gruffly. "The basement is sound-damped. No noise in or out. For the likes of you, anyway." Presumably the guards were exempted from the spell—they wouldn't be much use if they couldn't hear someone coming.

"What are you going to do with us?" Tane asked. "Why are we here?"

"No point wasting your breath on questions—there's no saving you now. Enemies of the Emperor are dealt with by His Mask, and he isn't known for mercy." There was a grim satisfaction in the guard's voice that Tane very much didn't like.

But he didn't let it stop him. "So the Mask is just an enforcer? Who is this Emperor?"

"That isn't for the likes of you or me, filth. The unworthy don't look upon the Emperor. It's enough that the Mask speaks with his voice. Shut your mouth."

"You mean none of you have *seen* them? You don't know who they are?" Again, that uncomfortable prickling in the back of Tane's thoughts. There was something there, something he hadn't quite grasped yet. "You're fighting for someone without even—"

"I said shut up!" The man uttered a short spell in the *lingua*—apparently he was exempt from the Astral isolation, too—and a sudden silver force shoved Tane away from the door. He landed painfully on his back against the cold stone floor.

The guard peered in through the opening in the door. "The next time you open this, it will go much worse for you," he said coldly, and slid the plate closed.

Indree rushed to Tane's side. "Are you hurt?"

"Probably bruised my tailbone, but I'm fine." Tane got to his feet again with her help.

"So we're prisoners of the Knights of the Emperor," said Indree. "An organization most people don't think exists. And no one will be looking for us—I didn't tell Durren where I was, for obvious reasons. I'm not sure how we get out of this."

"There's Kadka," said Tane. "She'll be looking."

"Will she? You said you argued with her, that she might not want to see you. We don't even know if she was going to come back to your office."

"She'll come," Tane said, and he believed it. "I once made the mistake of thinking she wouldn't, and then she climbed over the side of an airship hundreds of feet above the ground and saved my life. She'll find us."

Indree prodded her cheek with her tongue, and then nodded. "I wouldn't count her out yet, I suppose."

"There's something else, though," said Tane. "Why are we even alive for her to find? If the Mask wanted to deal with us, why not kill us at the office? It must have to do with luring us into the investigation to begin with. And how in the Astra could someone have gotten through my wards?"

"The Mask got through the wards on several Senate houses," said Indree. "You think yours are better?"

"Yes," Tane said without hesitation. "We had a list of people who were exempted from the wards at those estates. My exemptions are me, you, and Kadka. No one else. Which means we're looking at someone who's found a way to actually *ignore* a ward, not just to get on the list. You'd have to be dead already, or at least appear non-sentient to the Astra..." And then the prickling idea that had been forming at the back of his thoughts took shape all at once. "Spellfire, no."

Indree raised an eyebrow. "What—"

Before she could finish, shackles of silver-blue energy shimmered into existence around their wrists and ankles and yanked both of them hard toward the rear of the cell. Tane struggled against it, but in an instant his back was against the wall, his limbs pinned.

The door swung open, and a figure close to nine feet tall stooped to pass through, draped from head to foot in a black robe. It had no face, only a mouthless brass mask with slits for eyes and a crowned staff etched down the center.

The Mask turned back to the guard at the cell door. "Leave us." The voice was deep and distorted, the same one from the illusory messages at the murder scenes. Before the man could respond, a massive brass-gauntleted hand pushed the door closed. The giant figure stood alone before Tane and Indree and looked them up and down, narrow eye-slits glowing faintly from behind with silver-blue light. "Tane Carver. A pleasure to finally meet you properly."

Tane held his chin up, tried not to let his voice shake. "We've met. Or at least, I've met the man speaking through the mask. Or do you prefer 'The Emperor Who Will Be'?"

The Mask only regarded Tane silently, but Indree twisted her neck to look at him. "What are you talking about?"

And Tane knew as he said it aloud that he was right—it was the only thing that made sense. "There's only one way to get through all those wards and detection spells, including mine. The same reason we needed the crawlers to get access to the Audlian estate. The Mask isn't a sentient being, Ree. It's an automaton. A golem. And only one man could make a golem this advanced."

Indree's eyes widened with realization. "Endo."

And finally the Mask spoke again in that rumbling, distorted voice. "Very good, Tane." One hand reached up, palmed the delicately etched mask, pulled it free. Behind, two silver-blue lenses like eyes glowed in the center of a brass face-plate. Metallic irises contracted to adjust for the new light. Just like Endo's crawlers.

"Well," said Tane, "I suppose this means I'm not getting paid."

CHAPTER TWENTY-ONE

———

"TELL ME," **ENDO** said in the Mask's deep, warped voice, "what gave me away? I would like to know what mistake sentenced you to death."

If someone had told Tane ten years ago that one day he would feel so betrayed by Endo Stooke, he wasn't sure if he would have laughed or flown into a rage. And yet here he was. He'd fallen for the act, even started to feel some kinship toward the earnest, brilliant young man. *I can't believe I let him fool me. A decade hating him wasted just because he looked at me wide-eyed and told me how clever I am.*

But whatever he felt, it could wait—right now, he needed to stall for time. *Hurry, Kadka. I'm not ready to die just yet.*

Tane's hands trembled against their shackles, but he kept his voice steady. "There were plenty of clues. The way the Mask passed through wards. The lack of Astral trace at the scenes. The artifacts built with no regard to cost, like your chair and your crawlers. Disappearing with active illusion, the way only a gnome could—or maybe a golem with a gnome in control. I should have seen it sooner. But I didn't, not until I learned that no one had ever *seen* the Emperor in person. That's when things started falling into place. Your followers aren't the most accepting sort. They wouldn't take you seriously if they'd seen you in your chair. So you made yourself a stand in."

"A disappointing necessity," Endo said. "If I was going to recruit men like Talain Nieris, I needed a guise. They would never have followed someone so young, someone they saw as... limited. As 'the Mask', my reach has grown greatly. You would be surprised at some of the men and women who count themselves Knights of the Emperor."

"But *why*?" Indree demanded. "Why do all this? You killed your own *brother*."

There was no emotion in the automaton's blue lenses, and the voice was too distorted to read. "Who would believe I was the killer, with him as the first victim? My brother was a necessary sacrifice. The world is out of order. The magical have surrendered too much of their rightful power. That must be remedied."

"That's it?" Tane said. "You're just a true believer?" He didn't buy it. He couldn't help but notice that although Indree was right there beside him, the Mask barely spared her a glance. *This feels more personal than he wants to let on. Can I use that?* He couldn't be sure yet—he had to keep playing things out. "Then why drag me and Kadka into this? Why all the taunts?"

The automaton replaced its mask, adjusted it, and then looked at Tane again through narrow eye-slits. "You killed Talain Nieris. In every way that matters, at least. A great man, who devoted everything to the cause, and you stripped him of his mind and his magic. And in doing so, the two of you became a symbol to the non-magical, making them believe they might stand up to their betters. I couldn't allow that."

Tane shook his head. "No, not that. That part is obvious enough. But why not just kill us? You could have walked through my wards at any time. Why lure us into investigating?"

"Killing you might have made you martyrs," said Endo. "That was never my intent. I wanted Thaless to see you fail. I wanted you humiliated, not dead. And I must admit, there was a certain appeal to besting the son of the man who took my legs."

That was something. A hint of motivation beyond dispassionate plotting. *And he's still answering questions. Why? It feels like boasting. He wants me to know how he beat me.* Which made it easier to stall for time, at least. "So you mentioned us in your messages, knowing we'd get involved." Tane paused, remembering. "And it was you who first nudged us toward Deepweld, wasn't it? You *meant* for us to see you there that night."

"Yes. I knew that the automaton's size and the names on the list of ward exemptions would lead to Noana Uuthar."

"And her sudden shift in the Senate," said Tane. "You were the one blackmailing her. Setting up a lead for us to follow. Her secret made her look guilty. An easy scapegoat."

"But not as easy as I expected." It was hard to distinguish tone behind the automaton's uncanny voice, but there might have been a hint of respect there. "I'll grant you that much. I thought you would find the evidence against Uuthar and stop there. When the next victim died, all of Thaless would have seen your failure. Their precious Magebreakers accuse the wrong woman—a senator, no less—and the real killer strikes again when no one expects it. Your reputations would have been suitably ruined. But you didn't take the bait. I hadn't anticipated that you would speak to Talain. Or that he would give you something useful out of that smouldering ruin of a mind."

"All of this, just to discredit Tane and Kadka?" Indree said incredulously. "That's… you're insane. How could that possibly be worth it?"

A low, distorted chuckle through the mouthless mask. "You misunderstand, Inspector Lovial. Destroying the

Magebreakers was a happy confluence of events, but I had much larger goals. Operating in the shadows is fine and well, but there are limits to the influence one can attain that way. My Knights and I are ready to step into the light. Eliminating these magicless pretenders to the throne is a fine way for an Emperor to announce himself, don't you think? Already I have the Senate discussing changes to their outdated restrictions on the Protector's office, and when I kill the first elvish candidate in centuries, it will serve as a signal to the right-minded that our time has come. Speaking of which, I have an appointment at the Audlian estate that I cannot miss." The Mask turned to Tane once more. "A shame it came to this. I would have let you go, when it was over. As I said, I only wanted you shamed—alive or dead is immaterial. But now you know too much."

"Then do it," Tane said defiantly, and prayed to the Astra that he'd read the situation correctly. *He won't end it now. He's got something to prove. I hope.* "Don't you think you've taunted me enough?"

Endo regarded him for a long moment with the Mask's eyes, and then shook his head. "No. Not yet, I think. I want you alive when I kill Faelir Audlian. I want you to know how badly you've been beaten before you die." The huge automaton turned toward the door and pulled it open. Before leaving, those silver-blue eye-slits turned back one last time. "But I won't keep you waiting very long."

CHAPTER TWENTY-TWO

***

KADKA LED THE way, following an ever-fainter trail of ink spots through darkened passages. Whenever they came to a dead end, Iskar let them through by twisting a bolt or pressing a brick or some other trigger. True to his word, he knew the secrets of the tunnels—and there was no shortage of them.

Gradually, the ink marks became scarcer and farther between. Kadka had to choose which path to take at some forks by gauging what dust and debris seemed most recently stirred—or sometimes just by guessing. They doubled back more than once. But inevitably, no matter how far between, she would find another drop or smudge of ink, however small. That made little sense to her. The Mask—if it was the Mask who had taken Carver—had to be able to see in the dark, and no one could miss a growing ink stain forever. How had it not been noticed sooner?

After more than an hour, they came to another dead end, an apparently unfinished passage. The brick walls ended in ragged edges, giving way to raw stone. Somewhere under the far edge of Stooketon, if she'd judged the distance and direction properly—and she rarely got such things wrong.

"Had to go through here," she said over her shoulder to Iskar. There was no ink, but she'd passed a small drop-let a short way back, and there hadn't been a fork in the tunnel since. "Open it."

Iskar frowned, and his silver tail slapped against the floor. "Hrm."

"What?" Kadka turned fully around to face him. "Is problem? We need to move fast. Carver is in trouble."

"I... I don't know that there is a way through. I'm not aware of any passage here. If there is, it wouldn't go through the stone, but maybe..." He moved a silver-clawed hand along the brick wall to one side, then the other, tapped with the back of his knuckle at a few points. Finally, he shook his head. "I don't know, Kadka. I'm sorry."

"There is a door. Must be." Kadka pushed past him, started prodding bricks with her fingers. "Is no other way."

"Maybe they took a wrong turn, doubled back?" Iskar suggested.

She shook her head. "No. No sign of it, and never did before. Must be here. *Must* be." She balled up her fists and slammed them against the wall; fragments of old brick crumbled away, but no door opened. "Only used passages you know before. If you don't know this, must be end of trail. Mask's hideout. Carver is in there. We need to get *in*."

Iskar put a hand on her shoulder. "Kadka, I don't think—"

A sound came from behind, brick grating against brick. Kadka put a finger to her lips, spun to face the other wall.

A narrow line of light appeared there, ziz-zagging be-tween bricks, and growing wider.

Kadka grabbed Iskar's wrist and rushed down the hall, ducking around the next corner. She yanked Iskar against the wall with her, and they both pressed their backs against the brick.

Moments later, a massive shadow stepped into the fork in the tunnels. A dark robe covered its body, but it was some nine feet tall.

The Mask.

Kadka held her breath. If she'd picked the wrong passage—if the Mask turned their way—her chances of getting to Carver fell substantially.

Instead, the figure turned in the other direction, moving away from them into the dark.

As soon as the Mask was out of earshot—and she knew she was cutting it close—Kadka sprinted back down the tunnel. The brick had sealed shut once more. "*Desh-ka!*" she swore. Taking a step back, she hurled herself shoulder-first at the wall, ignored the pain of the impact, and did it again.

"Kadka!" Iskar caught up with her, grabbed her by the shoulders. "You'll only hurt yourself!"

She struggled against his grip—he was nearly as strong as she was. "Carver needs help. Can't stop."

"Then we need to find another way," Iskar insisted. "You're no good to him with a broken shoulder."

Kadka relented, stopped fighting him. "*What* other way?"

He sighed. "That I don't know. I could keep searching for a trigger, but that could take time Mister Carver might not have. And we can't simply knock on the front door. I wish I could be more use to you."

But something he'd said perked Kadka's ears. "Maybe we do go in front door."

"What do you mean?"

She was already moving back down the hall. There'd been a hatchway to the surface a short way beyond the last fork. "Stooketon is above, and main disc lines far that way." They were crossing the fork now, and she gestured down the passage to her right, where they'd hidden from the Mask. "So passage must go to basement somewhere. Just need to find what basement." She reached the ladder to the surface, started to climb. "And I am good at directions."

Iskar hesitated. "Kadka, I… I'm not sure I should. Someone might see."

Kadka paused on the ladder to look down at him. "No one will see. Is late, and dark. Please. Might need more strength than I have alone. I know you have secrets that make you hide. Is not for me to ask. But are they worth Carver's life?"

Iskar looked up at her for a long moment, and then, "No, I don't believe they are." He grasped the rung above his head and started up.

There was no one in sight when she emerged—it was late enough that the alley and the surrounding streets were deserted. She'd been right in her estimate of their location. They were at the far side of Stooketon, very near the Gryphon's Roost. Kadka hurried along the streets, tracing the lines of the maintenance tunnels in her head. It was only a few blocks to the spot, a windowless storehouse among several others like it at the very edge of the district.

"Here," she said. "This is place."

A single door led into the building. She tried the handle. Locked.

"How are you going to get through that?" Iskar approached from behind.

"Door isn't problem," said Kadka. Carver had taught her that. In a city of magic, no one relied on physical security. "Between two of us, should be strong enough. Problem will be ward behind it." That, she had no solution for.

Iskar took a deep breath. "I can deal with the wards."

Kadka cocked head. "Thought you had no magic?"

"I don't. I have… it's difficult to explain, Kadka. But I can get you through any ward you might face."

"Good. Help me with door."

Iskar grabbed her shoulder before she could turn away. "Wait. I… I cannot help you fight if it comes to that.

I will not harm anyone. I hope I can explain it to you in a way that you will understand, one day, but there is no time now. Please believe that I have good reason."

There wasn't time to ask more. She either trusted him or she didn't, and she decided in that moment that she did. "Is fine. Just get me in."

"No hesitation at all." Something glimmered in Iskar's bright blue eyes—admiration, maybe. "If we are dealing with the Knights of the Emperor, there will almost certainly be mages on the other side of that door. But you would face them alone."

"Carver is not perfect, but he is my friend. Maybe best one I have. If he needs me, I come. Always." She beckoned him forward. "No more talk. On three, we kick."

Iskar just nodded, and moved into position beside her.

"One. Two. Three!"

With a great crack, the door slammed inward under their feet. It opened into a curiously empty storehouse. A staircase descended into the basement on one side of the room, and in the opposite corner across a mostly bare floor sat a stack of chairs and several folding cots. Two of those cots were already laid out, though, and occupied. The figures in them stirred at the noise, and started to rise.

Instinctively, Kadka stepped forward, and met an invisible wall. A ward, just as she'd expected. "Quickly!" she said. She drew her long knife from behind her back, dropped a shorter blade from her sleeve into her empty palm with a flick of the wrist.

"Move aside," said Iskar, and centered himself before the door. He breathed deep, and then deeper still. His bare silver chest swelled. And then he opened his jaws wide, and exhaled with a terrible roar.

White hot flame gushed in a torrent from his mouth.

The fire spilled forth so bright that Kadka could hardly bear to look, rolling against the invisible ward like a great wave. Even from behind Iskar, the heat was almost unbearable; she took a step back to escape the pain on her bare face.

This was dragonfire. She knew it without doubt. Not a sad lick of flame like Sivisk had breathed at her, but *true* dragonfire, the kind so many kobolds boasted of but none possessed. Or at least she'd assumed none did, until now. She didn't know *how* he was doing it, what truth lay behind his evasiveness and secrecy, but just then she didn't care. All that mattered was that he was breathing dragon fire, and it was better than anything she'd ever seen. Better than magic.

Or at the very least, stronger.

Silver-blue light flared in the empty air across the doorway as the ward struggled against the white of the flame, and then Kadka *felt* something shatter—as if she could hear crystal breaking, but without any true sound.

"Go," Iskar panted as the flames died in his mouth. He bent, bracing his hands on his knees. "The way is clear."

But Kadka was already moving. She'd felt the magic break, and that was all she needed. The ward had stopped the flame from catching inside, but the outer doorway was still smouldering, uncomfortably hot to pass through. It didn't matter. She was through before Iskar finished speaking.

Two figures in black executioner's masks stood to face her, clearly hesitant to get any nearer the source of the white flame. One had retrieved an ancryst pistol from somewhere, and the other was already chanting magic words. A third was just emerging from the stairwell to join them.

"Only three?" Kadka felt the corners of her mouth rising. "You should have taken someone else's friend."

She met them grinning, knives in hand.

———

Tane heard the guard leave, but he didn't know why—there were only footsteps rapidly climbing the stairs, and then nothing. Nothing made it in past the sound-damping spell on the basement.

He rushed to the small window in the door, slid the metal plate aside. No one was there. They'd been left alone. "Something's happening," he said.

"Could just be changing shifts," said Indree.

"I don't think so. He sounded like he was in a hurry."

Indree moved to stand beside him, and took his hand. Neither of them had to say why. It had been near an hour since Endo's automaton had left them there. Tane didn't know who was upstairs, but if the Mask had returned, they didn't have long left.

"I'm sorry, Tane." Indree's voice was quiet and sad. "This is my fault. If I hadn't talked you out of going to the Audlians… because of me we basically walked right up to the Mask's door and told him we knew what he was planning."

He squeezed her hand. "You did the best you could with what you knew. And even if we had gone straight to the Audlian estate, we didn't have the resources to help them very much. We'd probably have ended up asking Endo for his crawlers either way. Which was entirely *my* idea, by the way. So save some blame for me, if that's what we're doing."

"Right. I forgot. I guess it's all *your* fault, then." Indree offered him a shallow smile. "I'm not sure that makes me feel much better, but thank you. For trying."

A sound came from the top of the stairs. A door creaking open, inside the sound-damping spell. A heavy footfall, and then another. Someone large.

It was easier to look at Indree than to just wait for the end, so he did. "We never did get that dinner," he said.

Indree gave him a sad smile. "I wouldn't have waited if I'd thought we'd run out of time."

There was too much to say. Too many regrets, too

many things he'd done wrong. He took a step towards her, still holding her hand in his. Looked into those amber eyes that he'd missed for so long, and wished to the Astra that he'd been smart enough not to leave. "Ree, if this is it…"

"I know." She moved to meet him, and then her body was against his.

Their lips met.

Tane grabbed her by the waist and pulled her as close as he could. Her arms were around his neck, clinging just as urgently as he was. *Spellfire, I missed this. I missed her.* Together, they tried to stretch the moment as long as they could, tried to ignore what was coming.

It didn't last.

The cell door swung open. Tane squeezed his eyes shut, and held Indree tight.

A familiar laugh came from the doorway. "Wouldn't hurry, if I know you two are having so much fun."

Tane's eyes snapped open, and he looked to see Kadka standing just outside the cell, a broad, toothy grin stretched across her face.

"Kadka!" His face flushed red, and he and Indree separated abrubtly, avoiding each other's eyes. Tane crossed the room and threw his arms around Kadka's broad shoulders. "I knew you'd come. I knew it."

"He's not lying," said Indree, exiting the cell behind him. "He was annoyingly sure of it, really." She clapped Kadka on the arm. "I'll admit, I wasn't so convinced. But I've never been so happy to be wrong."

"But how did you get in?" Tane asked, finally releasing her. "There had to be wards on the place."

"Iskar." Kadka nodded over her shoulder. Behind her, the tallest kobold Tane had ever seen rounded the bottom of the stairs, bare-chested and silver-scaled. "He breathes fire, breaks the spell. Couldn't have found you without him." She looked at Tane with a glint of defiance in her eyes, her thick jaw thrust out stubbornly. Making a point.

Tane raised his hands in surrender. "Kadka, I'm sorry. Everything I said last night… I should have just listened to you. You see things more clearly than I do, most of the time. You're so much more than just the muscle."

Kadka relaxed her jaw, and smiled. "I know. But is nice to hear you say so."

Tane looked to Iskar, then, as the muscular kobold drew near. "I don't know if you know this, but I owe you an apology too. I misjudged you without ever meeting you, even when Kadka told me you could be trusted. I'm sorry. Thank you for helping us." There *was* something curious in Kadka's story, though, and he just couldn't help himself. "But… you breathed fire on the wards and they broke? I've read legends that say dragonfire can break wards and shields, but even if that's true, kobold fire is… usually a bit less impressive." Although if any kobold had ever truly looked like a descendant of dragons, this man did, standing tall with huge silver wings at his back.

"My ancestors' blood runs strong in me," said Iskar, but his eyes flicked downward. "I was glad to help, Mister Carver. But perhaps we can speak of this later."

Tane had questions, but he let it pass. The man had saved them, and he was right: there were more important things at hand. "Right. No time to waste. Where are we exactly?"

"Edge of Stooketon, by Gryphon's Roost," Kadka said.

"We're close, then." Tane jabbed two fingers at Kadka and Indree. "You two need to get to the Audlian estate right away. The Mask usually strikes after most of the manor is asleep, and Endo doesn't know we're free—if he thinks he can afford to bide his time, we might still have a chance to stop him."

"Endo?" Kadka cocked her head. "He is part of this?"

"It's him, Kadka," Tane said. "He's the Mask. Or, he *built* the Mask. It's a golem."

Kadka's eyes widened, but she accepted the revelation without argument. "Explains why it doesn't stop your trail." She pointed to the dark ink stain down the side of Tane's trousers. "Only does what spells say to, yes?"

"Exactly," said Tane. "And its instructions right now are to kill Faelir Audlian. Tonight. Endo sent it out near an hour ago."

"I just sent to Durren for backup," Indree said, a distant look in her eye. "Even he's not stubborn enough to ignore us if I give him my memory of Endo confessing. But if we're at the edge of the Roost, we're closer to the Audlian estate than the Yard is."

"Should move fast then," said Kadka. "Have to do something with mages upstairs—they will wake soon."

"The Silver Dawn can deal with them," Iskar offered. "Our agents will secure this place until the constabulary can arrive. I'll see it done. You three get where you need to go."

"Wait." Indree's cheeks went red when she looked Tane in the eye; he felt his do the same. But she didn't let the embarrassment stop her. "Us two. You didn't say three. You said us two."

Tane nodded. "It's probably going to be a fight if you catch the Mask, and I'm useless against him. And they'll never let Kadka in alone. You're going to need your badge to get in. It has to be you two."

"That's not what I'm asking," Indree said, and now there was a hint of concern in her voice. "Where are *you* going?"

Tane gathered his nerve; his fingers went to the brass watch case in his pocket. "Well," he said, "somebody needs to have a talk with Endo."

CHAPTER TWENTY-THREE

———

"SO WHAT IS plan?" Kadka asked as she and Indree hurried down the street toward the Audlian estate. It sat atop a hill at the end of Riverview Avenue, a massive manor looking down over the surrounding city, isolated by a tall iron fence. The protective detail that had swarmed the grounds in previous days had thinned to a pair of guards on the gate and a few patrols across the property, visible in the dark by the light of their lanterns.

Endo's machinations had done their job. With Noana Uuthar and her son in custody, the Senate houses felt safe lowering their guard.

Indree spoke between breaths, easily matching Kadka's quick pace. "Backup is on its way," she said. "They're already at the Stooke house, but we're further from the Yard here, and we can't afford to wait. We'll go straight in. We might be able to evacuate the Audlians to protective custody before the Mask attacks. If not... We'll hold him—it—off as best we can." Her hand went to the empty holster where her pistol usually hung. She'd given it to Carver when they'd parted—it wouldn't do any good against a golem—but Kadka recognized the nervous instinct.

"Won't get past us," Kadka said as confidently as she could. She didn't bring up that the Mask had beaten her once already.

"I almost believe that, coming from you," said Indree. "You seem to have a habit of improbable rescues. I'm glad you're here."

"You too. Seen you fight before." Kadka grinned a forced grin, but just doing it made her feel a little bit better. "Your magic and my muscle, can't lose."

Indree didn't look entirely convinced, but she nodded. "I just hope we're not already too late."

They were nearly at the gates now, and the guards stepped forward to meet them, two elven men in Audlian blue and gold. "What business do you have here?" one man asked.

Indree produced her badge. "Constable Inspector Indree Lovial. The Audlians are in danger. You're going to tell Daalia Audlian we're here, and then you're going to let us through that gate."

Neither guardsman was stupid enough to mistake the tone in her voice—Kadka admired the authority Indree could project when she needed to. "One moment, Inspector Lovial," the elf who had spoken first said. "I'll notify the family."

Less than a minute later, they were through the gates, running up the hill toward the manor.

The guards at the door had already been notified to let Kadka and Indree in without delay. They passed through the doors and into a vast foyer with a stark marble floor and a pair of symmetrical curving stairways at the far end that led up to the second floor landing. It seemed a waste to Kadka, like most of the giant manor houses she'd seen the past few days. She lived in a cramped room in Porthaven that would have fit in this space four times over, and she'd grown up in Svernan longhouses where every inch had a purpose. This was just pointless emptiness to pass through.

Daalia Audlian waited inside, just before the stairs. Or at least, Kadka assumed it was Daalia Audlian—she'd never met the woman. An older elf with a simple robe wrapped around her body, she looked as if she'd just been going to bed, or perhaps just awoken. She wore no ornament or jewelry, and her long grey hair was unbound and unbrushed, but even so she had the dignified bearing of a powerful woman. An elven man stood beside her in a silken nightrobe, his blond hair rumpled and messy. He appeared far less collected than she did, and far more annoyed. Four guards stood with them, two on either side.

"What is the meaning of this?" the man beside Daalia demanded, rubbing bleary eyes. "Do you know what time it is?"

Daalia frowned at him. "You're being rude, Saelis. Inspector Lovial was instrumental in bringing down Talain Nieris, and if I'm not mistaken this is Kadka of the Magebreakers. I'm inclined to trust that they wouldn't trouble us without good reason." She faced Indree and Kadka. "Forgive my cousin. He's always grumpy when he wakes. I'm told you believe we're in danger?"

"I know it for a fact, Senator," said Indree. "I was taken captive by the Mask tonight, and he told me himself that he means to kill your nephew. We need to check on Faelir right now."

"Taken captive by the… but the Mask was arrested! How could you—" Saelis Audlian was still sputtering when his cousin cut him off.

Daalia pointed at the pair of guards on her right. "You two, join the men on the front door. And tell the others we may have an intruder on the grounds. I want everyone on alert. The rest of you, come with me." And then the head of House Audlian hiked her robe above her knees, turned, and sprinted for the main stairway. Straight to action. Kadka respected that.

They stopped at a door on the second floor. Daalia reached it first, and she was already calling her nephew's name as she turned the handle. "Faelir!"

Kadka tensed, half-expecting to see the huge silhouette of the Mask standing over the bed, crowned spike in hand. She'd be ready for him this time, she hoped. Her hand slipped behind her back to grasp the hilt of her knife. Beside her, she heard Indree muttering magical words under her breath.

The door swung open. Light spilled into the darkened bedroom.

There was no one inside except a young elf man, sitting up in bed and blinking at the sudden brightness from the hall. "Aunt Daalia? What's going on?"

Indree answered first. "We have reason to believe an attempt is going to be made on your life, Senator Audlian." It seemed every one of these elves was a senator of some sort. "We need to get you into protective custody at Stooketon Yard as soon as possible. Get dressed. Quickly." She ushered everyone out of the room and closed the door—not all the way, just enough to give Faelir some privacy—then turned to Daalia. "I assume you have a coach of some sort? I'd suggest we get your family on it with an escort of guardsmen and get you away from here as quickly as possible. There are more constables coming, but we can meet them on the way. The Mask is going to come looking for Faelir here, and your wards won't stop him. The sooner we're off the grounds, the better."

"Whatever you think necessary, Inspector Lovial," said Daalia. Her eyes went unfocused for a moment. "I've sent for the carriage to be brought around, and called back the guards patrolling the grounds. That should be sufficient escort."

Faelir stepped into the hall, still blinking against the light. He was a young man, at least by elf standards—he looked about Carver's age, although Kadka knew he had to be in his sixth decade, if not older. He had fair hair like his father, and sharp, solemn features. And apparently, he was the first magicless elf born to a Senate house in more than a hundred years, although that seemed to Kadka a curious thing to care so much about. "Is someone going to explain this to me?" he asked.

"The Mask is coming," said Indree. "If you want more details, you can have them on the way. Come on."

They marched quickly back down the stairs and through the foyer—Kadka and Indree in the lead, the Audlians behind them, and two guardsmen at the rear.

Indree paused for a moment just before the big front doors, and turned to face the others. "Once we walk through these doors, we don't stop until we reach Stooketon Yard. If you feel like slowing down, I suggest you remember that the Mask won't. Any questions?"

There weren't any.

"Good," said Indree. "Kadka, take the lead. If we run into trouble, I'll need space to get my spells off."

Kadka pushed open the heavy double doors with both hands.

She was just in time to watch the last of the guards fall.

A hooded giant in a black robe stood over a half-dozen prone bodies, holding a crowned spike of solid bronze in one hand. A faceless brass mask turned toward the door, and silver-blue eye-slits found Faelir Audlian's face.

The Mask advanced in utter silence.

Kadka's knives were in her hand at once, but instead of attacking, she backed off a step and tried to recall everything Carver had told her about automatons—any weaknesses she might exploit. All she could come up with were strengths. It would implacably follow whatever instruction it had been given, so there was no intimidating it, no scaring it off. It was strong, and tireless, and lacked any vital organs for her knives to find. It was made of brass, which would dampen the effects of spells—the metal wasn't strictly magic-proof, as far as she understood it, but no spell could pass *through*, which considerably dulled the impact of any attack Indree might make. It had artifacts that let it mimic spells of its own without even needing the words. She didn't know what victory against this thing even *looked* like.

And it had already beaten her once.

Indree spoke several sharp, fast syllables in the language of magic, and silver-blue energy encircled the Mask, clasping massive arms to its sides. "Get them somewhere safe!" she shouted over her shoulder to the two guardsmen left behind.

Kadka heard retreating footsteps behind her, but she didn't look back. There was no time left for hesitation. She couldn't let Indree do this alone. With a running leap, she launched herself at the Mask.

The golem strained against Indree's spell, and the silver energy stretched and thinned. It wouldn't hold long. Knives weren't going to do much, but strength could. Kadka grabbed the Mask's arms in a bearhug just above waist level—as high as she could reach—and gripped tight, hoping to give Indree a chance to bolster her magic. As long as they kept it bound, they were buying the Audlians time to escape.

It worked, for a moment. The combined might of Indree's spell and Kadka's grip held the Mask's arms in place at its sides, kept the artifacts in its hands from finding targets.

And then, in the corner of her eye, she saw a silver-blue flash.

The Mask discharged a torrent of silver force from its left hand, directly at the ground beneath their feet. The strength of it tore Kadka's grip free, threw her up and away to land hard on the ground in front of the doors. The Mask hardly moved at all; its size and weight and brass construction absorbed the bulk of the impact.

Eyes still blurry and unfocused from the fall, Kadka

pushed herself up on one arm, watched as the Mask shattered Indree's spell with a powerful surge of its arms. The golem barrelled forward, crossing the distance in huge strides. Kadka rolled aside to avoid being trampled, and Indree spun out of the way at the last moment.

The Audlians and their guards were on the second floor landing now, at least, with a decent head start. Or so Kadka thought.

Until the Mask jumped.

It reached the center of the foyer, bent its knees, and sprang into the air. Glyphs on the bottoms of its feet flared, and the golem soared into the air, impossibly high, arcing toward the second floor balcony. It was only then that Kadka remembered Endo mentioning the apparently groundbreaking levitation spells he'd woven into his chair.

So now they were fighting an unstoppable golem who could all but fly.

The Mask landed lightly on the balcony, with almost no sound. The guards moved to block its advance, short swords drawn. It simply stowed its spike at its waist, grabbed one man in each hand, and lifted them off the ground as their blades rang harmlessly off brass. Neither of them went limp, though. The dazing artifacts that the golem had used to kidnap Carver and Indree apparently weren't in play. That was something. Tane had said that the power drain on those was substantial—perhaps too much to sustain for a longer fight.

With almost casual ease, the Mask threw both men over its shoulders and off the edge of the landing. They struck marble with a sickening crunch.

From the first floor, Indree was chanting another spell, and as she finished a shield of translucent silver spanned the mouth of the hall at the top of the stairs, separating the golem from the Audlians. "Move, Kadka! It won't hold long!"

Kadka pushed herself up and ran for the stairs, climbing them three at a time. The Mask pounded huge fists against the magical barrier again and again. She leapt onto its back and wrapped her arms around its neck just as the barrier shattered. Her weight made next to no difference. The golem drew its bronze spike once more and strode down the hall after the fleeing family, carrying Kadka like she was nothing.

She might as well have been, for all she was doing to slow this thing down. They weren't going to be able to beat the Mask this way. Not with muscle, or force.

Which meant she needed to find another way. If there was a flaw in all magic, like Carver always said, she had to find it.

The Mask caught up to the Audlians all too quickly, but it had no eyes for anyone but Faelir. It bowled past Daalia and Saelir, grabbed the young elf, shoved him against the wall. Faelir raised his hands in futile defense as the Mask drew back its spike to jab at his face. Desperate, Kadka moved her hands over the eye-slits on its mask and pulled back hard. Carver and Endo had talked about automatons using their lenses to see, like eyes. She hoped that was true.

The blow missed by a sliver as Faelir jerked his head aside. The Mask didn't strike again, instead reached back to ball its fist in Kadka's shirt and tear her free. She grabbed at it, trying to find purchase, and gripped its black hood.

It wasn't enough. The Mask hurled her against the wall, and she struck hard, knocking the breath from her lungs. But the hood tore away too, still clutched in her fist. Suddenly the golem's head was exposed, a smooth brass oval with a single seam outlining a square hatch at the back.

A hatch like Endo's crawlers, where the scrolls that governed their actions were held. The one she'd seen had gone inactive when those scrolls were removed. If she could just get the Mask to stay still long enough to jam one of her knives in that seam, she was sure she could pry it open.

From halfway down the hall, Indree uttered a spell and grabbed the Mask's raised arm in a lariat of Astral force just before it stabbed down at Faelir Audlian's head once more. Saelis grabbed his son by the arm, shoved Daalia ahead, and the three of them were running once more, heading for the far end of the hall where another stairway led back down to the first floor. The Mask yanked against Indree's restraint, breaking free to aim one last thrust at the back of Faelir's head as he passed out of reach. It came close enough to stir the young elf's hair, but didn't quite find purchase.

Always the head. That was something else Carver had called out before. If it was a symbol for their lack of magic, the victims should have been stabbed through the heart, he'd said.

But what if it wasn't a symbol? Maybe an automated assassin couldn't judge for itself whether someone was dead or just unconscious. Maybe its instructions needed to be specific enough to make certain. The heart was unreliable, easily missed, but a spike through the brain…

The Mask pursued its fleeing victim down the hall. Indree caught up with Kadka, pulled her to her feet. "Are you hurt?"

Kadka ignored the question. "You see how Mask always goes for head? Sees spike there, maybe it knows victim is dead. Job is done."

"You have an idea? I'd be glad for one of those right now." Indree started after the Mask once more.

Kadka ran alongside her, pointed with her knife toward the back of the Mask's head as they chased it down the hall. "See seam there? Need to get that open to stop it. Just need distraction."

Understanding came to Indree's eyes, and she nodded emphatically. "I can make that happen. Be ready." She spoke the words of a spell, and a silver-blue cord wrapped around the golem's waist, slowing it down. The Audlians made the stairs at the end of the hall, moved quickly out of sight as they descended. Indree shouted after them. "Find some place to hide!"

The spell didn't hold long—each time, the Mask broke free faster as Indree's endurance ebbed. But it was enough for Kadka and Indree to close the distance. They were only a few yards behind when they reached the stairs themselves.

This stairway was clearly for the servants and guards, narrower and less impressive than the ones in the foyer. They switched direction at a landing halfway down; as they rounded that corner just behind the Mask, Indree quietly started to mutter the words of a spell.

Below them, Faelir Audlian ran by the bottom of the stairway, apparently alone. The Mask leapt down the last ten steps in a single bound, raising its spike. Kadka poured on the speed and threw herself after, exiting the stairway into a small servant's hall that led to the kitchen on her left. To her right, a door onto the grounds had been left open.

Faelir stumbled away in terror, and then his back was against the wall. The Mask raised its spike, and struck.

The spike tore through Faelir's face, pulping skin and crunching bone.

Desperately, Kadka hurled herself onto the Mask's back one last time, wrapped one arm around its neck. The Mask ignored her, didn't resist at all. Its primary goal was to kill its target; nothing else mattered. It drove the spike through Faelir's head until she heard it strike the wall behind.

Kadka jammed her knife into the seam at the back of the Mask's head, and put all her strength against the hilt. The hatch wrenched open, revealing three tightly coiled scrolls of spellwork. She jammed her fist into the hole and tore one free from its copper clasps.

Beneath her, the golem ceased moving. The faint silver-blue glow of its eyes died, and it dropped heavily to its knees. Kadka leapt free as it collapsed to the floor with a massive crash.

It was over. They'd done it. They'd broken the Mask.

Just not the way she'd imagined.

She looked to the limp body of Faelir Audlian, pinned against the wall on a bloody spike.

The body shimmered, colors fading into silver. Faelir vanished as the illusion blinked out, leaving only the crowned spike staked into crumbling plaster.

On the landing above, the sound of Indree's muttered spell ceased, and she descended the rest of the way to join Kadka. "How's that for a distraction?" she said.

Kadka turned to her with a wide, triumphant grin. "Does the job." She crumpled the glyph-covered scroll in her fist, and let it fall atop the Mask's massive, motionless frame.

"Is it over?" Daalia Audlian's voice, from outside.

"Not until Endo Stooke is locked up," Indree answered. "But you're out of danger." She and Kadka left the manor through the open door to the grounds.

Daalia, Saelis, and Faelir huddled together against the wall just outside the door, alive and well. Beyond them, Kadka could see the nighttime lights of the city spread out below the hill where the manor sat—not as impressive as the view from the top of an airship, but still decent.

Daalia Audlian stood, quickly recovering her dignified bearing. "Endo Stooke? Is that who was behind this? That is… hard to imagine."

"Is true," Kadka said. "Who else builds thing like that?" She pointed through the door, at the great sprawl of the Mask.

Daalia nodded slowly as she considered that. "An automaton that advanced… I don't know how you two stopped it. We are in your debt. Anything in my power—"

A massive, roaring explosion shattered the air, swallowing her voice.

"Get down!" Indree shouted, and threw herself in front of the Audlians.

Daalia ducked her head and pressed herself back against the wall as great pillars of silver fire gouted into the air across the darkened city below. The light burned painfully bright against Kadka's sensitive night vision even from so far away, but still she leapt to join Indree, ready to shield the Audlians with her body.

But there was nothing to shield them from. The fires were far away, six points of searing silver spread over the city. There was nothing to do but watch them burn. And as the pillars of silver flame reached their full height, a ghostly image of the Mage Emperor's crowned staff appeared in the sky above each spot, glowing silver-blue against the night sky.

"What in the Astra…" Indree breathed, looking up at the sigils in horror. "What *is* this?"

Kadka didn't have an answer for that, but she was a good judge of distance and direction. It didn't take her long to identify the locations: one at Audlian's Crossing, where protestors gathered before the Brass Citadel; two each in the poorer districts of Porthaven and Greenstone.

And one more.

Not terribly far away, a crowned staff floated in the air above Stooketon. A fist of dread closed around Kadka's heart.

"Don't know what it is," said Kadka, and pointed at the sigil over Stooketon, silver flames burning hungrily below. "But that one is Stooke house. Where Carver went."

CHAPTER TWENTY-FOUR

BLUECAPS HAD ALREADY surrounded the Stooke's townhouse by the time Tane got there. Two dozen men and women in blue uniforms and caps had erected a perimeter of glyph-etched brass pylons topped by copper spheres. A barrier of silver-blue energy spanned the gaps between them, shimmering against the dark and blocking anyone without the proper badge from going in or out.

"*They should already be there.*" Indree's voice in his head. She'd sent for backup before they'd parted. Her tone was purposefully brisk—no indication of the fact that they'd kissed less than a quarter hour before. "*It's not far from the Yard.*"

"*They are,*" Tane sent back. "*Already have their pylons set.*"

"*Good. Don't even think about going in after Endo without a good dozen of them in front of you.*"

"*I heard you the first five times. I'll be good.*"

"*You'd better be. I expect to see you again when this is done. I have to go now—we're almost at the Audlian estate. Good luck, Tane.*" The pressure died in his ears, and she was gone— very likely to face down the Mask. He tried not to think too hard about all the ways that could go badly. He couldn't afford to be distracted just now.

As he approached the townhouse, Tane reached back to tuck his vest over the pistol sitting in the back of his waistband. Indree had given it to him, but he wasn't certain the other bluecaps would approve. He didn't much like carrying it, but he had a feeling he was going to need every edge he could get before the night was over.

A blue-clad ogren woman waved him down as he drew near. "Mister Carver," she said in a lovely, sonorous voice. "I'm Inspector Vathaa. Inspector Lovial said you'd be coming." She was large enough that she had to bend at the knee to hand him a brass badge. "This will let you through the perimeter, if need be. I'm glad you're here. Things have become… complicated."

"How so?" Tane asked, pinning the badge to his waistcoat. "Is Endo inside?"

"He is," said Inspector Vathaa. "Our divinations con-firm two Astral signatures in there: Mister Stooke himself, and his mother. The problem is, he won't let anyone through the wards, and he's threatening to harm the senator if we try. I've been trying to negotiate, but he's not responding. And Astrally disassembling the house wards could take hours."

Tane raised an eyebrow. "And you think I can do something to help."

"I hope so," Vathaa said. "Just before you arrived, Mister Stooke told me that he would speak to you, and only you. I don't know what changed, but he seemed to know you'd be here. And from what Inspector Lovial says, I gather you might have some insight into his mindset that I don't. I'd like you to convince him to let some of us go in with you. If we can get close, we can take him down."

Tane shook his head. "Won't work. He'll never agree to it." If Endo wanted him inside, it was for one reason: to settle a very old score. He wouldn't let the bluecaps get in the way. "But you're right. Someone has to get in there. And he'll let me in if I go alone." Which was exactly what he'd promised Indree he wouldn't do.

But a senator's life was at stake now. *And she knew it had to go this way. She wouldn't have been so worried about it otherwise.*

"I can't let you do that, Mister Carver. It's against protocol, and Chief Durren—"

"Isn't here. Look, Ree—Inspector Lovial—was put in charge of this case by the Lady Protector, right? And she brought me on board. I'm not a civilian, I'm a professional consultant. And I know how to deal with Endo." That was a lie, but he didn't think the inspector would be checking for those just now. "Right now, the important thing is getting Senator Stooke out of there. If I go in, I might be able to get those wards down for you, if nothing else. Let me help."

Vathaa hesitated for a moment, and then nodded her head. "I shouldn't, but Inspector Lovial *did* say we should defer to your knowledge of the situation." She turned to the bluecaps holding the perimeter and raised her voice. "Mister Carver is going in. Let him through."

The constables gave her quizzical looks, but stood aside without argument. The badge Vathaa had given him allowed Tane through the perimeter shield, with a hair-raising tingle like passing through a ward. On the inside of the shield, a broad half-circle of empty space surrounded the Stooke's townhouse. It felt isolated, as if he'd stepped out of phase with the rest of the world. He could still see and hear the bluecaps on the other side, but they were somehow distant now despite their closeness. He was on his own.

He approached the door, but before he could do anything to signal his presence, he felt the pressure of a sending build in his ears.

"*Tane. You are full of surprises, aren't you? When my Mask saw your friends arrive at the Audlian estate, I knew you'd be along soon.*"

"*Then you must also know we've told everyone the truth,*" Tane sent back through the open Astral channel. "*This is over, Endo. Indree and Kadka are going to stop the Mask, and you can't hole up in there forever."*

"We'll see, won't we? In the meantime, why don't you come in and have a friendly chat? After all, we've become so close." The door swung inward. Endo said nothing more, but the pressure in Tane's ears remained—the channel was still open.

Tane wasn't keen on passing into the entry hall—he'd been ambushed by crawlers there once already—but he took a breath and stepped across the threshold. Death by automaton just inside the door was too impersonal. Endo wasn't going to do anything to him until they were face to face.

As soon as he was inside, the outer door closed behind him, and the inner one opened into the house proper. *"You haven't seen my workshop, have you?"* Endo's voice sounded in his head. *"I think you'll like it, considering our shared interest in the workings of magecraft. End of the hall to your right, please."*

Tane considered stalling, taking the time to search for wherever the Stookes kept their central warding artifacts, but really he'd only told Vathaa he'd try so that she'd let him in. The truth was, Endo was smart enough to have that room thoroughly secured. Instead, he turned right, just as he'd been told. A door waited for him at the end of a short hall, slightly ajar.

Taking a long, shaky breath, Tane brushed his fingers over the watch case in his pocket, and then reached back to grasp Indree's pistol. Keeping his hand hidden behind him, he pushed the door open and stepped into a workshop lined with long tables and littered with artifice debris: brass and copper and gold and silver and gems of all kinds.

Endo was waiting inside, his chair facing the door. The earnest little gnome Tane was familiar with had disappeared—his face was hard, and his eyes were cold. On the floor beside him, Umbla Stooke lay prone and bound, cyclopean brass spider-crawlers clasping her wrists and ankles with their segmented legs. One perched on her chest, holding a sharp-pronged claw at her throat. By the terror in her eyes, it was more the claw keeping her silent than the gag in her mouth.

"Let her go, Endo," Tane said. At the sight of him Umbla Stooke's eyes widened, and a muffled shout started under her gag.

"Quiet, Mother," Endo said, and his crawler pressed its claw slightly harder against her neck. She fell silent.

"You can't win here, Endo," said Tane, moving closer. "This will go easier on you if you cooperate."

Endo smiled without any real mirth. "Now Tane, you can't really have thought I would believe that. After what I've done, there is no 'easy' sentence. No, I think I'll wait this out."

"That's about what I thought you'd say." In a fluid motion, Tane drew Indree's pistol and aimed it at Endo's chest. "So let's define 'easy' as 'still alive'. Make a move I don't like, or utter a word of the *lingua*, and I can take that option away." Which was assuming Endo hadn't already cast a shield, or any other active magic that would turn and ancryst ball aside. *He's an artificer more than a combat mage. If he was already focusing on a spell, he'd show it. And he can't cast faster than a pistol shot.*

"I don't think you will," said Endo. "If you'll permit me to show you something without pulling the trigger?" He raised a hand from his lap, very slowly. In it, he held a small brass artifact. His thumb rested on a copper plate etched with glowing glyphs. "The instant this little device ceases to sense my Astral signature, my crawler will cut mother's throat. And if you think your aim sound enough to hit the crawler, consider that you'll have wasted your only shot—what will be left to stop me casting a spell?"

Tane kept the pistol steady. "First your brother and now your mother. Why? What is it you want? You can't think you'll still get it." Something felt wrong, and that sending pressure was still in his ears—it was hard not to try to shake his head clear, though he knew it wouldn't help. Endo was still keeping the Astral channel open, which meant he could send a burst of pain or a sudden image at any moment. But for some reason, he hadn't yet.

Endo laughed bitterly. "My dear brother. Do you have any idea what it was like to see her"—he jabbed a finger at his mother, there—"treat him as the favorite, the heir apparent? To pretend to be the meek little brother when I could do things he couldn't dream of? To watch them—and everyone else—look down with *pity* at the poor half-gnome with no legs, when magic gave me back far more than I ever lost? And then to learn that Ulnod was working with the Silver Dawn for non-magical rights, when it was a magicless fool who *took* my legs from me!"

Tane edged slowly to one side, hoping Endo was agitated enough not to notice. He had to get closer to Umbla Stooke if he was going to do something about that crawler. *I need to keep him talking, keep him distracted.* "It was a mage who made the error on those spells, Endo. The accident wasn't my father's fault. If he'd been allowed to have the magical education—"

"But he didn't!" Endo shouted. "It should have been a mage checking those spells! A mage might have caught the mistake! If we weren't so concerned with making the non-magical feel useful, your father would have had nothing to do with such a delicate artifact! And now his *son* has the gall to *pretend* at magecraft, making people like him believe they might do the same!" He took a breath, gathered his composure. "You would try to teach the blind to see, but they will never have true vision. The magicless look at me, and all they see is that I cannot walk upon the ground like they do. They never stop to think that if I needed to, I could *fly*."

"So this is all still about the accident, when you get down to it," said Tane. He almost felt like he could understand. The same experience had shaped them both, even if Endo had gone too far. "I spent a long time obsessing over it too. I ruined almost everything good in my life dwelling on the past. I still regret it." That was hard to face even now. So much time lost with Indree. And Allaea— he'd never even had the chance to apologize to her. "You have such a brilliant mind, and you're wasting it trying to change something that's already happened."

"I couldn't expect you to understand," Endo said. "You have… surprised me, I will admit, but still, you have no magic of your own. There is a natural order to things, and we have tried to subvert it in the Protectorate for too long. It is time things were put right."

Tane edged further toward the senator as Endo spoke, and it was only then that he noticed something strange.

Endo's shadow was wrong. It had looked right from the front, but from this angle it appeared to be cast by a light that wasn't there.

And that sending pressure was still strong in his ears.

"Spellfire," Tane cursed, and swung his pistol toward the crawler at Umbla Stooke's throat. He was close enough now that it was an easy shot. A silver flash, and the little brass automaton backflipped through the air and landed on the ground under one of Endo's worktables, several legs broken beneath it.

"Ah," said Endo. "I suppose the game is up." He laughed. "Did you *really* think I would sit here waiting for you just to explain my motivations in elaborate detail? I had my Knights put a contingency plan into motion as soon as I sent the Mask for you and Inspector Lovial. I'm afraid you've wasted quite a bit of time, Tane. And you don't have much of that left." His image shimmered into silver and then dissolved completely, leaving behind an empty chair.

He'd never been there at all. He'd been sending an illusion from the moment Tane had entered.

But the chair wasn't actually *entirely* empty. A four-sided pyramid of brass about the size of Tane's head sat upon the seat, with a round clock face set into the side. The hands glowed silver-blue, Astral images cast on clouded glass, and they were counting down. Only some two minutes remained. Beside that sat a small copper lined mimic vial. *That's why the diviners sensed him inside. He's been buying time to get away, and I fell for it.*

Though the image had gone, Endo's voice was still there. "*I'd hoped to announce my claim to the throne more elegantly, but it seems your friends have disabled my Mask. Senseless destruction will have to do. Goodbye, Tane.*" At last, the sending pressure abated.

There was no time to be relieved that Indree and Kadka had dealt with the Mask. Whatever that pyramid-shaped artifact was, it wasn't good, and there wasn't long left on the clock. Tane rushed to Umbla Stooke's side, battered the crawlers from her wrists and ankles with the butt of Indree's pistol.

As he freed her arms and legs, she managed to spit the gag from her mouth. She was staring, terrified, at the artifact in Endo's chair. "You have to stop it!"

"No time," said Tane. "We need to get out of here."

She shook her head. "You don't understand! He's set it to go off if we try to leave! And there are more around the city, set to activate when this one does!"

"More of what? What *is* it?"

"Spellfire!" she said, and at first he thought she was just swearing. But then, "It's a spellfire detonation! It's going to burn us alive!"

Tane's heart froze in his chest. He rose convulsively, spun on his heel to face the device.

A minute and a half left.

He lunged for Endo's chair and the detonation artifact. The side of the pyramid opposite the clock was hinged at the bottom, latched closed with a copper press-plate. He recognized the design. It would be Astrally sealed—unbreakable, unless it sensed the signature it was set for.

Luckily, Endo had left him just what he needed.

Tane snatched up the mimic vial from the seat of the chair, and a pair of brass tongs sitting on the nearby worktable. Clutching the vial in the tongs to insulate his own Astral signature, he touched the mimic vial to the latch, and pressed inward.

The side of the pyramid fell open.

Tane knelt to examine the interior workings. Inside, the faces were lined with copper, and glyphs in the *lingua* were etched over every inch, from top to bottom. A sapphire array was mounted at the back, held in copper clasps. Just above that was the clock face—the silver-blue hands oriented themselves to the perspective of the viewer, so it was perfectly readable from the inside as well as out.

And it showed just over a minute left.

Hastily, he scanned the glyphs. It *was* a spellfire detonation—he'd hoped the senator had gotten it wrong somehow. When the time ran out, the artifact would release a pillar of spellfire large enough to consume the house and everything else within the prescribed area. And there was no restriction to what it would burn—only the plain circle glyph for 'all things'.

There were more of them, too, just as Senator Stooke had said. Endo must have been pressed for time, because the spellcraft here was set as a template for a number of other detonations. The others would have much simpler glyphs, linking back to these ones. Faster to make a primary artifact and base the rest on it than to create and etch five in a few hours. If Tane hadn't been less than a minute away from death by spellfire, it would have been satisfying to know he'd at least forced Endo to scramble.

But if I can stop this one, I stop the others too.

Which was easier said than done. Endo had included tamper-proofing and redundancies everywhere. Scratching out any of the glyphs would set it off, or trying to remove the gems powering it. There wasn't much he could do except speed up his own incineration.

Which didn't really need speeding up. Only thirty seconds left.

"*Do* something!" Umbla Stooke yelled from over his shoulder. "There's no time!"

"There's nothing I *can* do! If I try to change anything, it kills us both!"

Except maybe that wasn't quite true. There was nothing to stop him from *adding* to the glyphs, as long as he didn't overwrite anything. Endo had used up all the available space, so there was no room for entirely new glyphs, but...

He glanced at the clock face.

Just under twenty seconds. He might still make it, if he was fast.

Tane whirled, frantically searched the worktable, tossed through piles of scattered parts. *Where is it?* He was sure he'd seen... there it was. A copper-tipped engraving wand, half hidden under a dirty rag. He grabbed it, pressed the activation glyph on the grip, and knelt before the pyramid.

It was only then that he remembered Indree's sending locket. He could have at least said goodbye to her. Told her to thank Kadka for him. Maybe even come up with some convincingly profound last words.

Five seconds. No time for farewells. *Astra, let this work. Let me see them again.*

As the clock ticked toward zero, he etched a single line.

The room exploded into silver flame.

———

"Tane?"

Tane coughed as he came back to consciousness, and he felt something come out, a fine grit that lined the inside of his mouth and lungs. His entire body ached. He blinked open his eyes, looked up to see Indree and Kadka kneeling beside him.

And looming large in the night sky directly above their heads, a towering image of the Mage Emperor's crowned staff.

Kadka clapped him on the shoulder, and he winced from the force of it. "Carver! When we saw fire, I thought… Is good to see you alive." She offered an arm, helped him to his feet.

Tane's leg nearly buckled under him, and he leaned against her for support. "What—" He started coughing again, and grey dust issued from his mouth. It looked like ash. Actually, now that he looked, he was covered in it, from head to toe. A huge ash-filled hole that had once been the basement was all that remained of the Stooke townhouse, and the homes on either side were gone as well. Everything below the crowned staff in the sky had been burned to nothing—all that remained was ash covering melted metal and stone. "What happened?"

"Spellfire detonations," said Indree. "Six of them, across the city." She pointed up at the Mage Emperor's sigil. "And one of those above every one."

"How many dead?" Tane asked, dreading the answer.

"About twenty counted so far, mostly from the bridge at Audlian's Crossing," said Indree. "But it could have been much worse. The spellfire must have been set to only burn inanimate matter. It incinerated buildings in an instant, and the bridge, but it didn't touch a living soul. What deaths and injuries we have are from when the bridge and floors gave way."

"Explains why I hurt so much. I must have fallen into the basement when the floor burned up."

"That's the most common story," said Indree. "Endo must have been making a point, but he could have killed so many more people. I don't see why—"

Tane shook his head. "It wasn't him. He was going to burn everything. The only thing I could do was change the glyph on the template. A half-circle on the downward side."

Indree's eyes widened. "All things not sentient. By the Astra, Tane, you saved a lot of lives."

"I was mostly trying to save my own," he said, and coughed up another cloud of ash. "What about the senator?"

"She's alive, but badly hurt in the fall," said Indree. "We've already sent her to the mage-surgeons."

Tane was about to ask more when a sudden pressure filled his ears. He knew who it would be even before the voice came.

"*You are a hard man to kill, it seems,*" Endo said mildly in a voice only Tane could hear. It sounded hollow, as if sent from a great distance. "*And more resourceful than I anticipated once again. But still, my sigil looks grand in the sky, doesn't it? It should have been above the Audlian estate, but I think my point has been made.*"

Kadka noticed something was wrong instantly. "Carver? What is it?"

"Endo," he said. Along the open Astral channel, he sent back, "*Every bluecap and Mageblade in the Protectorate will be looking for you. You can't escape. Not after this.*"

"*I already have. But we will meet again, Tane Carver. I promise you that.*" And then the pressure died. The sending was done.

"What is he saying?" Indree demanded. "Keep him talking! I might be able to trace him through the Astra!"

And Tane could only shake his head. "We're too late. I think he's gone."

CHAPTER TWENTY-FIVE

"THIS IS A disaster!" Chief Durren shouted, pounding a fist on his desk. "Dozens dead and injured, and no sign of the criminal responsible for it. Any evidence we might have found in the Stooke's townhouse is burned to ash. What *do* you have for me, Inspector Lovial?"

Tane stood with Kadka and Indree in the chief's office at Stooketon Yard. After a long night trying to track down Endo, they'd been summoned to report in the early hours of the morning. He leaned against Kadka—he'd twisted his ankle badly when the floor of the Stooke house had been incinerated under his feet, and it was still painful to stand on his own.

"Very little," Indree admitted. "We've closed the ports and rail stations, but I suspect Endo is already out of our reach. A small Stooke vessel left the harbor earlier tonight, not long after Tane and I were taken captive by the Mask. He was gone before we even knew who we were looking for."

Durren's face was growing redder by the moment. "And you'll have to answer for that! We might have apprehended him if you'd just brought this to me instead of going off on your own with these two—"

Kadka interrupted him with a loud bark of laughter. "Is joke, yes? We all pretend you would listen to us when we tell you truth?"

"I should have you thrown in a cell for interfering in this investigation!" Durren exploded.

"Of course you should," said Tane. "Because then you can blame us for everything, and you come out clean, right?"

"No." Indree rested her fists against the desk and leaned forward to look Durren in the eye. "Because I won't stay quiet if he tries, and he knows that the people won't stand for it if they hear the famous Magebreakers were jailed unjustly. You were never going to listen to anything Tane brought you, Durren. We did what we had to do."

"You... you are insubordinate, Inspector!" Durren sputtered, flushed all the way up to his thinning red hair. "There will be consequences!"

"Fine," said Indree. "I'm done trying to work around you. I joined the constabulary to help people, and if you won't let me do that, maybe I'm better off elsewhere."

Durren looked like he might explode, but as he opened his mouth, the door swung inward, and another voice cut him off.

"I think not."

Lady Abena strode into the office, a slender elven Mageblade at her side. All eyes went to her.

"I... Your Ladyship, I thought you were on the Continent," said Indree.

"I was. When I received your messages, I cut my trip short. The Hesliar's top speed is really very impressive." Lady Abena approached Durren's desk. "I understand that emotions are high in the wake of such a terrible tragedy, Andus, but I think Inspector Lovial is to be commended for her part in saving Faelir Audlian and stopping the Mask. She is not responsible for the actions of Endo Stooke, and because of her and her friends, we at least know who our enemy is. I'm sure you wouldn't argue that fact."

"Of course not, Your Ladyship," Durren said, struggling to hold back a scowl.

"In fact," said Lady Abena, "recent events have made me consider appointing an official liason between the constabulary and my own office, with a direct channel to me at all times. I believe Inspector Lovial would be the ideal candidate. If she will accept the position?" She turned to Indree with a raised eyebrow.

Tane couldn't help but smile. It was a clever move. Durren's position might be unassailable due to his political connections, but he couldn't touch Indree while she was liason to the Lady Protector.

"It would be an honor, Lady Abena," Indree said. Tane wasn't sure how she kept a straight face—if it had been him, he'd have been full-on smirking at the chief constable.

Durren opened and closed his mouth a few times, and then, "Your Ladyship, I'm not certain—"

"That you can afford to spare her?" Lady Abena finished for him. "Oh, I won't take her away from her duties. But when particularly important cases arise, she will oversee them and report to me."

Durren deflated visibly. "Of course, Your Ladyship."

"Now, I think you'll agree we three have much to discuss, concerning Mister Stooke." Lady Abena smiled at Tane and Kadka. "Once again, Mister Carver, Miss Kadka, the Protectorate thanks you for your diligent service. I'm certain we will speak more later, but for now, I hope you'll excuse us?"

Tane nodded. "Come on, Kadka. I'm sure Chief Durren is *eager* to work out the details of this new arrangement."

Kadka didn't bother to hide her laughter as she led him out.

———

Kadka walked Carver toward the exit, helping him keep himself upright. She chuckled to herself as they entered the waiting room at the front of the Yard, still picturing the indignant look on Chief Durren's face when they'd left his office.

"Kadka! Mister Carver!" Iskar raised a hand, and then stood from his chair and crossed the room to meet them.

"Iskar?" Kadka cocked her head. She hadn't expected to see him. Not that she was complaining—he was as pretty as ever, silver scales gleaming in the building's magelight. "Why are you here?"

"The constables had questions after they secured the storehouse," he said. "And afterward, I wanted to make sure you had both come out unscathed."

"You are still there when constables come? Thought you would leave it for others. Is hiding done, then?"

Iskar nodded, a glimmer of passion in his blue eyes. "Most of the victims tonight were of the Silver Dawn, or non-magicals come to fight for their rights. It's clear who the targets were. If our enemies are willing to be so brazen, I don't think I can hide any longer." He gave Kadka a meaningful look "And… perhaps I learned something of a lesson in bravery tonight."

Kadka smiled. "Was nothing." She gestured to Carver, still leaning against her. "He gets into trouble, I save him. Happens more than you think."

Carver laughed. "I wish that wasn't so true."

"Well I am very glad she did," Iskar said solemnly. "I'm told it was only thanks to your quick thinking that more didn't die. Thank you, Mister Carver."

"I was just trying not to burn to death," Carver said. "But you're welcome." He offered his hand. "I should have realized this earlier, but any friend of Kadka's is someone I trust."

Iskar returned the handshake. "I feel much the same."

"Mind you," said Carver, "I'd still like to ask you about what you did to those wards on the storehouse. I didn't think that was possible, and I'm a bit of an… enthusiast where getting around spells is concerned."

"Leave him, Carver," Kadka scolded. "Is for him to say or not say." She was more than a little bit curious herself—it was *dragonfire* they were talking about—but people were entitled to their secrets.

Iskar's tail swished nervously against the ground. "I take no offense, but… perhaps another time, Mister Carver. You understand, I must see to my people after everything that's happened." She didn't have to be Carver to read in his body language that he was uncomfortable with the topic—there was something there he didn't want to talk about.

"Is fine," said Kadka, before Carver could embarrass anyone any further. "Go, if you need."

"Yes, I suppose I should." Iskar hesitated, gave her a long look. "Kadka, I do hope that… even if you don't choose to speak for the Silver Dawn, I would very much like to see you—"

"Don't need so much talk," Kadka reached behind Iskar's neck with the arm that wasn't supporting Carver, and kissed him solidly on the snout.

Iskar's eyes widened, and then his hand found her waist, and he was returning the kiss.

Carver squirmed away with a groan. "Come on, don't make me part of it."

Kadka snorted a laugh through her nose, and drew back for air. "You could learn something. Saw you kiss Indree." She pointedly wrapped her now-free arm around Iskar and pulled him tight against her, enjoying the firmness of his bare silver chest, running her fingers down the ridges on his back. One last time, she pressed her mouth against his.

And then she pulled away. Best not to let it go on for too long—he'd been living underground for a long time, after all, and she didn't want to overwhelm him all at once.

Or maybe it was too late for that. Iskar was staring at her with wide blue eyes, a dumbstruck half-smile showing teeth at the corners of his snout. He opened his mouth, apparently came up with nothing, and closed it again.

"See you soon, dragon man," Kadka said, and then offered her arm to Carver and led him away from the speechless kobold.

She was still grinning as they left the building.

CHAPTER TWENTY-SIX

———

TWO DAYS LATER, Lady Abena came to the office with Indree and an escort of Mageblades.

"Come in," Tane said, ushering them through the door. "Er, we don't have much in the way of seating. You can have my chair, Your Ladyship. Behind the desk." He flushed when he caught Indree's eye, and looked away. They'd been in contact via sending, but he hadn't seen her in person since the day Endo had escaped. She'd been busy with her new duties.

And they still hadn't talked about the kiss.

"Thank you, Mister Carver," said Lady Abena, stepping into the office. She waved away the first Mageblade to try to follow her in. "Stand guard outside. I'm sure the wards on this room are sufficiently secure."

"Updated for the possibility of automatons," confirmed Tane. "I know you asked Chancellor Greymond for the University's help in fixing the city's wards—she brought me on to consult yesterday. It's complicated if we still want to allow other artifacts, but I think I have it figured."

"Excellent," said Lady Abena. "I had a feeling you would find your way into the process." She seated herself in the chair behind his desk and nodded to Kadka, who was leaning back in her usual seat with her feet up.

Kadka grinned her welcome, and then swiveled her head toward Indree. "New job goes well? Make Durren's face redder every day?"

"Most days," Indree said, and moved to stand beside the Lady Protector's chair. She had a package under one arm. "It's been busy. We're still dealing with the damage from Endo's attack. But it's not nearly as bad as it could have been." She looked to Tane with a slight smile. "Thanks to you."

Tane rubbed the back of his neck. "Any sign of Endo yet?"

Indree shook her head. "We've got patrols scouring the Channel and every road, but I don't think we're going to find him. He'll have gone to ground by now."

"But that is not why we're here," said Lady Abena. "Unlike the Nieris matter, there is no reason the Protectorate cannot thank you two for your service in stopping these killings. We come bearing gifts." She nodded to Indree, who placed her package on Tane's desk. "Firstly, a token of appreciation, commissioned under Inspector Lovial's guidance."

"Open it after we leave," Indree said, a glint of mischief in her eye.

"And secondly," said Lady Abena, "a matter I think has been overlooked for too long." She reached into her coat and pulled out a roll of papers, which she unbound and spread on the desk. "Miss Kadka, if you would look these over."

Kadka cocked her head curiously and removed her feet from the desk to lean forward over the papers. She frowned, trying to puzzle out the Audish words, and glanced to Tane. "Carver? Is what I think?"

Tane looked over the papers, and his eyes widened. "These are citizenship papers."

"You weren't born within our borders, but few native citizens have done as much for the Protectorate as you have," said Lady Abena. "I thought it only fair. Of course, it is your decision. You only need sign your name."

Kadka didn't hesitate. "Where is pen?"

Tane pulled open a desk drawer and handed her a pen and inkwell. She snatched them up, signing her name in a messy scrawl at the bottom of the papers. Then, she looked up at Lady Abena. "Is done?"

The Lady Protector gently took the pen, and turned the papers toward herself. She signed across from Kadka's name in a much neater hand. "It is now. Welcome to the Protectorate, Miss Kadka."

"Congratulations, Kadka," said Tane, laying a hand on her shoulder.

"Is my fight now," Kadka said softly, and though Tane didn't know what that meant, he could have sworn he saw a glint of wetness in her eye before she blinked it away. "Thank you, Ladyship. I will not let you down."

"I don't expect you will," said Lady Abena. "And we may need your help again soon. Mister Stooke is a brilliant man, and his recent demonstration will, unfortunately, draw those of a certain mindset to the Knights of the Emperor. He has, it seems, managed to take with him a large portion of the Stooke fortune, and his house has trade connections all across the Continent. Even as a fugitive, I suspect he will not find himself lacking for resources. You two have as much insight into the man as anyone—I hope we can rely on your assistance in dealing with him."

Tane and Kadka shared a glance, and nodded their assent at the same time.

"You can count on us," said Tane.

"I knew we could." Lady Abena rose to her feet. "Now, we must be on our way. There is still much to do, and I'm sure Chancellor Greymond would prefer it if you kept at work on the new wards. Inspector Lovial?"

They were on their way out the door when Tane finally mustered up his nerve. "Ree, wait."

She turned, with a half-smile that said she knew exactly what he was going to ask. "Yes, Tane?"

"Maybe we could get that dinner tonight?"

Indree's smile broke full across her face. "I think we've waited long enough. I'll see you tonight." She nodded to the package still waiting on the desk. "And don't forget to open that." Again, that spark of amusement in her eyes. Then she was gone, and the door swung closed behind her.

Kadka grinned toothily at him. "Takes you long enough to ask."

"Shut up," said Tane, but he couldn't stop smiling.

"Wipe off funny look and open present," Kadka said, tapping the package. "I want to see it."

Tane picked the package up, hefted it in his hand. It was heavy, probably metal, flat and rectangular in shape. He tore off the wrapping to find an engraved brass plaque, held it up to read.

And groaned.

"What? What is it?" Kadka stood and craned her neck over, trying to get a look.

Reluctantly, Tane put it down on the desk for her to see. "I wonder if I can give it back."

Kadka cackled loudly as she read it. "Have to use. Is gift from Lady Protector. No choice now."

The plaque was clearly intended to replace the unfinished one on the office door. It was lovely work, engraved at the center with Audland's rearing gryphon, and inscribed underneath with the words, *In honor of courageous service to the Protectorate.*

Which wasn't the part that bothered him. Now he knew what Indree had found so amusing—the name inscribed *above* the gryphon. A name he was apparently stuck with.

Magebreakers Consulting and Investigation.

ABOUT THE AUTHOR

———

Ben S. Dobson is a Canadian fantasy author. When he isn't writing to indulge his lifelong passion for epic tales, he can probably be found playing Dungeons and Dragons, or watching a Joss Whedon show, or something equally geeky.

If you're interested in being notified when I release a new novel, you're welcome to sign up for my mailing list on my website.

For more information, check one of these places:
Website
http://bensdobson.com
Facebook
http://www.facebook.com/bensdobson
Or, contact me directly by email here:
bensdobson@gmail.com

Made in the USA
San Bernardino, CA
01 December 2019

60687237R00144